T0196437

Angie of the Garden

J.E. Hall

authorHOUSE®

AuthorHouse™
1663 Liberty Drive
Bloomington, IN 47403
www.authorhouse.com
Phone: 1-800-839-8640

First published by AuthorHouse 5/31/2012

ISBN: 978-1-4685-5729-9 (sc)
ISBN: 978-1-4685-5730-5 (e)

Library of Congress Control Number: 2012903485

Printed in the United States of America

Any people depicted in stock imagery provided by Thinkstock are models, and such images are being used for illustrative purposes only. Certain stock imagery © Thinkstock.

This book is printed on acid-free paper.

Because of the dynamic nature of the Internet, any web addresses or links contained in this book may have changed since publication and may no longer be valid. The views expressed in this work are solely those of the author and do not necessarily reflect the views of the publisher, and the publisher hereby disclaims any responsibility for them.

CHAPTER ONE

Hollis Simms was lounging on the veranda of Fairhaven on a quintessential summer day. The barely perceptible breeze moving lazily through the majestic trees did not rustle the *New York Times* enough to hamper his ability to read the words. Hollis was alone, as his wife and daughter were visiting friends on this morning. He truly felt like the master of his domain. Taking a sip from his cup of coffee, he gazed out over the well-kept grounds.

Fairhaven had been constructed in the early 1800s. There had been many renovations over the years before his wife Olivia had purchased the mansion for them to live in. At that time there was only Hollis and herself, so the 30 rooms their new home provided seemed excessive. The arrival of their first and only child did little to change that perception. Still Olivia Reese had been accustomed to living in elegance. She would not allow marriage to alter her standards.

"Mr. Simms!"

A familiar voice interrupted Hollis's reading. Frank Martin, the man responsible for the appearance of these aesthetically pleasing acres, came running up to the porch.

"There's a wino sleeping on the lawn," he breathlessly informed his employer. "Should I call the cops so they can get his drunken ass out of here?"

Hollis was tempted to say yes since he was reticent to do anything that would interfere with his perfect Sunday morning. Calling the authorities was the most expedient way to remedy the situation, but his curiosity would not allow him to choose that option.

"I'll have a look first, Frank."

The two men walked towards the west side of the mansion. They came upon a stocky individual in a three-piece suite lying on the grass there.

"He doesn't look like a wino to me," Hollis observed with a barely perceptible smirk on his face.

"I know he don't. But people ain't always what they seem. I think we should call the cops."

"But Sam may be offended if we do," Hollis told him.

"Who?"

"This is Sam. You've met him before, only he didn't have a beard at that time. He also wasn't behaving like a dipsomaniac."

"It's a good thing I don't know what that means, or I might be offended," the intruder said.

Then he opened his eyes and continued.

"My name is Sebastian, not Sam. After all these years you should know that."

"You should have been named Sam. You're sturdy and dependable, for the most part, anyway. I've always associated those qualities with that name. So why are you one week early for my surprise party?"

Sebastian sat up and laughed. That Hollis would discover his wife's plan was to be expected.

"Olivia's not going to be happy when she finds out that you know about the party."

"That's the way Mrs. Simms usually is," Frank observed.

"As for my reason for coming early," Sebastian continued as he stood up. "I was hanging out with some friends on the island last night. I lost track of the time, and had them drop me off here. But then I noticed that it was three o'clock in the morning. I slept on the grass because I didn't want to wake you. I've lost my job. And Clare threw me out of the apartment."

"I'm sorry to hear about the job," Hollis said, "and Clare as well. I've always liked her."

Sebastian looked away for a moment. Hollis was accustomed to dealing with people who were experiencing emotional problems. Even so it was always more difficult when it came to consoling someone he knew personally.

"Why don't you go inside and take a shower? I have some clothes you can borrow. Olivia and Belle aren't here. We can have a few bloody marys."

Sebastian turned and looked at his older brother. Hollis always found the right thing to say.

"Do you still make them as strong as you used to?" he asked.

"No. They've gotten stronger over the years," Hollis responded.

Frank returned to the cottage on the grounds of Fairhaven where he lived with his family. Hollis went inside the mansion with his unexpected guest. As he walked up the long spiral staircase and observed the beautiful design sculpted into the ceiling, Sebastian once again marveled at the fact that his brother lived here. That had become possible when Hollis married Olivia Reese. Though Doctor Simms was a successful psychiatrist in his own right, only the staggering wealth of the Reese family could have provided them with such a magnificent palace to dwell in.

Sebastian finished his shower and put on the sweat suit that Hollis had provided. He then walked through the narrow archway to join his brother in the study. The bloody mary Hollis had promised him was on a table beside a vacant leather chair. His host occupied the one next to it. The large stone fireplace that dominated the room was dormant now. A painting by Jackson Pollack hung on the wall near the large window.

"So tell me what happened," Hollis said as his brother sat down next to him.

"Do you remember Jason Fields?"

"I remember the name."

"He's the Vice President of Research at McDivet Investments." Sebastian nearly choked on the last two words. "I've worked for him for the last several years. I analyzed companies to determine if they were worthwhile investments for our customers and submitted my reports to him. One of those companies was called 'Let Us Shop.'"

"I've never heard of them."

"That's not surprising," Sebastian said. "They were an Internet company. Their customers submitted a list of groceries online and LUS delivered them to their homes. The plan was to start out by offering the service for food only, and then expand into other consumer needs. I thought that the average person would find the cost too prohibitive. Jason disagreed with me though. He recommended it to our brokers. Many of our clients lost significant sums of money on their investment. At first he acknowledged that the debacle was his responsibility. Then when the time came to explain the losses to his superior he changed his mind. Jason asked me to take the fall."

Hollis recognized the expression on his brother's face. He was still reliving the initial feelings of outrage and betrayal he had first experienced over a month ago. Hollis had many patients who had sustained similar emotions for even longer periods of time.

"And you wouldn't?" Hollis questioned him.

Sebastian stood up and walked over to the window. The younger Simms absent-mindedly held onto the blue velvet curtains as he looked out over the spring vista before him.

"Of course not," he finally replied. "I wasn't the one who fucked it up. But Jason presented it to his superiors as if I had to save his job. I was out on the street two weeks later."

"I'm sorry, Sam. That was a raw deal."

"I looked around for a couple of weeks, but there was nothing out there for me. Not only had I been fired, but it happened at a time when the bears have overrun the street. So I started wondering if I should do something else with my life. I'm only 37. I could still change careers pretty easily."

"I gather Clare didn't see it that way."

"That's an understatement. She accused me of giving up on our future, and asked me to leave. Since the apartment was originally hers I had no choice."

"So what are your plans now?" he asked Sebastian.

Sebastian turned and faced Hollis.

"I'm still working on it."

"Why not stay here? We have enough room to put up an army."

"But won't Olivia object to having one of your unemployed relations in the house?"

"You're family. It won't be a problem."

Sebastian returned to his chair and took a sip from his glass.

"I appreciate the offer. But I have a better idea. Why don't I stay in the old house? That way I won't be interfering with your daily routine."

At first Hollis seemed troubled by his brother's suggestion. Sebastian was perplexed as to why, but didn't question him about it.

"That's a great idea," Hollis finally agreed with a smile. "It is a bit musty, though. Frank and his family moved out of it a year ago. Olivia has wanted to tear it down, but I've resisted her attempts to do so. For sentimental reasons, of course."

"I know what you mean. I guess when you are in my situation it's good to be able to go home, at least for a while."

They walked to the old caretaker's house with their bloody marys in hand. Frank, who had been informed of Sebastian's intentions, arrived there ahead of them. He was opening the windows to let in the fresh air at Hollis's request.

"Are you sure Olivia won't mind?" Sebastian asked once more.

"She'll love having you here," Hollis assured him.

"That's because she just loves to mind," Frank observed with a grin.

"I have some work to do tomorrow morning," Hollis told his brother. "But in the afternoon we can play some golf if you'd like. I have a spare set of clubs, though I'm sure they're not as good as your own."

"It's the only way you'll ever beat me," Sebastian said with a grin. "That sounds great."

Hollis put his hand on Sebastian's shoulder.

"Courage, my friend," he told him.

Olivia returned home and found Hollis once again reading the paper on the veranda. The warm sunlight of early spring bathed the awakening grasses in a soft pleasant light. Her husband appeared to be the picture of containment.

"You're still reading, love? You certainly know how to take advantage of a day off," she said to him.

"I was interrupted earlier," he told her. "We have company."

For a moment Olivia feared that one of the people she had invited to the surprise party had confused the dates. Her husband put her mind at ease when he continued.

"My brother Sam is here," he explained. "It seems that he's had a run of bad luck. He's going to stay with us for a while."

Olivia gave him a stern look. This was not because she objected to having his brother as a guest. Hollis had every right to open their home to whomever he pleased. Olivia, though, had always been responsible for running the household. Her husband should have informed her of his intention to offer the invitation before asking Sebastian to stay.

"I would have discussed it with you first," Hollis said after seeing her displeasure. "But he showed up unexpectedly."

"What kind of *bad luck* has he had?"

"He lost his job. And Clare threw him out."

"You know your family is always welcome in our home," Olivia assured him. "But in this case I would like to know if Sebastian intends to make destitution a way of life."

"Of course not. He just needs some time to collect himself."

"He can use the guest room at the end of the west wing."

"He's staying in the old house."

"That's certainly appropriate. I'll have one of the staff prepare it for him."

"Sam greatly appreciates it and so do I," Hollis said as he stood up and gave her an affectionate kiss.

"Perhaps if he stays here long enough you'll actually learn his name," Olivia responded with a pleasant smile as she walked into the house.

Sebastian spent part of his week shopping for clothes. He had no desire to retrieve his belongings from the apartment in Manhattan. That would have meant seeing Clare, and his wounds were still too raw for such an encounter. Sebastian purchased casual clothes, with the exception of the suit he intended to wear at Saturday's party.

The day of Hollis's birthday dawned bright and clear. The temperature was unseasonably warm for early April. Olivia had originally intended to get Hollis away from the house by asking him to take care of a matter at their attorney's office. Now Sebastian's presence provided another, and more desirable, option. She insisted that her husband spend the day on the golf course with him. After presenting him with a new Mercedes convertible for his gift, she sent Hollis and Sebastian off to the Oak Hollow

Country Club. Then Olivia began to prepare the house for her husband's party.

"Your wife is certainly good to you," Sebastian observed as they drove through the winding roads of Old Westbury.

"I can't help but agree. Not only did Olivia present me with this car, but she also insisted that I play golf today. I get to play twice in one week, which is a rarity for me. And my daughter bought me the *Star Wars* anthology. It truly doesn't get any better than this."

"I know it's brand new but can I borrow it?" Sebastian asked him.

"Sure. The car is yours whenever I'm not using it."

"I don't mean the car. I meant the anthology."

"You're a man who truly appreciates the finer things in life," Hollis replied with a laugh.

They played 18 holes and then retired to the clubhouse for a drink. Many of the other members stopped at their table to wish Hollis well. He knew some of them would be at his home later that evening but managed to conceal his knowledge. The older Simms introduced the younger one at every opportunity. Nonetheless, Sebastian still felt uncomfortable.

"I guess we're heading in opposite directions," he remarked. "You have a career and a family, and I've got nothing to show for thirty seven years of living. I'm on my way to becoming one of your patients."

"That is a tad dramatic, wouldn't you say? You're experiencing what psychiatrists refer to as a life problem. Or, to express it colloquially, you've had a shitty month. My patients, unfortunately, have deeper problems than that."

"I know. I'm just feeling sorry for myself. Does Olivia still believe you don't know anything about the party?"

"I think so. But it's very difficult to deceive her for long. Not that I've ever tried to, of course," Hollis said with a devilish grin.

"I really appreciate your help. If I can ever do you a favor, I will."

"I'm glad you feel that way, because I'm going to ask you to do one for me tomorrow."

"I didn't mean right away!" Sebastian pretended to object. "The favor I'm repaying is still being granted. You should let me take advantage of it for a while before I have to repay it."

"You ungrateful transient!" Hollis raised his voice in mock anger. Then, in a normal tone, "I believe that Paul Nustad will be attending the party tonight."

"I remember Paul. He's an historian from Boston, right?"

"Yes. I gave him an old diary to research for me. I've been waiting patiently for two years for him to do it, but Paul being Paul, he's never gotten around to it. The man can tell you what happened on any given date for the last five thousand years but he can't remember what he's supposed to do today."

"Is that the diary you dug up when we were kids?"

"Yes. I was overturning the garden for Dad when I found it. You were only about 7-years-old at the time. I'm surprised you remember."

"I'll never forget how you fell in love with its author."

"Well, I had reached the age when females were becoming very intriguing to me. And the woman who wrote the diary traveled on the Oregon Trail in the 1800s. She must have been a very courageous person to overcome the hardships described in her writings. So I was understandably smitten. Anyway, I'd like to have it back. And I don't trust the mail, or even the overnight messenger services. Would you go up to Boston with Paul and bring it back for me?"

"I'm many things big brother, but an ingrate isn't one of them. I'll be glad to help you out."

While driving back to Fairhaven they passed the estate of Mildred Price. She was over 60-years-old, and had recently lost her husband of 40 years. Her chauffeur was giving Mildred driving lessons. She had never driven a car before, the widow Price's attempt to do so at this late stage of her life being part of a sincere effort to become independent. The inexperienced driver came to the end of the driveway that led to her home. She just barely managed to stop before reaching the road. Hollis saw her coming, and applied the brakes in front of the gate to her estate.

"Hello Mildred," he said. "I'm glad to see that you're becoming more comfortable behind the wheel."

"Well, you're just being generous, Hollis. I think I've taken several years off the life of Henry."

The lack of color in the chauffeur's face was a testament to the truth of her statement.

"Courage, Mildred," Hollis said with a kind smile. "You've only just begun. Give yourself a chance to become acclimated to driving a car."

"I'll try, Hollis. Thank you for your encouragement."

Mildred Price intended to back up and turn around; only she put the car in drive instead. Sebastian's complexion suddenly bore a striking resemblance to the butler's. Hollis was unaffected. Mildred managed to avoid hitting her neighbor's birthday present.

"You should be telling everyone else on the road to have courage," Sebastian pointed out as they drove away. "That lady is a menace."

"It gives Mildred something to do while she's adjusting to the loss of her husband," Hollis told him. "She'll never go out on the open road."

"You must be grateful for that. I would be if she was my neighbor."

Hollis turned onto the long driveway leading up to his home. There was no indication the Simms had visitors that evening due to Olivia's having the guests park their cars in the back of the estate. Doctor Simms gave Sebastian a knowing look and walked through the front door. A large crowd of people yelled "happy birthday" in unison. Hollis played the role of one caught unawares, and his performance was convincing. His brother, who knew the truth of the matter, was impressed. Yet one person in the room saw through his deception immediately.

"Are you surprised my love?" Olivia asked him after she greeted him with a long kiss.

"Absolutely," Hollis replied in an earnest fashion.

Annabelle was the next to greet him. His 16-year-old daughter was starting to take on the appearance, if not the continence, of a young woman. His pride in her was evident as the two of them embraced.

"Did we fool you daddy?" she asked him.

"Completely," he replied with a smile.

"I'm glad to hear that you can still play golf. At your advanced age I thought the physical exertion might be too much for you."

His friend Paul Nustad made that observation. Hollis was particularly glad to see the historian.

"How good of you to come, Paul."

"It was no trouble at all. Your house happens to be situated between Europe and Boston."

"Did you make any interesting discoveries on your trip?"

"I did find some new information about Henry the Eighth."

"A wife we didn't know about?" Hollis asked.

"I can't reveal it until my paper on the subject is published. But you'll be one of the first to read it. I'll send you a copy for your birthday present."

"That's far from the most personal gift I've ever received. But fortunately for you it's the thought that counts," Hollis replied. Then he said to everyone in the room. "Thanks for coming, my friends. I have to put on some proper attire for the occasion. Make yourself at home."

Hollis went upstairs to change. When he emerged from the shower his wife was waiting for him.

"So when did you find out about the party?" she asked him with an even grin.

"I never could put anything past you," Hollis replied while drying his neatly styled chestnut brown hair. "Over the last month I noticed that your phone conversations suddenly turned to whispers whenever I entered the room. I'm not suspicious by nature, but after a while even someone like me starts to wonder."

"I'm glad you didn't think I was having an affair."

"Now you've put a devil of an idea into my mind," Hollis replied with a laugh.

"Then I'll remove it," she responded as they embraced. "You're more than enough for me to handle. Enjoy your party, dear."

The guests had congregated in the ballroom on the second floor. There was a balcony in the spacious room that had once been used by the musicians performing at the formal affairs held at Fairhaven by previous owners. Olivia had opted to use smaller bands for her parties, and they sat in chairs at one end of the room. Annabelle Simms sat in the empty balcony above the crowd with her friend Celia Upton. They had known each other since they were three. Annabelle, or Belle as she was more often called, observed the guests coming into the room and gave Celia her opinion of them.

"See that creepy looking man with the dark glasses and the beard standing over there?" she asked while pointing to the guest.

"Oh, yeah. Who's that?"

"That's Harley Fox. He's supposed to be some kind of Hollywood big shot. He wants mother to help finance one of his films. I wouldn't give the creep 21 cents. But mother seems to think it's a worthwhile investment. Sometimes I think he wants to hit on me."

"Oh, how gross!"

The two girls giggled loudly.

"Oh no, here comes trouble," Belle said with real distress in her voice. "Here come the itty old bittys."

The "itty old bittys" were Miss Nora Novak and Miss Wilimina Simms. They were too older women (just how old no one could be sure) who were the aunts of Hollis Simms. Their physical stature had been reduced by the passage of time, while their penchant for meddling in the affairs of their favorite nephew and his family had increased over that same period. On their last visit the two ladies had politely, but incessantly, taken Annabelle's parents to task for allowing their daughter to have the side of her nose pierced. Belle wore a beautiful but not overly large diamond there.

"Really, Hollis, the child looks like an aborigine," Wilimina told him. "Only the savages of this world would do something like that to their body."

"I can't help but agree," Nora chimed in.

Olivia was furious. Belle threatened to replace the small diamond with a large ring. Hollis acknowledged their indignation and addressed his aunts on their behalf.

"While I'm not a body piercing enthusiast I must say that my daughter's taste in jewelry in no way reminds me of the objects worn by primitive tribes. Still, you can rest assured that if I notice Belle taking an interest in such things as human sacrifice or cannibalism I will put my foot down. No child of mine is going to eat another human being."

The ladies ceased their complaining.

Sebastian walked into the room wearing his new suit. He took note of the jester and musician that were carved into opposite sides of the heavy wooden door. The two figures represented the musical merriment the ballroom would provide for the guests on this night.

"There's my Uncle Sebastian," Belle told her friend. "I should start calling him Uncle Loser. He lost his job and his girlfriend threw him out."

"Why did he lose his job?" Celia asked her.

"I'm not sure. But he showed up here after going on a bender. He might be an alcoholic."

"Having him around must really suck for you," Celia said sympathetically.

"He's living in the old groundskeeper's place, so it's not too bad. I just hope he doesn't go on a drinking binge one night and break into our house. I can't even imagine what he might do."

Belle's dramatization of her domestic situation was interrupted by Hollis's entrance into the crowded ballroom. He immediately looked up to the balcony and waved. Annabelle's father knew where his daughter liked to be during the Fairhaven social functions.

"Well, hello there old man."

Hollis turned and found Elliot Reese standing behind him. Olivia's father was a distinguished looking man whose appearance belied his age. The 70-year-old entrepreneur had started out with one pharmacy in his early 30s. That had grown into a large pharmaceutical chain, which he sold for an unspeakable amount of money later on. After that he spent his days investing in other companies and running a charitable foundation. His daughter, and only child, assisted him in the later. Elliot had always been pleased with Olivia's choice for a husband. In an era when many young men seemed to lack a real purpose in their lives, Hollis Simms had impressed him with his dedication to psychiatric medicine. He was determined to help those who suffered from psychological afflictions, and to become the best at his chosen occupation, not merely competent. Though Elliot had tried he could not find a flaw in the young man who had asked for his daughter's hand in marriage. He was convinced that Hollis Simms was truly interested in Olivia herself and not the wealth the Reese family had accumulated.

"Thanks for coming, Elliot." Hollis shook his hand.

"So how does it feel to be 46-years-old?"

"Not bad at all. I can honestly say that I have just as much energy as I did at 45."

"There's a phone call for you, sir. A Miss Clare Johnson," one of the servants told Hollis.

"Excuse me. Be sure and have something to eat. The chef has an excellent reputation."

Hollis walked into the study and closed the door. He picked up the phone.

"Hollis? This is Clare. Happy Birthday!"

"Thanks so much for calling. How have you been?"

"I'm fine," she replied in an unconvincing tone. "I guess you heard about what happened. I'm sorry that I missed your party, but it's just not a good time for me to see Sebastian."

Hollis paused for a moment. The doctor wanted to console Clare without making it sound like professional advice. This called for a more personal touch.

"Olivia and I understand. I know things are difficult now, but my brother seems to have been badly used. It's just going to take him a while to get over it."

"I know. But it's been over a month, and Sebastian has just given up on his career, and himself. And as far as I'm concerned he's given up on us, as well."

Clare fought back tears as she said those words.

"Sam isn't a quitter," Hollis assured her. "He'll come around."

"Could you do me a favor? Tell him that he can come by and get his things whenever he wants."

"I will. Let's get together for lunch sometime."

"That would be nice. Goodbye, Hollis, and happy birthday."

He hung up the phone and rejoined the party. Hollis mingled with the guests before being drawn to the dining room by the succulent aroma emanating from there. His wife had acquired the services of the chef from the Four Seasons Restaurant in Manhattan. The food he prepared had everyone's taste buds brimming with anticipation.

Elliot Reese had also found his way into the dining room. Much to his chagrin he had discovered that Olivia's mother was also attending the party. She and her husband took separate vacations, and in fact seemed to spend most of their time apart. Jacqueline Reese almost never appeared at the same social functions as her husband. Elliot found himself standing behind his wife as the server put a generous portion of duck ravioli on her plate.

"Hello Jacqueline," he said with little enthusiasm.

"How nice to see you," she replied in the same fashion. "How have you been?"

"Not bad. I'm glad I ran into you. I want to use the East Hampton house on the Fourth of July. A…. acquaintance of mine would like to spend the holiday out there."

Jacqueline placed her plate on the table so she could address Elliot, hands on hips.

"I always use the beach house on the Fourth. And that's not going to change just because one of the tarts you run around with wants to go to the Hamptons."

"You will not impugn the character of my friends!"

Elliot picked up the plate of food and was about to throw it at his wife when Hollis intervened. He had observed their encounter from a distance, making his way over to them when he noticed that Jacqueline's nostrils had begun to flair.

Now I know why they call it "duck" ravioli the man serving the food thought to himself with amusement. *When someone is about to throw a plate of it at you it's time to duck.*

"Elliot, please," he said while taking the food away from him. "There are many hungry people here tonight. We can't waste the ravioli just to settle a disagreement."

The two combatants withdrew. Olivia came over to find out what had caused the commotion.

"Don't you think it's time they got a divorce?" Hollis asked her.

Olivia did not see fit to pry into her parents' relationship, so just what they intended to do about their dysfunctional marriage was not within the realm of her knowledge. She only knew that they loved her.

"A guess a divorce would be too messy," she replied.

"As opposed to your mother wearing a plate full of duck ravioli?"

Olivia went off to find her parents. Hollis prepared a plate and sat down at one of the tables. He had already savored his first few bites when his meal was interrupted.

"Every day should be your birthday," John Block said as he took the seat next to him. "I don't get to eat like this very often."

"Thanks for coming Dr. Block," Hollis said as he reached out and shook his hand. "I was just thinking about you."

"I find that hard to believe. I think the food is the only thing on your mind at the moment."

"I cannot tell a lie. You're right. But I was thinking about you earlier this evening. I have a new patient with an irrational fear of bald people. Her phobia is a hindrance to her career, and social life as well. The patient doesn't feel she can wait for long-term treatment to find a solution to her problem. I'm going to use behavior modification."

John Block had always believed in the traditional approach to psychotherapy. This method required many sessions over a very long period of time. As a result the patient incurs a very high cost, both in the analyst's fees and the time required to achieve peace of mind. Hollis often followed Block's teachings and prescribed long-term treatment. Yet he was not hesitant to use behavioral therapy as well. This technique spends less time investigating the history of a patient, focusing instead on changing his or her behavior. Many of his patients found this approach preferable to the traditional method. They had experienced positive results in a relatively short time.

"So she isn't interested in finding out what caused the phobia?" John asked him.

"It's a question of time and money. My patient doesn't feel she has enough of either for prolonged treatment. I'm having her sit on the subway next to a bald person at every opportunity. She is to increase the length of each successive encounter incrementally."

"I'm sure you'll be successful. Though there will probably be some people who will receive the wrong impression. They'll think your patient has a *thing* for bald men. You know I've always believed in your ability, Hollis. I felt that way even after you started using a more expedient approach. So you're 46 now. You'll catch up with me one of these days."

"Excuse me, but I couldn't help overhearing." A third person joined their conversation. "He should just prescribe medication. It's all about chemicals, gentlemen."

Alec Collins had arrived. While John Block would best be described as a mentor and friend, Alec most closely fit the one word description of *colleague*. Olivia had invited him because they often saw Doctor Collins at work-related social functions.

Alec Collins believed in the pharmacological approach. He prescribed drugs to ease the suffering of his patients. Block claimed that this practice only covered up the symptoms of much deeper problems. Hollis agreed with him in many instances, though in some he recognized the urgency of bringing severe symptoms under control. The three of them had spent many hours debating the merit of each approach.

"I hate to talk shop at these things," Alec said. "But since the two of you have already started I feel obligated to join you."

"You might at least wish me a happy birthday before you do," Hollis pointed out.

"That's right! That's why we came here today. I even remembered to bring a present, which I've placed on the table with your other gifts. Now that I've dealt with the amenities, what do you think about the San Diego conference?"

"I take it you mean what do I think about the fact that we're both speaking on the same day?" Hollis responded.

"Exactly," Alec said with a grin.

"It should be interesting," Hollis replied in kind.

Both men hoped to be the second one to speak, as that would mean having the last word.

"I just hope you don't carry on about how human emotions are more than just a series of chemical reactions in the brain. Because that's all they are," Alec said confidently.

Hollis's reply consisted only of a confident expression on his face implying that he would prove his rival's statement incorrect. This gave Alec something to consider for the rest of that evening, and during the weeks remaining before the conference would be held. He could not imagine what Hollis had in mind.

"I'd like to speak with you alone, gentlemen," John said as stood up. "Someplace private, if you don't mind."

Hollis led the two men into his study. He closed the door behind them.

"The first order of business is to give you your present, Hollis. Happy Birthday."

John Block handed Hollis a wooden walking stick. The hand carved present featured a fearsome wolf's head on the handle.

"That will come in handy if you're ever attacked by a wild animal while strolling around the grounds," Block pointed out. "You can use it to beat the beast into submission."

"Why thank you, Doctor Block. It's beautiful."

"You can defend yourself against the squirrels now, Hollis," Alec said with a laugh.

"I have an announcement to make," John told them. "I've decided to retire."

John Block was the head of the psychiatric department at Mullins University Hospital. He had also been a teacher, and had two former students on his staff there. Block now looked at both of his one-time pupils carefully. Hollis and Alec had been taken aback by his announcement. Simms was the first to speak.

"Why, Doctor Block, you never gave any indication that you were thinking of leaving. I can't imagine working at the hospital without you."

"The world's moving too fast for me," John replied with a grin. "No one has the time to do things the way they ought to be done. That's just my opinion, of course. I'd like to do some traveling. I'll still see patients as a private physician. But it's time for me to slow down and enjoy myself."

"Congratulations, Doctor Block," Alec said as he shook his hand. "You've had a very long and distinguished tenure."

"The staff will vote on a replacement. As the two senior psychiatrists I'm sure it will come down to a choice between the two of you. It's no secret that I think quite highly of you Doctor Simms, and you, Doctor Collins. I just hope no one asks me for advice as to who they should vote for. I don't think I'll be able to oblige them."

"I guess we should start brown nosing immediately, Hollis," Alec suggested with a grin.

They were interrupted by Olivia's entrance.

"I invite all these interesting people, but you come in here and talk about your work all night." Olivia feigned annoyance as she spoke.

"You know I prefer boring people," Hollis told her. "That's why you invited Alec, too. I do appreciate it."

"This is a wonderful night," John kissed her hand.

"The food was delicious," Collins, who was never one to engage in pretenses, added.

The four of them returned to the ballroom. Olivia called to someone in the crowd. Harley Fox walked over to join them. Hollis had never met him before, but was aware of why he was here. Olivia introduced him to the three psychiatrists. Each took note of the dark glasses he wore.

"So my wife tells me you're interested in producing a movie," Hollis said to him.

"That's right. I want to tell the real story behind the Civil War. Not like that *Gone with the Wind* crap."

"I rather enjoy that movie," Alec remarked.

"He also has something to ask you," Olivia said to her husband.

"I know the guy who produces *The Robin Wainscot Show*. It's one of those day time talk shows," Harley explained while barely hiding his disdain for the genre. "His name is Johnny Mueller. He's looking for a psychiatrist to become a semi-regular on the show. I suppose you'd just listen to the people in the audience, and maybe the guests, complain about their problems. Then you'd tell them how to straighten out their lives. You should give him a call."

"Think of what that would do for your career," Olivia said enthusiastically

Doctor Simms did not believe he belonged on a talk show. Hollis took his profession very seriously and he strongly suspected that the people who put on *The Robin Wainscot Show* did not. Then he caught just a glimmer of jealously on the face of Alec Collins, which was enough to make him appear to be interested in Harley's suggestion.

"I appreciate your telling me about this opportunity. I'll have to think about it. Do you know how I can get in touch with Johnny Mueller?"

"Here's his number." Harley handed him a card. "You can reach more people in ten minutes then you have during all your years of being a shrink. Think about that."

"And now I have to steal my husband from you. The waltz they're playing is too beautiful to sit through. I must have this dance."

Hollis was not an enthusiastic dancer, but he did find it pleasurable to hold this slender woman in his arms. His wife moved gracefully to the music as he managed to do a passable job of keeping up with her movements. The large chandelier above them sparkled as they moved across the floor.

"Doctor Block is retiring," Hollis told her. "I'm one of the candidates to replace him as head of the department."

"That's exciting, darling."

"I could use the challenge. There have been some days recently when psychiatry felt more like a job than a calling."

"Everybody gets into a rut now and then. Now you have a chance to lead the department, and be a television star. Are you excited about Harley's suggestion?" she asked.

"I'm not sure that being on a talk show would suit me. I've barely enough time to see my regular patients. And now I may have additional responsibilities at the hospital. Where would I find the time?"

"You could work something out. Harley thinks you'd be perfect for the show."

"Harley met me for the first time tonight," Hollis pointed out with a smile. "So how would he know? Besides, I think he really believes your money would be perfect. Perfect for him, that is. I will think about it, though."

"Did you see how jealous Alec was?" Olivia took pleasure in seeing his reaction to the producer's proposal.

"Was he really? I didn't notice," Hollis replied facetiously.

The early morning hours found Hollis sitting at a table with Sebastian and Paul. The other guests had said their goodbyes. Soon after that Olivia retired for the evening. The three men were sharing a bottle of brandy.

"So how's my diary?" Hollis asked the historian. "Did you ever get to research its author?"

"I am sorry. The last two years have just been impossible for me. I promise to get to it as soon as the spring semester is over."

"Which is what you promised last September, only then it was going to be after the fall semester was over. I can't wait any longer. I'm sending Sam with you to bring the diary back here. I'll have to find someone more reliable to research the life of Angelica Barton."

"I would be offended, if you weren't telling the truth," Paul replied with a grin. "I can send it back to you by courier. There's no reason for Sebastian to come with me."

"I don't trust the mail or any other delivery service," Hollis told him.

"I don't mind," Sebastian told him. "It will be a short trip."

"Very well, then. My flight leaves at nine thirty tomorrow. I expect there will still be seats available on it. I apologize for not doing as you asked, my friend."

"There's no reason to," Hollis responded. "I know you're a busy man. I'm just very curious about Angelica Barton. I'd like to know if it's a true account of her life."

They spent another hour discussing other subjects. Then Paul stood up to leave. He once again wished Hollis a happy birthday, and also apologized for a second time. Hollis walked to the front door with the two men.

"I'd like to make a copy of the diary," the historian said as they stood on the porch. "I'll have one of my student aides start researching it right away. I tried to have one of them work on it last year, but the aide left before he could begin working on the diary. Maybe this one will get the job done."

"Fair enough," Hollis agreed.

"I'll see you tomorrow," Sebastian said as he shook Paul's hand.

"You're really interested in this woman," Paul observed as he opened the door of the taxi that was taking him to his hotel. "I wonder why."

Hollis Simms did not reply. Sebastian answered for him.

"She was his first love. Hollis has been infatuated with her ever since he was a kid."

He embraced his older brother and walked towards the old house.

And even more so now, Hollis thought to himself as he watched the two of them leave, *because I've met her.*

CHAPTER TWO

The old house had been the boyhood home of Hollis and Sebastian Simms. Their father was the caretaker at Fairhaven when Thomas P. Owens owned the estate. The residence provided for John Simms and his family was a very simple affair, which suited his personality very well. He was a man of the earth, not one to concern himself about the lack of splendor in his house. Simms could coax the most ragged looking plant into becoming a thing of beauty: this was enough to satisfy his aesthetic needs. John also managed to inspire his sons to find their full potential, though he had hardly imagined his oldest child would one day reside in the mansion that was visible from the front window of his home.

His firstborn had been an insightful individual from his earliest days. John and Martha would never forget the day when a very young Hollis announced that his Aunt Alice was with child. She had been keeping it a secret, and had yet to show any outward signs of her condition. Still the five-year-old boy could sense the anticipation being harbored by his aunt. From that day on they paid particularly close attention when Hollis spoke. John Simms continually told his oldest son that this ability should be used in a constructive fashion. Hollis took his words to heart, and decided to become a psychiatrist.

Sebastian Simms also benefited from his father's presence, but to a lesser degree. This was due to the fact that he was a stubborn child, and was resistant to any suggestion that did not fit his perception of what constituted the correct approach to accomplishing any given task. While Hollis could be reasoned with, Sebastian often refused to acknowledge the validity of any differing point of view. As a very young boy Hollis's brother had insisted that he could be a more successful fisherman by using chocolate for bait. The obstinate child reasoned that since he preferred the taste of candy to worms his prey would surely be more attracted to the former than the latter.

"I spend more of my time convincing that boy I'm right than I do earning a living," John lamented after once again failing to persuade his youngest son that chocolate bars were not suitable fish bait.

"He's just a little headstrong," his wife told him.

"Yeah, like the ocean is just a little wet."

In spite of his frustration their father lived to see them both graduate college with honors. Hollis became a doctor, while Sebastian entered the business world. The older Simms boy established a successful practice while his younger brother rose through the ranks of a Wall Street investment firm until he received a better offer from another one. Sebastian remained single well into his thirties, while Hollis had married at the age of twenty-five. He made what his friends and family considered to be the most desirable catch any man could make.

Hollis met Olivia Reese at a dinner dance that was being held for a charitable organization. They had been placed at the same table by chance. The two strangers suddenly found themselves alone shortly after the affair began when the other guests who were to sit with them abruptly left.

"I guess we're not very good company," Hollis observed with a grin.

"Those people had only come for a cameo appearance, not to spend the evening," Olivia replied. "I think we'll do very well without them."

They were immediately attracted to each other. After the affair ended the two of them spent the rest of the evening dancing and conversing in a Manhattan nightclub. The young psychiatrist asked for her phone number after the evening was over, and Olivia obliged. A friend informed Hollis about the social stature of Olivia Reese the next day. He had never heard the name, and had only half believed it until being a guest at her parents' home shortly after.

How their relationship had so quickly blossomed into love was one of the most intriguing and enjoyable mysteries of their lives. He was the analytical type, who looked to find rationalizations for virtually all human behavior. She had no interest in explaining the actions of others, and simply judged people's conduct as being either inappropriate or acceptable. While Hollis enjoyed good restaurants and smart clothes, Olivia's standards were well beyond anything he had ever imagined. Neither of them could comprehend their unexpected union, even when they were standing in front of the priest on their wedding day.

John and Martha Simms could hardly believe their eyes either, for the ceremony was being held on the lawn of Fairhaven. Olivia had purchased the estate to be the newlyweds' home. The heirs of the late Thomas P. Owens sold it to her soon after their engagement was announced. John Simms lived to see his oldest son move into the estate. He did not live much longer than that, unfortunately. After retiring from his chosen occupation several years earlier, Hollis's father succumbed to a stroke in Florida. His wife lived long enough to see Sebastian, who was seven years Hollis's junior, graduate college. Then she too passed away.

After three years of living at Fairhaven, Olivia decided to build a more modern residence for the groundskeeper. Hollis agreed with the idea, but asked that the old house remain standing. He was normally not a sentimental man, but these circumstances made for an exception. Olivia agreed, though she felt his boyhood home was well on its way to becoming an eyesore. Even so the woman that ran Fairhaven was willing to tolerate it for her husband's sake.

Hollis had set up his office in a room that was in a turret-shaped section of the main house. He often mused about one day putting a large gun on the top of it to protect him from any dissatisfied patients looking for retribution. Doctor Simms could look out the window and see the garden near the old house in the twilight. That was where he had found a leather-bound book containing the story of the most inspiring person he had ever encountered, albeit, at the time, through the written word alone.

Hollis came across the diary of Angelica Barton at the age of 16 after his father asked him to turn over the soil in the garden near their home. Sebastian assisted his older brother, though he was often more of a hindrance than a help. Hollis was all but finished when his shovel struck a metal object buried in the ground. He picked it up and opened the container. There was a book inside, which contained the account of a woman who had traveled west in the 1800s. Hollis became infatuated with Angelica. To no one's surprise, Sebastian enjoyed teasing him about his first love. Hollis had no defense against his taunts, for the 16-year-old boy was truly smitten with this woman from the past. Even as he grew older, Hollis would occasionally peruse through the diary to rediscover the sense of adventure she had provided for him.

As an adult, Hollis often sat on the large rock in front of the garden. He thought about all the summers that his father had planted vegetables behind the wrought iron fence erected by the original owner of Fairhaven. There were always several tomatoes lying in the windowsill in the groundskeeper's house to take advantage of the sun during the hot August days. Hollis spent many hours here fondly remembering his life at Fairhaven as a young boy. Olivia had turned it into a rose garden after she purchased the estate.

There were so many new experiences for me back then he would muse. *I couldn't wait to see what the next day might bring.*

He was also attracted to the garden by the "grand old man", which stood just outside the iron fence. This was a 60 foot high cooper beech tree that had been transported over Long Island Sound by the previous owner of the estate. The tree's circumference was over 17 feet. Hollis and Sebastian loved to disappear into its low lying branches for hours at a time when they were boys. Frank was the first to refer to the Beech as the grand old man after being told that the tree was estimated to be over 100-years-old. The only way to determine the exact age was to count the rings on the inside of the trunk. This could only be done after its demise, an event that no one was eager to see transpire. One summer the old man had a fungus, and those at Fairhaven feared the tree would be lost. Frank worked feverishly with a specialist Olivia hired to save the beech.

"Can't kill nothing that won't die," Frank remarked after they succeeded.

He refused to trim back the branches that encroached on the garden after the tree's near death experience. As a result, some of the plants received little or no sunlight. Since all the inhabitants of Fairhaven were so grateful the beech had survived, there were no objections to this. Doctor Simms found that sitting in the presence of a living thing which had persevered for over a century had an uplifting effect on him. He was about to meet the spirit of a living being who had survived for just as long.

Hollis enjoyed walking the grounds of the estate after dinner. Simms was doing so one evening when he came upon the garden. The doctor walked up to the gate with the intention of going inside, but stopped as soon as his hand grasped the handle to open it. Hollis had caught a brief glimpse of a woman in black with long, flowing hair in the darkness. The image barely lingered long enough for him to realize that someone was there. She was like a wisp of translucent vapor carried by the gentle breeze passing through Fairhaven on that evening. A sudden burst of light consumed the woman, and she was gone. Hollis stood there for a long time after but saw nothing else unusual. He finally attributed the experience to his imagination and walked away.

Three days later Hollis walked past the garden once again. There was a half moon in the sky, so he could see much more clearly on this evening. As Hollis approached the garden he saw a flash of white light illuminate a figure near the rose bush in the back. The woman was bent over and seemed to be searching for something. He carefully moved closer.

"Hello there," he said in greeting. "Can I help you?"

The stranger looked up at him with a startled expression on her face. She backed away from Hollis, and much to his amazement, disappeared into the darkness beyond the confines of the fence. A flash of blinding light superseded her departure. He stepped inside and examined the place where the apparition had appeared to leave the enclosure. The iron fence was still intact. There was no logical way to explain what he had seen.

Hollis Simms believed that there was more to existence than that which could be detected through the five senses. He was certain one had the opportunity to move on to another level of conscientiousness after this life was over. Hollis did not believe in ghosts, however. He reasoned that if a person could come back to revisit the places and people from their former lives, the world would have been inundated with such visitors long ago. Most people would have many things left to say to those they loved, and those they despised. The recently departed would also be expected to have a strong desire to visit the places dear to their hearts. Since the accounts of their appearances were so rare, Hollis decided they could not be real. Yet now he felt obligated to reconsider his position on the subject.

For several nights he returned to the garden without seeing the woman. Hollis was about to write off the experiences as being the result of a fatigued mind when she appeared once more. This time Hollis stopped well short of the fence. He watched her search the ground for several minutes before speaking. There was a phosphorescent glow about her that faded after several moments.

"Hello there. Can I help you?"

The woman raised her head and stared at Hollis with the most piercing green eyes he had ever encountered. Her dark hair was now in long braids, and was in striking contrast to the apparition's pale, grayish skin. She wore the attire of a house servant. This was in conflict with a theory Hollis had been formulating in his mind. He was anxious to find out who the interloper was, but knew that his attempt to do so should not be too abrupt.

"You look as though you've lost something," he continued. "Perhaps I can be of some assistance."

The woman in black moved backwards, but did not disappear. The apparition seemed to be floating along the ground instead of walking on it. She carefully observed her questioner.

"What's your name?" Hollis finally asked her.

"Well, sir, I do not think it would be appropriate to give you my name. You are the stranger here. Are you a friend of Mr. Ellsworth?"

Hollis was delighted to receive a response. He thought about pretending to know the person she had mentioned in order to convince the woman he belonged here. Yet that would be dishonest, and therefore an unacceptable way to begin a relationship.

"I'm not familiar with him. Who is he?"

"Only the owner of Fairhaven," she replied with an incredulous grin.

"I'm afraid you're mistaken. My wife and I have owned this estate for over twenty years. My name is Hollis Simms."

The woman looked at him with a bewildered expression on her face.

"Mr. Ellsworth has sold his home? Then I am the trespasser. I apologize, sir. I will leave at once."

"There's no need to do that," Hollis quickly replied. "You're welcome here. I'd just like to know your name."

"Angelica Barton, Mr. Simms."

She was the author of the diary.

She thinks that Ellsworth still owns Fairhaven, so Angelica must also believe that she's still in the 1800s. I wonder if this spirit knows she's dead, Hollis thought to himself.

"The trees here remind me of home," Angelica told him. "Especially that one. I played in a tree just like it as a child."

She pointed to the grand old man, which had been here during Angelica's lifetime.

"You're from Boston, aren't you?" Hollis asked with a smile.

"How did you know that?"

Hollis was about to mention the diary, then thought better of the idea. This woman might not be comfortable with the idea of someone knowing her innermost thoughts. He would have to gain her trust first before broaching that subject. The doctor came up with another explanation instead.

"I recognize your accent, even though it's not very pronounced."

"That's because I've lived in many different places," she explained. "But I was thinking of Boston when I mentioned home before. The beautiful trees here remind me of the ones that Mayor Lyman had planted along the commons when I was a girl."

There was a distinct melancholy in her voice as she thought back to the days on Tremont Street. Angelica Barton had lived in a townhouse there with her father and nanny. Her mother had died while giving birth to her only child. As a young girl she clung to her father, which became increasingly difficult to do as the years went by. Reginald Barton was a man on the rise. He was an attorney who won some very important cases for some equally important people. As his reputation grew his services became in ever-greater demand. Young Angelica saw him less frequently as time went by.

She found her solace in the long afternoons at the Boston Common. Angelica and her friends could often be seen running along the promenade amongst the more casual adult walkers. In the winter they would slide down Flagstaff hill. There was nothing in her early years that compared with the sensation of flying down the steep slope with the frigid air roaring by. These activities filled her days, and made the absence of the child's father tolerable. Then his new found success took the Boston Common, and her friends, away from Angelica.

Reginald Barton decided to spend some of his newly acquired wealth. He bought a mansion on Beacon Hill. The move from Tremont Street to Mount Vernon Street did not involve any great distance. Nonetheless it made his daughter feel as though they had journeyed to the other side of the world. This was due to the fact that Reginald insisted she find new friends in the mansions next to their own while forsaking her old companions. Angelica brooded for a long time, and made few acquaintances among her contemporaries there to spite her father. She was now 16, and was becoming a very strong willed, some would even say difficult, adolescent. In contrast the potential friends who lived in the houses next to her own struck Angelica as being mere contrivances of their parents. Tension grew between father and daughter: the only time there was any affection between the two was when attending Sunday Mass. Angelica loved the emotional release the hymns provided, and could imagine herself as a little girl once more with her then doting father's baritone voice singing the praises of the lord at his daughter's side. Still, she could not help but realize that Reginald had become like the beautiful blue dress he had given her several years before. Angelica loved the garment but had outgrown it, just as she was now outgrowing her father as well.

In Angelica's opinion the only redeeming feature about their new home was a red-haired chambermaid named Cassia Johnson. She was Angelica Barton's age, and had been hired with several others to maintain the much larger home on Beacon Hill. This young girl had an imagination to match Angelica's. She also had a fondness for the wilder side of life. That his daughter had formed such a close personal relationship with one of the servants would have distressed her upwardly mobile father, but he didn't have the time to notice it.

Angelica was reading Godey's Lady's Book one evening when Cassia knocked on the door of her room. She had been invited to the birthday party of another Beacon Hill girl, but claimed to be ill in order to avoid going. Cassia was aware of her ruse, and had come with an alternative suggestion about how to spend that Saturday night.

"We can go down to Ann Street," she suggested. "They'll be dancing down there for sure."

Ann Street was part of the waterfront district. Angelica had never been there, but she had heard all about the raucous nightlife there. The area was notorious for its barrooms and bordellos. While they were filled with disreputable characters, many hard-working souls like Cassia went there for the fiddle playing and spirited dancing. She was fond of the whiskey as well.

Angelica had missed a birthday party for the daughter of one of her father's closest associates. Reginald Barton would be outraged if he discovered that she had gone to Ann Street instead. A year ago or more the threat of his wrath would have stopped her from accompanying Cassia. Presently his influence had become greatly diminished, however. Angelica left the house with the chambermaid.

The bawdy noise from the waterfront reached their ears long before the two women arrived at their destination. Cassia and Angelica entered the first saloon they came to, immediately joining the large crowd of people who were dancing there. The chambermaid fit right in with the other patrons, but her companion drew stares as she danced across the room. They could see that the woman in the striking green dress was unaccustomed to such places. She attracted many suitors, who were very generous when it came to offering her drinks. Angelica politely turned down most of them, as she was not used to spirits at the time.

"Isn't this the best time you've ever had?" Cassia breathlessly asked after a long session on the dance floor.

"It certainly is," Angelica agreed.

A man who was sitting at a nearby table caught her attention. He was a powerful looking individual with a kind face. Angelica asked Cassia who he was, but she had never seen him before. Fortunately for Miss Barton the object of her curiosity walked over and asked for the next dance.

"You don't come here very often, do you lass?" he said to her after they finished dancing and sat down at a table

"No, this is my first time."

"Mine too. I'm from Nantucket."

"Are you a whaler?"

"Yes, ma'am. And what do you do?"

Angelica had never been asked that question before. A woman from a well-to-do family was not expected to do much of anything, of course. Yet that did not make her lack of an answer seem any more acceptable to Angelica.

"So what's your name?" the man asked after realizing he would not receive a reply to his first question.

"Angelica Barton."

"I'm Tom Shanahan. Would you like a taste of my beer?"

Angelica accepted, though it was not her drink of choice. She had been sipping whiskey for most of the evening. They danced a while longer and then Tom suggested that they get some air. Angelica let Cassia know she was leaving. The chambermaid smiled when she saw the whaler.

They walked along the docks and enjoyed the fine summer evening. Tom spoke about his adventures at sea, his exploits soon capturing the young lady's imagination. Angelica could feel the raw power of the mighty ocean as the whaler described his experiences on the water. She then discovered that he was a religious man. The whaler believed only God could protect a man who ventured out on the ocean.

"You're in a little boat on top of a bottomless sea," Tom told her. "And there's a giant monster just below the waves. It could shatter our boat with a flick of its tail. And we're foolish enough to try and kill the beast. That's when you better have the good lord on your side, or you're good as dead. There's not any hope for the lot of us without the lord."

Tom could see he had made an impression on her. He looked into Angelica Barton's eyes and smiled. Their first kiss followed.

"Would you mind if I call you Angie?" he asked her softly.

"Why, of course not."

No one, not even her father, had been that casual about addressing Angelica. Tom Shanahan had managed to create an intimacy between them she had never known before. Their first loving embrace took place against the backdrop of Boston Harbor. Though this was not the first time she had experienced such a moment, it still felt that way to Angelica Barton.

The first man she had kissed was named William Conners. He was working at her father's law firm and had impressed Reginald Barton. He believed William was someone who would become successful in life. His daughter, in her father's opinion, could not hope to do better. Angelica had reluctantly agreed with him at first, but Tom Shanahan had now changed her point of view. The rebellious spirit Angie possessed demanded that she fight for the whaler from Nantucket.

"Yes, I've been to many places," she told Hollis as her thoughts returned to the present.

Hollis understood her statement. Angelica's diary contained a narrative of her travels in addition to the vivid description of how Tom had won her heart. She intended to present him to her father, and deal with Reginald's disapproval by insisting on marrying him. Then, inexplicably, Tom Shanahan left for the western frontier. The young woman wrote of the pain and anguish she experienced after his departure, but did explain why he had abandoned her. There was no further mention of William Conners, though Hollis had always attributed that to her lack of interest in the law clerk.

With the appearance of Angie Barton's ghost he could now discover the reason for Tom Shanahan's defection. Hollis was also curious as to how her diary came to be buried on a Long Island estate.

"How did you meet Mr. Ellsworth?" he asked her during one of their early encounters.

"I work for him. I'm one of his chambermaids."

She turned and walked to the back of the garden, vanishing before his eyes.

That the bright, energetic author of the diary Hollis had found in his youth could come to such a station in life was quite beyond his comprehension. Doctor Simms was determined to learn the reason for this, and also to discover how the young woman's journey on the Oregon Trail had ended. The diary stopped abruptly after Angie reached the Hastings Cutoff, which was far from her final destination.

Hollis Simms sensed that this woman was suffering from a malaise. He was familiar with this condition from his work with a number of other people. The psychiatrist saw Angie Barton as a potential patient. He believed something traumatic had happened to her, and was confident he could help this visitor from the afterlife overcome her current inertia.

All these things contributed to Doctor Simms' decision to accept the fact that the sprit of Angelica Barton had returned to Fairhaven. He knew she was looking for the diary Sebastian was bringing back from Boston. Hollis intended to read through it once more before attempting to treat her.

I can't believe this is really happening, Hollis thought as he looked out at the garden from his office one evening after the white light had appeared once again. *But I guess you can't kill something that won't die.*

CHAPTER THREE

ebastian Simms arrived in Boston. His ride from the airport
through this New England City was an enjoyable one for the
visitor from New York. He had his first glimpse of the city's skyline,
followed by a view of Fenway Park and the Boston Garden. After arriving
at the university the two men walked across the campus to Paul's office,
engaging in casual conversation along the way. Sebastian observed the
students sitting in large groups on the new spring grass. There were also
solitary figures taking advantage of winter's retreat. Simms recalled his
own days as a college student. He envied their freedom and the fact that
these people still had a virtually unlimited number of options available
for their futures.

With his seniority Professor Nustad could have taken any one of
the offices in the history department. Yet Paul chose to remain in the
small office where his career had begun. To say it was disorganized fell
considerably short of doing justice to the numerous piles of papers and
hopelessly cluttered bookshelves. Sebastian suddenly wondered if his
brother's prized possession had been lost forever.

"Look at all these messages," Nustad complained as he sat at his desk.
"These people knew I was going to be away. Why did they call me?"

"They wanted to make sure you had something to do when you came
back."

"And you want the diary," Paul said as he stood up.

Despite the chaos all around him the professor located Angelica Barton's journal with no trouble. He removed it from a stack of books, and then looked at it as though seeing it for the first time.

"There was something I needed to tell you," he said with a perplexed expression on his face. "Well, it will come to me. In the meantime I'll make a copy of it. I promised Hollis I'd have it researched. And I always keep my promises, even if it may take me a very long time to do so. Come with me."

They went down the hall to the Xerox machine where Paul encountered several of his colleagues. They were all anxious to hear about his trip, so Sebastian spent a considerable amount of time listening to Nustad's account of what he had discovered in Europe.

"Thanks for your patience," the professor said to him after he finally began to copy the diary.

"No problem. You really seem to enjoy your work."

"History has always been a passion of mine. Unfortunately, most of the students don't feel the same way. They don't believe that places and people from long ago have any relevancy to their lives. But every so often you get one or two who really make it worthwhile."

He finished duplicating the journal and they returned to his office. Sebastian intended to make a stop on the way back to Fairhaven so he was anxious to leave. Sensing this, Paul intended to send him quickly on his way. Then the professor suddenly remembered what he wanted to tell Sebastian about the diary.

"I had a graduate student start researching it last year. Jack was a bright fellow, but he transferred to a school on the West Coast before making much headway with the diary. But he did learn something about the man who was courting Angelica Barton. His name was William Connors, as I remember. He was found dead near the Charles River. The man she loved, a whaler named Thomas Shanahan, was suspected of being involved, but no charges were ever filed against him. He left for the western frontier soon after, though. Angelica followed him. I don't believe that information is in her diary."

"I'm sure Hollis will be very interested to hear about it. Thanks."

"Jack also found out where Angelica is buried. She's in an old cemetery at the south end of town. Your brother might want to visit it one day."

Paul drove Sebastian back to the airport. Simms thanked him for the diary and then boarded the shuttle to New York. His next destination was going to make for an emotionally difficult experience. He tried to think of something else as the plane climbed into the clear blue sky. Sebastian did not succeed. He then tried reading some passages from Angelica's journal, but they failed to distract him.

Simms arrived at the door of the apartment that Clare had shared with him for the past five years. Sebastian hesitated when he heard someone inside. He expected her to be at work at this time of day. The former occupant thought about leaving, but then realized this moment could not be avoided indefinitely. Sebastian put his key in the lock and opened the door.

Clare was sitting on the couch using her lap top computer. Though they had lived together for years, the two of them now looked at each other with the expression they usually reserved for strangers. The silence between them was unbearable. Sebastian finally spoke.

"I thought you would be working," he said apologetically. "I just came by for the rest of my things."

"I decided to work at home today. Come in."

"So how have you been?"

"Good. I've been working like a dog, though. I spoke with Hollis on his birthday. Did he tell you?"

"Yes. He really appreciated the call."

"What's that in your hand?"

Clare had noticed the diary. Sebastian did not want to risk leaving it in his car.

"Oh, this is something Hollis found when we were boys. It's the diary of a woman who traveled to the western frontier. He had loaned it to a friend, and I picked it up for him. I have a lot of time on my hands these days."

"Well, you don't have to!"

Sebastian cursed himself for making that remark. Their strained, but cordial conversation suddenly became unsustainable. Clare tried to reign in her emotions once more, but there was no way to restore the civility between them. Sebastian quickly went inside and gathered up the rest of his possessions. Clare tried to look away when he returned.

"I'm sorry about everything," Sebastian told her as he placed his key to the apartment on the coffee table. "But I can't just eat shit and rollover for a paycheck."

"So don't!" Clare turned and faced him. "You can get another job! You still have a chance to save your career. What happened...well, it happened. You just want to give up on yourself. And by doing that, you're giving up on us, too."

Her eyes pleaded with him to reconsider. Sebastian walked over and kissed Clare's forehead. Then he walked towards the door.

"We can work this out. I'll call you," he told Clare without turning to face her.

She remained mute as he left the apartment.

Sebastian started driving back to Fairhaven. He felt as though everything valuable in his life had suddenly been taken from him by some stealthy thief in the night. A bagel shop caught his eye and the wounded man walked inside with the diary in hand. Food had managed to quell his despair during the other crises of his life. Sebastian believed a hot bagel could do so now. He ordered one with a cup of coffee before sitting down at one of the tables. The bewildered expression on his face caught the attention of the owner.

"You must have had a rough day," he said to Sebastian.

"I just got back from a trip. So I'm dragging."

"My name is Sam Turner. I own this place. My coffee will pick you up. It's stronger than battery acid, but tastes a hell of a lot better. I know how you feel. The manager of the store quit on me, and I haven't had a moment's peace in three weeks."

Sebastian suddenly noticed the *help wanted* sign behind the counter. Until that moment he had been aware of nothing, due to his draining encounter with Clare.

"Why did he quit?" he asked the owner aloud. Then to himself *you probably tried to force him to take the blame for a batch of bad bagels. You swine!*

"His wife wanted to move to Florida."

Sebastian Simms did something now that was just as spontaneous as his walking into the bagel shop had been. The former investment analyst suddenly saw an opportunity to show his former lover just how disinterested he was in having a career. Sebastian did not understand why he felt compelled to make this point. The younger Simms intended to have Hollis explain his behavior one day.

"I'd like to apply for the job," he told Sam.

"Okay. Come in the back. I'll give you a form to fill out."

Sebastian completed the paperwork and waited for Sam to review it. The owner of the bagel shop was understandably surprised that someone with the applicant's background would be interested in the position.

"You could do much better. I can't pay you much, especially compared to what you used to make."

"That's fine, Sam. I just want to do something simple, without all the political bullshit."

"Well, why not? If it turns out that you're really hiding from the FBI or something, then at least we'll have the excitement of watching your capture. And believe me, this place could use it."

Sebastian drove back to his brother's house. He presented the diary to him, and received a grateful smile in return. Hollis went into his office and the younger Simms followed.

"Paul said to tell you there had been some research done on it," he informed him. "It seems the man who had been courting the diary's author was found dead near the river. Another man whom she really loved was suspected of murdering him, but never charged. Paul said he left for the frontier anyway, and Angelica Barton followed him."

"Very interesting," Hollis replied. "Let's have a brandy to celebrate the return of Angie's diary. Then you can join us for dinner."

"Paul did make a copy of it," Sebastian told him. "So he might have some more revelations for you later on."

"I hope so," Hollis said thoughtfully as he handed him his glass. "There are many things I don't know about the young lady."

They finished their drinks and joined the rest of the family for dinner. Olivia was very affable towards her unexpected houseguest. She asked him about his trip, and then politely inquired about his plans for the future.

"I've accepted a position," he responded proudly.

"That's good to hear. Where will you be working?" Olivia asked him.

"I'm now an employee of The Always Fresh Bagel Shop. I start tomorrow."

"You're working at a bagel shop?" she asked him incredulously.

"You're really on the way up, Uncle Sebastian," Annabelle remarked.

Hollis was as surprised as the other two people at the table. He recovered quickly, however.

"There is dignity in all work," the doctor observed.

"Absolutely," Sebastian concurred.

"Well, perhaps a change will be good for you," Olivia remarked before leaving the room. "I've some phone calls to make. It's good to see you again."

Annabelle soon followed, and made a point of rolling her eyes towards the ceiling as she did so.

"I must say I'm surprised," Hollis said.

"Well, like you said, there's dignity in all work."

"True. But this is like an airline pilot deciding to run a ride at an amusement park."

"I just want to get away from the financial markets for a while. Besides, even if I wanted to get back into investing, there aren't many opportunities around right now. And I have a black mark on my resume."

Hollis Simms struggled against his inclination to offer professional advice. He had dealt with many patients over the years who had abandoned their chosen paths in life due to a single setback. In Hollis's experience the one constant among them was the remorse these people felt years after making their decision. He did not want his brother to find himself in that situation. Yet Hollis also did not want to treat Sebastian in the same manner as he would a patient.

"You're about to give me advice," his younger sibling said with a wry smile. "I appreciate it, but it isn't the right time. I just want to do something uncomplicated now."

"Understood. Allow me just one question, though. Do you know anything about bagels?"

"They're round, there's a hole in the middle of them, and they're delicious. What else do I have to know? That's the beauty of this job."

"You know your product," Hollis said with a grin.

"I'll find an apartment in town, since I know where I'll be working."

"You're welcome to use the old house for as long as you want, Sam. I have to review some cases for tomorrow. Have a good night."

"You too."

Sebastian walked back to his current residence and turned on the television. There was nothing to be found there that was intriguing enough to clear his mind. So he decided to explore the attic instead. Sebastian used a long pole to open a trap door in the ceiling and then climbed up to it on a ladder. The Simms' possessions had long since been removed from the attic, with one exception. Sebastian found an old chess set there. He removed it from its case. The pieces inside were the ones that the Simms brothers had played with during their youth. All the emotions that had been generated by recent events suddenly overwhelmed him. Sebastian Simms cried for the first time in many years.

When I was living here as a boy it seemed like there was nothing I couldn't do he thought in despair. *What happened?*

The sound of the front door opening forced him to regain his composure.

"Sam?" the voice of Frank Martin echoed through the house.

"I'm up in the attic, Frank."

The groundskeeper climbed up the ladder to join him. He was carrying a six pack of beer, and offered one to Sebastian. The current occupant of the house gladly accepted.

"I just wanted to say hi to my new neighbor."

"That's nice of you. I don't know how long I'll be here, though."

"Where did you used to live?'

"In Manhattan. But I lost my job and my girlfriend kicked me out."

Frank shook his head sympathetically.

"A woman ain't never happy to hear that the money is gone. Why did your boss throw your ass out?"

"It's a long story. The guy I worked for needed someone to blame for something."

"That's why I like working for Mr. and Mrs. Simms. They just tell you what they want. There ain't no bullshit about it."

"I'm hoping that working for Sam will be the same way."

39

"I thought you were Sam," said Frank with a puzzled expression on his face.

"No, Hollis thinks that's my name, but it isn't. The Sam I'm talking about owns a bagel shop. I start working for him tomorrow."

"Oh. What's this?"

"It's a chess set. Hollis and I used to play up here all the time. It brings back a lot of memories," Sebastian said in a distinctly melancholy tone.

"Oh, yeah. My grandma used to play. I never really knew what she was doing with those knights and kings and shit. But she taught me a little."

"Would you like to play a game?"

"Sure. You'll kick my black ass, but what the hell."

Soon after the game began Sebastian discovered that he had been lied to. Frank knew more than just a little about the game of chess. He had managed to acquire the advantage just as the beer ran out. The groundskeeper offered to get some more.

"That's a good idea," Sebastian agreed, "because I'm the one who's getting his ass kicked. I need the alcohol to numb the agony of my defeat."

"Oh, hell, I'm just getting lucky. I'll be right back."

Sebastian stood up and walked over to the window. The garden was visible from his vantage point. He saw Hollis standing outside the wrought iron fence, and another person standing inside. This unfamiliar figure was a woman dressed in black. There was something unusual about her appearance. The woman's skin was an unearthly grayish-white, and it seemed to reflect the light from the half moon shining down on the garden.

Sebastian turned and moved quickly towards the trap door. The exit from the attic was suddenly closed before he reached it. Frank Martin had returned.

"What are you doing? Let me out of here!"

Frank did not reply. Sebastian heard him leave through the front door and then watched through the window as he returned to his home.

Hollis Simms had returned to his office with the intention of preparing for the next day's sessions. He began to review the various cases, but his attention soon wandered to the garden outside the window. There was nothing out of the ordinary to be seen in the soft twilight. Hollis finished his work and then glanced outside once more. The darkness had fallen, and the moon was slowly rising above the trees. Suddenly there was a brief but brilliant flash of white light in the garden. Hollis caught a glimpse of a solitary figure illuminated by the dazzling streamer.

Angelica Barton had returned. She had not appeared for over one week, and Hollis had begun to fear that the apparition would never come back. He had devised a plan for their next encounter, and would now have the chance to implement it. Hollis could barely contain his excitement as he walked towards the front door.

Doctor Simms had decided to tell Angelica that he had read her diary. If the psychiatrist believed she would appear on a regular basis, he would never have tried to accelerate their relationship in this way. Given the unpredictability of her visitations, however, he saw no choice. Hollis would reveal to Angelica that he had found her chronicle, read it, and then loaned it to a friend for study. The doctor then intended to assure the apparition that he would get the journal back for her, but since his friend was out of the country, her missing writings could not be retrieved for quite some time. In the interim, Hollis hoped the lure of her recovering the diary would keep Angelica coming back to the garden, where he could delve further into the details of the woman from Boston's westward journey. Hollis could then use their time together to discover why she had become an ordinary house servant.

His approach also called for developing intimacy in their relationship by requesting permission to address her as *Angie*. According to her diary, Tom Shanahan had been the first to do so. Angelica had written about how his informal manner had affected her. Hollis thought at first she might misinterpret his request as an attempt to begin a romance. Then he reasoned that since Angelica Barton had not been of flesh and blood for over one hundred years, the thought of such a liaison with someone who was among the living would never occur to her.

Hollis started to walk outside when he realized that there was another matter to consider. The garden was close to the old house, which was where his brother now resided. Sebastian might catch a glimpse of the ghost. Hollis called Frank to ask for his help.

"I just want you to keep him occupied for a while. I have something to do outside, and I'd prefer to do it alone."

"Yes, sir, Mr. Simms, I'll keep his ass in the house."

"Thank you, Frank. And please call me Hollis."

"Damned if somebody didn't hit me with the stupid stick! You keep telling me that, and I keep forgetting."

Hollis walked out to the garden and smiled at the visitor there. Angelica looked up from her search, acknowledging his presence without smiling. The delicate roses that surrounded her were enveloped by the soft moonlight.

"Can I help you look for something?" he asked her.

"No, I don't think so. But it's kind of you to offer, sir."

"I think I know what you're looking for."

Angelica stopped looking at the ground, instead directing her gaze at Hollis. The piercing green eyes of the spirit struck him like a physical blow. Yet as he was accustomed to such reactions from his other patients the expression on the doctor's face did not change.

"Your diary was buried in the garden. I found it there many years ago."

Angelica Barton recoiled. The revelation that this strange man had a chronicle of her most intimate thoughts in his possession appeared to perturb the ethereal being. Then she looked into the eyes of Hollis Simms and saw only kindness there. That dissuaded her from disappearing into the night.

"I would like it back at once, sir. You only happened it upon by chance. It belongs to me."

"Why did you bury it?"

Angelica hesitated before responding, leading Hollis to believe her answer was not entirely truthful.

"A servant's quarters are not the safest place for one's valuables," she explained. "I put it here so no one would take my diary."

"I recently loaned it to a friend of mine to study. He's an historian, and was very interested in your journey."

Angelica Barton stomped her feet, and walked towards the back of the garden. Many who knew Miss Barton in her lifetime would have recognized that gesture, for she never hesitated to make her displeasure known. Hollis feared for a moment that she would leave Fairhaven forever. Much to his relief, Angelica turned to address him once more.

"I suppose you have read it as well. I can't blame you for doing that, since you did not know to whom it belonged. Please return it at once."

She used a demanding tone of voice, her eyebrows arched in striking crescents.

"The friend I loaned the diary to is traveling abroad at the moment. But I will get it back for you, I promise. In the meantime could you tell me why you left for the west? As I remember you never explained your reason, or reasons, in your writings. And if I may be so bold, what happened to Thomas and William?"

Angelica considered her response for several moments. She was about to reply when Sebastian Simms came running up to the garden. He had escaped the attic through a window, and then climbed down a tree next to the house. This means of exiting his boyhood home was very familiar to him, since he had often used it to defy his father's curfews. Angelica Barton was frightened away by his sudden appearance. To the amazement of Sebastian she walked towards the back of the garden and vanished into the night. Hollis was furious.

"God damn it! She might never come back!"

"Who...or what was that?" Sebastian asked him with an astonished expression on his face.

Hollis Simms turned and walked to the main house without saying a word. Sebastian went after him, following the doctor into his office.

He had rarely seen him angry. Hollis walked to the window and then returned to his desk. Doctor Simms repeated those movements several times. His older brother's agitated state was very disconcerting to Sebastian. The younger Simms was having difficulty coming to terms with what he had seen in the garden. Hollis had always provided a reassuring voice for him on the occasions when something unsettling entered his life. Now the psychiatrist seemed as rattled as his brother was.

"What was that?" Sebastian asked him once more in a bewildered tone.

Hollis sat in the chair behind his desk. He ran his hands through his hair and gathered himself before responding.

"I believe she is the spirit of Angelica Barton. That's the woman who wrote this diary," Hollis explained as he put his hand on it.

Sebastian was momentarily speechless. He fell into a chair, looking at him with an expression of disbelief on his face.

"Are you telling me that she's a ghost?"

Hollis nodded.

"I don't believe in ghosts," Sebastian told him, as if his statement would dispel the specter forever.

"Neither did I, until now. But this is the sixth time I've encountered her. I've searched the garden for any signs of a hoax. There are none. Therefore I've reached the only logical conclusion. I must say that though your timing left much to be desired I'm glad you saw her as well. I was beginning to wonder about my sanity."

"But the woman who wrote that has to be dead," Sebastian said as he pointed to the diary with a trembling hand. "No one could live this long."

Hollis stood up and looked out the window. He wondered if this beautiful spring night harbored any other surprises.

"I have always believed there was something for us after we die," Hollis said after sitting in the chair behind his desk once again. "My belief was always based on nothing more then intuition until recently. Now I have proof."

"Let's get a camera and take her picture. Better yet, why don't you get one of those people who research this kind of thing here to observe her? Then we'll find out the truth."

"No. She's not just a curiosity to me. I want to help her."

"Help her? How?"

"Did you have a chance to read her diary on the way back from Boston?"

"I thumbed through it."

"Well, I've read it many times. I've also had a great deal of experience with evaluating the emotional state of individuals. The woman who wrote this diary is not the same woman I met in the garden. Something happened to Angelica Barton during the long journey west, or perhaps after it was over, that changed her. It could be why the spirit we encountered roams the night. I'd like to help her find peace."

Hollis spoke about her as though she was a life-long friend.

"Wouldn't something that significant be mentioned in the diary?"

"Angie stopped writing in it before she reached California. Now I have a chance to find out why. I'd also like to know how she ended up at Fairhaven."

"Well, at least I know why you were so anxious to get the diary back from Paul. Have you told anyone else about her?"

"No. And I wouldn't have told you, either. Frank failed me. He was supposed to keep you occupied."

"He did his best. The son of a bitch even locked me in the attic. Fortunately I still remember how to climb trees. Did you tell her that you have the diary?"

"No. I told her I could get it for her, though. I also said it would take a while, given that the friend who has it is away. Angie knows that I've read it. Telling her that was a gamble, but I think it will pay off."

"Isn't lying to a patient considered a bad thing to do? I mean you could return her diary right now."

"It's a tool to ensure her return. This is a very unusual circumstance. I'm going to have to use a much different approach."

"How do you expect to collect your fee? Does she have any living relatives that you can present the bill to?"

"I never thought about it." Hollis smiled. "But then again I've never been as mercenary as you are, either."

"Me! I work in a bagel shop. You have to let me see her again. I don't believe she's really a ghost. Maybe I'll be able to prove it."

Hollis looked at him carefully. He could not in good conscience deny Sebastian such a remarkable experience. Yet he fully intended to provide Angelica Barton with the assistance that only those in his profession could give. Their conversations would have to be kept confidential.

"It won't present a problem for me if you observe her from a distance. But you can't listen to our conversations. Every patient has the right to privacy."

"Patient? Come on, Hollis. We both know she can't be real. How can you treat her like she's one of your patients?"

Hollis was momentarily embarrassed by his question. He knew his behavior would elicit this kind of a response from any reasonable person.

Doctor Simms had already admitted to himself that his initial acceptance of the ghost's reality was based largely on the infatuation he had experienced in his youth. Now after several encounters with Angie the doctor's empathy with this woman from the past had become the basis for his belief in her existence.

"I know this must sound bizarre to you," Hollis responded. "But I'm not going off the deep end, or losing my grip on reality, or whatever other cliché you care to use. Something extraordinary is happening here. I'm going to take advantage of this opportunity. As I said, you can observe her, but you can't listen in on the sessions. Now, if you don't mind, I have to finish preparing for tomorrow's appointments."

Sebastian was not pleased with the constraints Hollis had put on him. Nonetheless, he knew there was no point in trying to debate the matter. Doctor Simms was not at all flexible when it came to the welfare of his patients. Sebastian said good night as he walked towards the door. Then he remembered another question he had for his brother.

"Did you know Frank can play chess?"

Hollis looked up and smiled at him.

"Yes. I found out one day when he saw the chessboard in the living room. Frank told me he had watched his grandmother play, but that he didn't know very much about the game. He kept claiming to be a novice right up to the moment he defeated me. I suspect he did the same to you."

Sebastian exhibited the same expression as he nodded in reply.

He walked out the door leaving Hollis to his work. Doctor Simms created a file for a new patient that night. Her name was Angelica Barton.

CHAPTER FOUR

ollis Simms walked into the dining room one evening and found Olivia sitting there with a perturbed expression on her face. After glancing at his daughter he understood the reason for his wife's current demeanor. Annabelle was also seated at the dining room table, wearing a paper bag over her head. Hollis pretended not to notice it while taking his seat. He casually began eating his dinner without comment.

"Hollis, don't you have anything to say?" an exasperated Olivia asked him.

"Yes. This salad is delicious."

"I meant about our daughter."

He looked up and observed Annabelle.

"I see what you mean. I think it's quite an improvement."

Annabelle immediately removed the bag from her head.

"Daddy!"

"I was only kidding, dear," Hollis told her. "Now tell me why you're imitating a New Orleans Saints fan."

"A who fan?" his daughter asked.

"They're an NFL team. Years ago the Saints were so bad it drove some of the people who attended their games to wear a paper bag over their head."

Olivia rolled her eyes. Sports were, in her considered opinion, simply a waste of time.

"I just feel embarrassed by all this," Annabelle explained. "I mean, there are people starving in the world, and we have a banquet every night. There are people dying because they can't pay for drugs. And we have more money than we'll ever need."

"So you're embarrassed to eat with us," Olivia said angrily.

"It has nothing to do with you two," her daughter replied.

"I find that difficult to believe, since your father and I are the only other people at the table."

Hollis looked at Olivia with an expression that pleaded with her for restraint. Then he spoke.

"I understand what you're trying to say, Belle. There are many unfortunate people in this world without enough to eat. And there are many who cannot afford the proper care. We are very fortunate and do not take it for granted. Your mother, along with your grandfather, is trying to help those people who are in difficult circumstances. They run a foundation that supports various charities. In fact we met at one of its charitable functions. Perhaps you can tell Belle about the good work it does, Olivia. Your mother even spoke with President Clinton on one occasion."

She hesitated for a moment. The Reese Foundation had always been a very secretive organization. This was not because Elliot and Olivia were embarrassed by their generosity. They were instead concerned about being inundated by requests for financial aid.

"That's a good idea, Hollis. But of course you must promise to keep the details about the foundation's work confidential."

"You're afraid that the IRS will find out that the foundation doesn't give away as much as you say it does," Annabelle replied with a smirk.

Hollis fought the urge to laugh. His wife was not amused, however.

"That is not true," Olivia said and slammed the table for emphasis. "The reason is we can't solve every problem in the world. And if word got out about the causes we do contribute to the Reese Foundation would be besieged by requests from all the other organizations. Besides, we give plenty to the IRS as well. They're one of our favorite charities."

Annabelle rolled her eyes, but finished the rest of her meal in silence. She picked up her headgear and left the table somewhat mollified by her parents' response to their daughter's concerns. Hollis and Olivia had coffee in the living room afterwards.

"So how was your day, darling?" she asked him. "I haven't had the chance to ask you."

"Hectic, but not too difficult," Hollis replied.

There had been an emergency sandwiched between his regular appointments. One of his patients had found himself in a hopeless depression over his wife's defection. Hollis was concerned about the man becoming suicidal. Fortunately he benefited immensely from their emergency counseling session, and was able to overcome his despair. Hollis was not inclined to provide any of these details to his wife. The doctor believed in leaving his day outside the door when he returned home.

"I hope our daughter doesn't grow up to resent us," Olivia said thoughtfully after taking a sip of coffee. "Sometimes I think it's inevitable."

"I don't think she'll turn out that way. Belle is just reaching the age where she is beginning to understand the world around her. That makes her question who she is, and who we are as well. Your daughter will always love you, dear."

They enjoyed a long embrace. Hollis ran his fingers through Olivia's hair. She was already wearing her summer-cut, much to her husband's disappointment. He secretly missed his wife's longer locks. Hollis then excused himself and walked into his office. He started to prepare for the next day's sessions, all the while glancing out the window for a glimpse of Angie. Having completed his task the psychiatrist decided to walk outside. He saw a flickering light in the garden, and approached it carefully. Angelica Barton had appeared once more. This was his first encounter with her since Sebastian had interrupted them.

"It's a lovely evening, isn't it?" Hollis said as he approached the wrought iron fence.

"Yes it is, Mr. Simms."

Hollis started to move closer but quickly stopped when she withdrew. Angelica was apparently intent on keeping some distance between them. Hollis sat down on the large rock that was some twelve feet from the garden. The breeze created a pleasant rustling sound as it moved through the leaves of the grand old man.

"I think you should call me Hollis."

Angie ceased her pacing and eyed him carefully.

"You are a stranger, sir. The only thing I know about you is that you've acquired Mr. Ellsworth's home."

"I'm a psychiatrist. I help people who can't cope with their emotions."

"You must be a very accomplished one to own Fairhaven."

"My wife made that possible. Her family is very wealthy."

"Did they come by their fortune honestly?"

"Yes, they did. Her father started a chain of stores. He was able to sell them for a considerable amount of money."

"A chain?"

"By that I mean several stores selling the same products in different locations."

She studied Hollis intensely once more. Something in his demeanor apparently met with her approval. For the first time a faint smile crept across her formerly stoic face.

"I will call you Hollis," she told him.

"Thank you," he replied with a smile. "I would like to call you Angie."

She was taken aback by his forwardness. Then she recovered and took stock of this man from the present once more.

"You seem to have a way of overcoming a stranger's defenses," she observed with admiration in her voice. "Although I'm not really a stranger to you because you've read my journal. And I must say you've been rather forthcoming about the details of your own life. So I guess there would be no harm in your using my nickname. As you know, the first person to address me in that manner was very dear to me."

"Yes, I do. Whatever happened to Tom?"

Angie turned away and gathered her emotions. Even after one hundred years this was still necessary when she thought about Tom Shanahan. For this woman from Boston speaking of her lost love evoked an ocean's worth of memories, some painful and some sublime. She turned to face Hollis. The answer to his question emerged from her like a flood, a torrent of recollections colored with the emotions from those bygone days. She had apparently concluded that since Hollis had already become familiar with many of her innermost thoughts and desires there was no reason to keep most of the others from him. Angie began to tell her story.

Angie Barton told Hollis that she did not see Tom Shanahan for quite some time after their first encounter on Ann Street. As a whaler he spent many months, in some cases over a year, at sea. He had made that fact quite plain to the young woman from Beacon Hill on their first night together, but she had been too smitten by this larger than life seaman to heed his warning. To compensate for his absence, Angie spent the next several months enjoying wild nights on the waterfront. She was able to hold the modest amounts of liquor the men bought for the young woman with the striking green eyes, never letting any of them steal more than a brief embrace.

On other evenings Angelica was in the company of William Conners. She was genuinely fond of the clerk from her father's law office. He made an amicable and respectful beau. William wanted only to settle down to raise a family with Reginald Barton's daughter. Angie might have been persuaded before meeting Tom, but now her perception of what life could offer had changed forever.

Her father began to comment on how slow his prodigy was in concluding their courtship. He did not know that William had all but proposed to Angelica on one occasion, only to be put off in a firm but polite fashion. Reginald decided to speak with the young man himself. He was unaware of his daughter's true state of mind at the time, and would have been shocked to learn that a common seaman had captured her heart. Reginald Barton learned of his daughter's reluctance during a long conversation with William Connors. He intended to discuss it with her that evening, but upon arriving at the mansion Reginald discovered that Angelica was gone.

Cassia had delivered an urgent message from Tom earlier in the day. Having just returned from an extended journey, he was anxious to see Angie. Miss Barton replied by suggesting they meet at Christ Church, better known as the Old North Church. She did so for a romantic reason. The church's spire, in addition to sending a very important signal during revolutionary times, was also famous for guiding vessels into the harbor. Angie believed it would guide Tom to her as well.

They met there on a warm spring evening. The sailor inspired her with his tales of life on the open ocean. He was the man who stood in the front of the small whaling boat patiently waiting for the great beast to emerge from below the waves. When the leviathan finally appeared he threw his harpoon, daring to attack it despite the whale's overwhelming size. One twitch of its tail would have sent Tom and the rest of the men in the boat to their deaths. Still they had prevailed, returning from the ocean unscathed. Later Angie accompanied him to a secluded spot near the Charles River.

"Why did you stop?" Hollis asked after she became silent.

Angie had reached the point in her story where she had made love for the first time. Though the apparition felt very comfortable speaking to the doctor up till now this subject was much too personal to include in her narrative. The author of the diary almost blushed when recalling the night she became a woman. The experience had convinced Angelica Barton that only a man who regularly defied death could evoke the greatest depths of passion within her. Angie's feet had never touched the ground as she floated home to the mansion on Beacon Hill.

"We had a very pleasant evening," Angie finally said with a coy expression on her face.

Then she continued her story.

"You were out late tonight," the barrister had remarked when she walked through the door of the mansion.

"It was such a beautiful night. Cassia and I took a walk around the commons."

Her father was sitting in front of the fireplace. He motioned for her to sit in the chair next to his and Angie obliged him. Reginald Barton was a very intimating man, yet his daughter had never been frightened of him. This was especially true on this night. Her encounter with Tom had left Angie feeling as though she was invincible.

"I think Cassia is a good worker, and a nice person," Reginald told her as he produced a large cloud of smoke with his pipe. "But I don't believe that she's someone you should be socializing with. We've a reputation to uphold now. Do you know what I mean?"

The warm glow enveloping Angie vanished when her father denigrated Cassia. The verve that Hollis found lacking in her apparition was very much alive within Angelica Barton a hundred years before.

"I do not believe it is your place to choose my friends," she shot back. "Cassia is a fine person, and is not hindered by the pretensions plaguing the others on Beacon Hill."

Reginald was momentarily stunned by her reply. Angelica had never addressed him in such a caustic tone of voice.

"I am surprised you're even aware that you have a daughter," she continued. "I feel as though I've been living alone for many years now."

"I won't have you speak to me that way!" Reginald stood up and towered over her.

Angie stared at him without moving. Her father regained his composure.

"I know I've been inattentive, child. But I had the chance to further my interests and yours as well. We are looked up to in this town now. And there's a young man with a bright future who wants to marry you. William is going to follow in my footsteps. Why are you turning him away?"

She stood up and walked over to the fireplace. Angie was considering her next words very carefully, for she knew that admitting her love for a man who was below their social position would create a horrific scene. Angie was not yet ready to provoke such a quarrel. While she would never be cowed by the barrister, Reginald's daughter was well aware of how difficult life could become if she invited her father's wrath.

"Because I do not love him," she explained while turning to face him. "I won't marry just for convenience or to suit anyone but myself. Good night."

Angie left him, all the while expecting to be summoned back at any moment. Reginald Barton allowed his daughter to retreat to her room, however. He spent another hour smoking his pipe and wondering why Angelica was being so difficult. Reginald twirled his handle bar mustache as he contemplated his daughter's behavior.

During the next two months Angie spent most of her time at the mansion. Occasionally she would take long walks on Boston Common, but because of Reginald's interest in her activities she did not return to Ann

Street during that time. Angie did not want to risk making him suspicious unless it was unavoidable.

Then Tom Shanahan returned once more, inspiring her to throw caution to the wind. William had followed Angelica on one of those nights when she had declined his dinner invitation. He watched as she arrived at the church and met the whaler. William then followed them from a discreet distance as they walked to their secluded spot on the river.

Connors waited for them to leave. Angelica left without Tom Shanahan on this particular occasion. Her lover had decided to take advantage of the pleasant spring night and sleep by the river. The clerk now had an opportunity to confront the sailor alone. William watched her begin the long walk to Beacon Hill, and then approached Tom just before he closed his eyes.

"You are not to see that woman again, sir," he told him after Tom stood up.

Shanahan was not intimidated, being a much stronger man than the slightly built future lawyer was.

"And what business is it of yours, mate?" he responded.

"I'm Angelica's intended. We have a future together. You will not ruin it for her."

"Would you like a drink?" Tom asked him with a smirk on his face.

He bent down and took the cork out of the whiskey bottle with his teeth. William refused the bottle when the sailor offered it to him.

"So you think you're a better man than me?" Tom questioned him. "Well, I'm not saying that isn't so. But I've never heard Angie mention your name."

William looked at him with utter disdain.

"A young woman cannot be expected to accurately judge the quality of people," he replied. "That's why her father has chosen me for his daughter. I will marry her, and you will return to Nantucket. If you can't be persuaded by my words, perhaps this will convince you."

William Connors drew a gun from his coat, looking at Tom with an expression intended to convince him that he would use the weapon. Shanahan had not taken him very seriously up until that point. Tom now allowed his instinct for survival to dictate his actions. His outward demeanor did not change, yet his movements had a purpose William could not detect.

"That's a mighty nice gun, lad. And it's certainly given me something to think about."

He picked up the whiskey bottle as if to take another drink. Then Tom threw it at William while at the same time lunging at him, keeping low to the ground as he did so. William fell backwards as a single shot rang out. Tom Shanahan stood over him and realized he was dead.

"My God!" he said while wringing his hands. "I've killed this man!"

The sailor ran off into the night, believing that the authorities would never listen to his explanation for Conner's death.

Angelica Barton had a large breakfast the next morning. This had become her custom after spending an evening with Tom. Her father had left for the law office very early that day, as was his custom no matter what the night before had entailed. Angie was surprised to see his carriage return before she was done eating. He walked inside and looked at his daughter with a somber expression on his face.

"I've some terrible news for you, Angelica. William Conners is dead."

She looked at him in disbelief. Though Angie had never been interested in having a romantic relationship with William, she was fond of him. Tears began to flow down her cheeks. Reginald fumbled as he tried to find the words that would comfort his daughter. Her father could not, nor could he do so after the young man's funeral. Angie desperately wanted to see Tom, but he had returned to Nantucket for another voyage.

The following months were painful ones for Angelica Barton. The young woman tried to avoid all the places where she had spent time with William. This was extremely difficult to do, however, since many of those evenings had been spent in front of the large fireplace in the living room. The constant discussions about who his killer might have been did not help her forget his death either. The authorities had no clue as to who committed this terrible crime. The town was in an uproar, as would be expected when the life of a well-respected young man had been violently cut short.

Angie struggled to cope with her grief. For the first time that she could remember, Reginald was very attentive to her needs. This hardly compensated for the absence of Tom Shanahan, but was still greatly appreciated. Then on a beautiful mid-summer's eve Cassia delivered a note from her lover. Instead of meeting him at Christ Church, it said he would be waiting for her at the opposite end of town. Angie was breathless with anticipation as she made the short journey to meet him. He was sitting on a carriage block in front of a private residence when she arrived. The sadness in his eyes quelled her excitement.

"Is there anything wrong, my love?" she asked him after a hurried embrace.

Tom looked at her as if he was seeing Angie for the last time.

"I've done a terrible thing, lass," he said somberly. "I killed William Conners."

He gave a detailed account of their struggle.

"But it wasn't your fault," she said hopefully. "William had the gun. You just tried to defend yourself."

Tom shook his head sadly.

"It's not that simple, lass. They'll hang me for sure without even listening to my story. And your father will supply the rope when he finds out we've been together. I have to leave. I have to go somewhere so far away they'll never find me."

"Then I'll go with you," Angie said without hesitation.

Tom gently caressed her face and kissed her softly on the lips.

"You don't want that kind of life, girl. You're too fine for such a rough way of living. I'll be running for the rest of my days."

Angie felt him slipping away from her. She threw herself in his arms. Tom held her for a long time. Then a man came out of the house and spoke to the sailor in an urgent tone of voice.

"We'd best be going. We have to leave before they find out you're back in town."

"Get the horses and bring them here."

Angie was sobbing. Still she was able to gather herself and ask one question.

"Will you still think of me when you sail the ocean?"

"Oh, lass, I can't do that anymore. The good lord won't keep me safe now. Only a man who's at peace with God can ever hope to survive on the sea. I've killed one of the lord's own. I won't sail again."

After a long farewell kiss Tom was gone. Angie stumbled back to Beacon Hill beneath the flickering whale oil lanterns that lit the Boston streets. There she wept in Cassia's arms.

For several months after, Angelica was little more than a living ghost. She moved from room to room in the mansion with no discernable desire or purpose. Her father noticed this, mistakenly concluding that she was distraught over the death of William Conners. He sent other eligible bachelors to call on Angelica, but they were all rebuffed, some not in a very polite fashion.

Then another loss befell her. Cassia had become involved with a local man named Wyatt Flanders earlier that year. They soon became constant companions. One evening she hesitantly knocked on Angie's bedroom door and was invited inside.

"I'm no good at goodbyes," Cassia said. "Wyatt thinks we should go west to California. There's not much for us here, you know. I just hate to leave you, after you've been such a good friend and all."

Angelica got off her bed and embraced the house servant. Earlier that day she had learned that Tom had departed for the western frontier. A friend of his had informed her of this after a few drinks combined with some mild flirtations from Angie. Shanahan intended to settle in San Francisco. Angie was considering following the former whaler before her friend had knocked on the bedroom door. Now she looked at Cassia with her bright green eyes ablaze with anticipation.

"I'll come with you!"

Angie's friend was initially excited about her offer. Cassia would certainly appreciate having Angie with her as she ventured into the unknown lands of the west. Yet Wyatt had warned her about the dangers involved. She could not allow her dearest friend to risk her life.

"But Angie, you have everything here. You can marry any man in Boston. Wyatt and I are going on the trail for a better life. That's the only reason we'd ever go, because it's a dangerous trip to make. We wouldn't do it if there was something here for us."

In light of Tom's circumstance, Angie was reticent to explain why she wanted to travel west. Instead she gave a different reason for wanting to make the trip, though there was more than a grain of truth in it as well.

"I want some adventure in my life, Cassia. I can't just sit here on this infernal hill pretending to be alive. I want to feel the wind in my face, and see the places that few people have yet to see. Now I won't accept *no* for an answer. Tell me your plans."

"Well, we're leaving in a couple of months. Wyatt has a cousin in Ohio who's coming with us. We're riding to his place and then taking a riverboat to Independence. That's in Missouri. I'd love to have you with me. I'd be twice as brave with you by my side. But I'll have to ask Wyatt, of course."

"Tell him that I'm more than willing to share the expenses," Angie informed her with a smile.

Wyatt was eager to have Angie join them, especially since she would be taking her purse on the long journey. She said nothing to her father about her plans. Angelica knew the barrister would not only object to her leaving, but would also send someone after her if he knew where she was going. So Reginald's daughter silently slipped out of the house early on a Monday morning. She then took a horse and carriage from the barn. With a brief look back at the house on Beacon Hill, Angie began her long trek to San Francisco. Suddenly a loud siren assaulted her ears.

"What is that horrid sound!" she asked the doctor.

"It's the siren on a fire engine, or an ambulance. It tells the others on the road to give way. So you left without saying goodbye to your father," Hollis noted.

Angie jerked her chin at the mention of Reginald Barton.

"I saw no reason to make him aware of my plan," she coolly responded.

"Did you ever see him again?"

Angie looked away from Hollis, giving him only silence for her reply. Then she walked towards the back of the garden and disappeared into a blinding flash of light. This session had ended.

CHAPTER FIVE

A week went by without the ghost appearing. Hollis faithfully looked out his window every night but to no avail. He found himself becoming preoccupied with the disappearance of his most intriguing patient. Olivia noticed the change in her husband's demeanor.

"Did you hear me?" she questioned him as they sat at the dinner table one evening.

Annabelle had already finished her meal and departed.

"Excuse me," Hollis lifted his head and replied.

"I said you have to do something about the way Frank is speaking to the plants," Olivia said in an annoyed tone.

"Many people talk to plants. It's said to improve their vitality and growth."

"Frank doesn't just talk to the plants, he threatens them. One day I heard him tell the shrub by the front door that he was going to 'tear its droopy ass out of the ground and use it for a fucking bonfire if it didn't perk up.'"

"Well, it did. It hasn't looked this good since we moved here."

"I can't argue that, but it's simply inappropriate. Mrs. Hollander heard one of his exchanges and was quite shocked by the language he used."

Hollis smiled. He remembered the profanity laced tirade by Constance Hollander after discovering that someone had put a dent in her Mercedes.

Then Hollis quickly put her hypocrisy aside as she did a great deal of work for the foundation. He promised to speak to Frank about toning down his language when there were guests around the house.

"Maybe we should offer Frank's job to Sebastian," Olivia suggested.

"My brother isn't tough enough. The plants and trees would walk all over him."

They retired to the den for coffee. Hollis sat down in a soft red chair. He then leaned his head back and closed his eyes as Olivia occupied an identical chair next to her husband's. The rich brown paneling in this room provided a relaxing environment for the two of them after their respective trials of the day. Etchings of a feudal manor over the crackling fireplace invited their minds to drift into a far away time. Olivia chose to remain in the present, running her fingers through Hollis's hair. She was not sure where her husband's thoughts were at the moment.

"What is it, love?" she asked him. "I can't ever remember seeing you so consumed with your own thoughts."

Hollis had decided not to tell his wife about Angie. He knew her logical mind would produce a long list of reasons why this ghost from the past could not possibly be real. His wife was firmly anchored in the consensus view of what constituted reality. She would suggest Hollis seek the same help he offered to his patients.

"I have a case that is presenting quite a challenge for me," he answered her. "I thought we were making progress, but she has withdrawn. That troubles me greatly."

"Remember when you proposed to me? Do you remember what you said?"

"Yes. I said I would only marry you if you gave me the left side of the bed."

Olivia playfully punched him.

"You said that you wouldn't bring home any problems from your office. And now, Mr. Simms, I'm holding you to that promise."

Olivia kissed him. Hollis laughed and chased all thoughts about Angie from his mind for the moment.

"Do you remember the talk show Harley told you about?" she asked him.

"Yes."

"The host, Robin Wainscot, called here today. She wants to meet you. I think you should see her. It would be a nice diversion from your regular patients."

Hollis was not comfortable with the idea of practicing psychiatry on television. Still, visiting the host could do no harm, and would placate his wife.

"I'll call her back," he told her.

Hollis agreed to meet the talk show host for lunch. Sebastian accompanied him on the ride into Manhattan. He was meeting with some former co-workers at a restaurant there. This was the first time he would see anyone from McDivet Investments since being fired.

"Do I seem nervous to you?" Sebastian asked him.

"Yes, but it's understandable. You're revisiting a very traumatic experience."

"I don't really care about the firm anymore. But I am curious about what's been happening since I left."

"You really want to know if they miss you. Again, it's perfectly understandable."

"I suppose you're right."

Hollis dropped his brother off and drove to the NBC studios. He spoke with the receptionist before taking a seat. Simms observed the various posters on the wall representing the network's television shows. After a brief time Robin Wainscot appeared.

"Doctor Simms," she said in a husky voice.

"Ms. Wainscot. It's a pleasure to meet you."

They shook hands as she led him into her office. There were books and magazines strewn all over her desk. She unceremoniously deposited a large pile of them on the floor before taking her seat. Hollis did the same with the ones on the chair in front of the host's desk before sitting down.

"I've heard a good deal about your work," she began. "After Fox recommended you to our producer I checked up on you. I hope you don't mind."

"Not at all."

"You're regarded as a consummate professional by your colleagues. And they also see you as a humanist. Those two qualities just happen to be exactly the ones I'm looking for in the psychiatrist who will make occasional appearances on my show. I know you're at least a little bit interested because you're here. But are you interested enough to accept my offer?"

"To be honest, Ms. Wainscot, I…"

"The hell with the formalities, just call me Robin. Of course I'll insist on calling you Hollis in return."

"Just as long as you don't insist on calling me anything unflattering," he said with a smile. "I just don't know if I'm the one you're looking for. I'm not a showman. And I do take my profession very seriously."

The talk show host stood up and sat on the corner of her desk. She looked down on Hollis; though intimidating her guest was not Robin's intention.

"I know what most people think of talk shows," she said. "They think it's just a way for millions of bored housewives to kill the day. I'll confess that some of the things we do are not much more than a ploy to bolster our ratings. But having you appear on the show would be a way of offering the viewers something worthwhile. You could reach many people who are afraid to ask for help, or who simply can't afford it. I'll bet the people who wear the 'I'm glad that isn't me' expression after hearing about someone else's psychological problems are secretly saying 'that's just how I feel.' You can reach those people on my show. You'll come into contact with more of them by appearing on television then you ever would through your practice, or at the hospital."

Hollis was intrigued, even though he had already heard that line of reasoning from Harley Fox. This was because Robin had a sincerity about her that was lacking in the movie producer. Dr. Simms had been concerned that becoming involved with daytime television would diminish his reputation, but now he could clearly see a benefit from accepting Robin's offer.

"We don't even allow fighting on *The Robin Wainscot Show*," she added with a smile after watching the doctor mulling over the offer.

"I'm glad to hear that. I'm not very accomplished when it comes to fisticuffs," Hollis told her.

"Neither am I, which is why we don't allow it. It wouldn't be any good for the star of the show to get beaten up. Though come to think of it that might help my popularity."

"Do you intend to have people in the audience ask me questions? Or do you plan to have the people who wish to speak with me as guests on the show?"

"Johnny Mueller and I kicked that around for a while. He's our producer, as I think you know. We decided it would be better to have people call in with their problems, and to grant them anonymity if they want it. We thought the callers would be more likely to discuss serious problems that way. What do you think?"

"It sounds like a good idea. I would also want the calls taken in private before the show. It would allow for the caller's situation to be evaluated beforehand. Some might have problems that are too serious to be discussed before an audience, even anonymously. The person calling in may believe that he or she is comfortable with the arrangement, but deeply regret it later on."

"We thought of doing it that way. But we were only thinking of avoiding prank phone calls. You've come up with a better reason for talking to the callers beforehand. We'll tape the phone calls and play them back during the show. You can give some insight as to how you came to your diagnosis of the caller's problem while it's being played. We also thought you could take some questions from the studio audience as well."

Hollis had visions of becoming an advisor for the lovelorn. He assumed most of the problems presented to him from the audience would be of that nature, since the majority of the people would not want to reveal more serious problems if their identity was to be revealed. Robin understood his concern without being told.

"We can just stick with the phone calls, if you'd like. Now what do you think, doctor? I know we can't tempt you with money. You already seem to have enough of that. But like I said, you could reach a great many people this way."

"I'm very interested. I believe you're sincere about wanting to help people."

Robin paused before answering.

"I am sincere, Doctor Simms. You see as a child I was the little black girl that no one wanted to adopt. I went from foster home to foster home without a glint of love or hope in my life. By the time I was ten, Robin Grange was one messed up little person. Then the Wainscots adopted me.

They were a middle-aged couple who had overcome considerable obstacles to become financially, and socially, successful in Baltimore. The first thing they did was to send me to someone like you. I had developed attachment disorder from constantly being rejected as a child."

Hollis nodded with a sympathetic expression on his face.

"So I just want to give someone else a chance to receive the same kind of assistance that I did."

Robin looked over at the picture of her adopted parents. The talk show host physically resembled them, and could have been their daughter, which in the spiritual sense of that word she actually was.

"Let me have a couple of days to think about it."

"Certainly. Now let me show you the set. Then I'll take you to lunch. What's your favorite place to eat?"

"I already have one difficult decision to make. I'll let you choose."

She took him to one of the most exquisite places in town. Hollis witnessed firsthand what it was like to be a television personality. Robin was besieged by well wishers as she made her way to their table. Though he received only curious glances the doctor was able to imagine himself in her place. Hollis would never have admitted it to anyone, but the idea of being so well-known was becoming appealing to him.

"Do you miss your privacy?" he asked after they were led to their table, which was in a secluded corner of the restaurant.

"If you can find privacy in a public place, it means you're dead in my business," she replied with a laugh. "I hope they never get tired of asking for my autograph. But of course they will. Nothing is forever, Hollis."

"How did you get started?"

"I'd like to say it was because I was a good communicator. But it was actually because I'm a very nosy person. I could sit and talk for hours about what everyone else was doing, because until I received therapy, I rarely had the courage to do much of anything myself."

"I don't believe that."

"You're a nice man. But it's true. So have I convinced you to join the show?"

"I'll need some more time to decide. But I think that it would be an interesting experience for me."

"You simply have to say yes," Robin said as she lifted her glass of wine in a toast. "Otherwise the producer might not agree to pay for the lunch."

Hollis left the studio and picked up Sebastian. His brother was in a somber mood. They drove in silence for some time before he spoke.

"You know, people really suck," Sebastian informed him.

"You sound like Belle. Did your friends fail to show up?"

"All but one of them suddenly had other things to do. Apparently the higher-ups at the firm let it be known that no one was to associate with the pariah. Even Bill Kline, the only one who did come, insisted on going somewhere else to eat."

"I'm sorry. But I'm sure you're not really that surprised. Corporate politics can be very intimidating. Most of those people have families to feed."

In fact, Sebastian was not surprised at all. He knew how the game was played: anyone who was seen as being sympathetic to his plight would be putting their own future in jeopardy. Yet the former employee had managed to convince himself that the people he had worked with for so many years would rise above those concerns for one afternoon. Sebastian had envisioned several hours of reminiscing about the times when they had joined together to overcome obstacles. He had also expected Bill to fill him in on what had transpired at McDivet since his departure.

"Kline was so paranoid he could hardly finish his meal," he told his brother. "He kept looking around to see if anyone from the office was there. It was a complete waste of time."

Though he did not tell Hollis, there was one moment when Sebastian had his undivided attention. That was when he told Bill about his new job. He looked at Simms with an astonished expression on his face. Kline's reaction made Sebastian feel as though he had told him about his brother's ghost.

"So, that's enough about me. What is Robin Wainscot like?"

"She's a pleasant person. And I must say she draws a crowd."

"Are you going to do the show?"

"I told her I'd think about it. I'm tempted to give it a try."

"You should ask your ghost to be on the show. Then it would have the most viewers in the history of television."

"Angie is a patient," Hollis replied.

"I can't figure out how we wound up where we are. I'm working in a bagel shop, and you're not only rich, you're about to become a television star. But you're twice as screwy as I am. You actually believe that some woman from the 1800s has come back to visit you."

"My wife is rich," Hollis corrected him. "I'm only rich by association. Angie came back for the diary, so her being here makes perfect sense. Besides, you've seen her, too."

"I've seen someone, or something. But I'm not going to believe she's real until all other possibilities have been eliminated."

"Suit yourself," Hollis told him as they drove through the gates of Fairhaven. "I believe she's real. I only hope Angie appears again. She's never been away for this long."

A strange expression of longing came over the psychiatrist's face. Sebastian put his own troubles aside for the moment, carefully observing his brother. He had never seen Hollis this emotionally involved with anyone, except his wife and daughter.

Hollis accepted Robin's offer. He soon found himself being recognized on the street by the strangers passing by. The doctor was generous when it came to signing autographs, but he shied away from giving advice. Hollis knew he could do more harm than good by making a snap diagnosis, even for the most mild of psychological problems. Dr. Simms found it difficult to turn these people away, but as a professional there was no choice.

His daughter became his most enthusiastic fan. Annabelle invited her friends over to watch her father appear on *The Robin Wainscot Show*. His only child managed to convey the impression that she was proud of him without ever using the word. Olivia was also impressed by his success, though she made light of his new career at every opportunity. Still, his wife did not fail to notice how the dapper doctor swayed the callers and the audience with his thoughtful analysis of the problems that were presented to him.

Even Mildred Price drove over to Fairhaven to congratulate him. That was, in his opinion, the greatest compliment he had ever received, since the dear old lady risked both her life and her chauffeur's by doing so.

The only negative reaction came from Alec Collins. His peer made it known to everyone who was inclined to listen that Doctor Simms was sacrificing the dignity of the profession by practicing psychiatry on a talk show. He likened it to fast food, only now the product being offered would affect the mind, not the body. Alec wrote an editorial on the subject that appeared in The New York Times. Olivia and Annabelle were furious. Hollis simply shrugged.

"The man is entitled to his opinion. And I have to admit that his argument against doing the show has merit. Though I intend to avoid the pitfalls he mentioned."

Frank also railed against Doctor Collins. He watched his employer on television, even asking Hollis for his autograph, ostensibly for his daughter.

"You don't need no damn Ph.D. to know what jealousy is, Mr. Simms," he told the doctor after reading the article.

"If you don't start calling me Hollis I'm going to start calling you Mr. Martin."

"Oh, right, I keep forgetting. Do you want me to put some sugar in his gas tank the next time he's here?"

"No thank you. I appreciate the gesture, of course, but it would only prolong his visit."

"I didn't think of that."

Sebastian was also enthusiastic about his brother's success. He made sure the television set in the bagel shop was tuned to *The Robin Wainscot Show* whenever Hollis appeared on it.

His first day began with several calls from people who had life problems. These are difficult circumstances that can stress a person with even the strongest of emotional constitutions. Yet there is nothing psychologically wrong with the person who is confronting these dilemmas. The doctor could offer little more than his sympathy. He knew of no technique capable of removing their pain. Hollis began to wonder if he had made a bad decision.

Then a woman who could not cope with the passing of a distant relative called in. Hollis sensed immediately that there was more than the death of a third cousin causing her despair. He spent several hours casually probing the caller's history. The director kept signaling for Robin to put a stop to this much longer than anticipated conversation. She refused; the host instead mimed the words *we'll edit it later*. Wainscot was far too impressed with the Doctor's ability to analyze the caller's feelings to interrupt him. Doctor Simms detected guilt in the woman's voice and inquired about her past.

"So how did you decide to become an accountant?" he asked at one point.

"Well, I was thinking of playing the violin professionally, but my parents almost freaked. And they were right. There are relatively few people in the world that can pay their bills with a violin."

Simms saw the woman as someone who was greatly influenced by her parents. This suggested a scenario he was familiar with.

"When you were a child, did you lose someone close to you?" he asked her.

"Why, yes. My Aunt Fay died while visiting us. She was fine one minute, and then gone the next."

"How old were you?"

"I was six, I think."

"And how did the people around you react?"

"They were sad, of course."

"I meant how did they treat you?"

There was silence on the other end of the phone.

"Were your parents impatient with you?"

"There was one day when my mother yelled at me for spilling a pitcher of lemonade. She said…she said I caused all the problems in the house."

"And the most serious problem at that moment was the loss of your aunt. So she inferred you had caused it. You probably subconsciously believe you were responsible for your cousin's death as well, even though you've grown well beyond the little girl who caused all the problems in the house."

The woman on the phone let out a sob. When the studio audience listened to a truncated tape of the phone conversation there was not a dry eye among them.

"I can't tell you that the loss of anyone you've known, even casually, will ever be easy to understand, or to bear," Hollis told her. "But you should recognize that it wasn't your fault. Sometimes adults inadvertently give the wrong message to children, and often at the worst possible time."

The woman thanked him. Hollis gained a great deal of satisfaction from the session. His decision to appear on the show had been justified. Later that same day a conversation with another caller demonstrated the wisdom of his decision to talk with those seeking his advice before the show.

"Doctor Simms, I have an unusual problem that you may be able to help me with," the man began.

"Can you describe it to me?" Hollis asked.

"You're going to think I'm putting you on, but I'll tell you anyway. I'm being visited by a woman from the future."

For a moment Hollis believed he had received a waggish call. Yet there was something in the man's voice that imparted sincerity. Doctor Simms decided to continue the conversation.

"You've made an extraordinary claim. Can you substantiate it?"

"Not really. I don't have any physical proof."

"How long have you been seeing the woman?"

"About three years."

"And you've decided it's a problem only now?"

"Well, Doctor, it's not really my problem. My boss found some illustrations I drew of the future that were based on her description of it. I had to tell him where the idea for them came from. He thinks I should talk to someone about Avalor. That's the woman's name. I saw you on a commercial for this television show. I thought you might be able to help me. Can you?"

"So you're only contacting me because your employer instructed you to."

"Yes."

"And you'd be willing to have your call broadcast on television?"

"Sure. I've got nothing to hide."

The confidence of this caller impressed Hollis Simms. He was quite comfortable telling a stranger about the visitations, and was even willing to have millions of people hear his story. Doctor Simms believed this person would feel very differently after realizing the woman he mentioned was a product of his delusions. Simms knew Robin would certainly want to put him on the show; the entertainment value would be enormous. Hollis was only concerned with helping the caller, however.

"I think your situation deserves a different approach," he told him. "I'd like to see you in my office."

"What about the cost? My health benefits might not cover your bill."

"I won't charge anything for the first meeting. It will be a consultation."

"That's the right price, doc."

He provided the man with his phone number. Johnny Mueller summoned Hollis and Robin to his office after the call was completed.

"People, this guy is a gold mine," he began after the host closed the door behind them. "The people will eat this up with a spoon."

"Out of the question," Hollis responded. "The caller would be subject to ridicule if someone he knows recognizes him. This man needs confidential help."

"Doctor, I respect your judgment. But you also have to respect mine. This is what having you on the show is all about. I've got to have this guy."

Robin Wainscot had a diminutive physique, yet she still had a presence that could fill a room. The talk show host approached her producer and said:

"The doctor makes this call, Johnny. Nothing that has my name on it will stoop to ruining someone's life for a larger audience. Now back off!"

The tape of that particular phone conversation was quickly erased.

Two days later, Hollis greeted Gregory Hill with a handshake. He offered him coffee but the tall, muscular individual declined. The potential patient sat down without a trace of self-consciousness. Hollis had already read the questionnaire Hill filled out in the waiting room.

"You're a detective. That sounds like interesting work."

"It can be, sometimes. But you also have to deal with a lot of sleaze balls."

"You seem to have been blessed with perfect health."

"You're right about that. I haven't even had a hangnail in thirty-nine years. My only problem is that the boss thinks I'm a few bricks short of a load."

Gregory smiled when he spoke. Hollis was again impressed by his confidence.

"So tell me about this woman you've been seeing."

"Well, her name's Avalor. She's lives in the year 2151."

"When did you first see her?"

"I was walking through the park after a long day at work. It was in the middle of the softest spring shower I can ever remember. She was sitting on the grass. There was something unusual about her. I don't know if it was her eyes, or hair, but something about Avalor caught my attention."

"What was so special about her eyes and hair?"

"Avalor's eyes are a cooper color. And her hair has the richest texture you could ever imagine. She was wearing the most beautiful flowers I've ever seen in it. "

"Do you have a picture of her?"

"No, she doesn't like cameras. She does like my drawings of her, though."

"So, Gregory, what would you like me to do for you?"

"My boss, Dale Sterns, gave me a leave of absence. I had just been promoted to Chief of Detectives and was cleaning out my desk to move into a new office. Dale was helping me. That's how he found a drawing of Avalor I had made. I had it in my desk. I told him who she was, and now Sterns won't let me come back to work until someone like you says that I'm mentally stable."

"I believe that will be possible, if you work with me."

"I'd like to, but I just can't handle a large doctor's bill."

Gregory Hill intrigued Hollis. He decided to treat him for whatever price the man could afford.

"I'll submit a claim to the insurance company for your treatment. I'll take whatever they'll pay as my fee, and if they pay nothing I'll accept whatever you can afford."

"That's nice of you, doc."

"You can schedule an appointment with my secretary for next week. I'll see you soon. Bring your drawings with you the next time."

Gregory shook his hand and started to walk out of the office. Then he turned to face the doctor once more.

"You must really think I'm crazy if you're willing to lower your fee."

"Not at all. I'm just anxious to hear your story."

Hollis returned home, sitting on the porch to collect his thoughts before going inside. He replayed the session with Gregory in his mind several times before realizing why he found this case to be so unique. The detective was not seeking to change his life. Nor was Gregory Hill looking for someone to explain his extraordinary experience. He firmly believed a woman from the future had contacted him. The patient would expect Hollis to verify her existence to his superior.

I'll have to convince him that she's not real the doctor thought to himself.

Hollis Simms was so absorbed in his thoughts he failed to notice Sebastian as he walked through the archway and onto the veranda.

"I saw you on television!" he announced.

Hollis almost jumped out of his chair.

"I'm sorry to startle you. Did you get a chance to see it?"

"No, I'm going to watch a tape of it with Belle tonight. If I recover from the heart attack you just gave me, that is."

"When you were talking to that woman about dealing with death, why didn't you mention your ghost?" Sebastian asked him.

"I didn't tell her about Angie because it would have been inappropriate," Hollis answered his brother. "The appearance of a woman who lived over one hundred years ago would strain anyone's credulity."

"So you admit it is way out there."

"Of course. I never said it was an easily acceptable premise. I just happen to believe it's true. But to use such a tale to convince someone else that her departed relative still exists in another form would be irresponsible, even if the woman was a patient I had been seeing for a long time, and was someone with whom I had established a great deal of trust. There is also the matter of what was really troubling the caller. She was feeling guilty because of a childhood experience. Proving there is life after death wouldn't necessarily solve her dilemma."

"That makes sense. But are you ever going to tell anyone else about Angie? I mean a man in your position could cause quite a stir if you suddenly announced that you had met a ghost."

"Why would I want to cause a stir? I think there are enough things going on in today's world to keep everyone in a frenzy."

"But this is good news. You should be dying to get it out."

"Is that a pun?" Hollis asked him with a grin.

"Not an intentional one."

"I have thought about presenting a paper on Angie. But that's provided I discover why she is so troubled. If I share this experience with the masses, it will be done in a psychiatric context. I wouldn't do it to get myself on the front page of the Enquirer."

"There are a lot of people who would love to hear your story."

"Especially Alec Collins. It would guarantee that he would be named head of the Psychiatric Department at the hospital. I don't intend to do anything to help him in that regard. Besides, there are plenty of ghost stories around. Mine won't be missed. You sound like you're starting to believe in her."

"I'm still undecided."

"So you'd be willing to see me make a fool out of myself if she's not real."

"I was just wondering if you intended to tell anyone else, since you obviously believe she's from the spirit world. There isn't much else for me to do, except count bagels."

"Courage, my friend. Something will turn up for you. Of course, you could help it along by actually looking for another job on Wall Street."

"Who says I want to go back there?"

Hollis gave him a knowing look. Sebastian smiled back at him.

"You shrinks think you know everything."

Hollis smiled. He knew that his brother's statement was not true, because the doctor did not know where Angie had gone.

CHAPTER SIX

❦

S ebastian Simms stood behind the counter in the bagel shop watching his staff serve the customers. When the former broker first came here he found the young workers to be a refreshing change from the jaded, power hungry people one often encountered in an office environment. Yet now they only served to remind him of how far from his early aspirations he had fallen. This was a place where most people worked in order to earn fun money or to help with their college expenses. These young adults would be doing other things in the very near future. Sebastian, unlike them, had no other prospects.

Annabelle walked in with her friend Celia. His niece's companion did a poor job of hiding a smirk when she saw him behind the counter.

"Hi Uncle Sebastian," Belle said with a smile. "We're just dying for a bagel. Do you have any that are hot?"

When she addressed him Sebastian heard her say *Uncle Loser* instead of Uncle Sebastian. He had recently overheard Annabelle refer to him that way. In spite of this, he still managed to answer her enthusiastically.

"We sure do. April, take care of these two young ladies. And be extra careful, because this one is my niece," Sebastian said to one of the college students that worked for him. Then he said to Annabelle. "I have to step out for a while, honey. I'll see you tonight."

Sebastian went out the back door. As he walked to his car a sudden surge of determination came over him. He intended to drive back to the old house and make some calls. Though it would most likely be a very frustrating process, there would be no turning back for him now. Sebastian Simms was going back to Wall Street.

"I'll have to remember to thank Belle for this."

He drove thru the small town and stopped at a traffic light. In the distance he saw Frank Martin walking towards Fairhaven. Sebastian gave him a ride.

"I was just getting some oil to loosen up the lug nuts on that Hollander lady's car," Frank said. "She had a flat and didn't want to wait for the damn auto club to get there. With all her money she should just buy another car. It was a nice day, so I decided to walk to the store."

They arrived at Fairhaven. Sebastian dropped Frank off at the garage, and then passed the main house on the way to his current residence. His peripheral vision afforded him a view of Olivia Simms and Harley Fox standing on the mansion's long porch. Though he only had a brief glimpse, Hollis's brother sensed they were engaged in an intimate conversation. Harley's arm was around her waist. The expression on Olivia's face also suggested to Sebastian that they were involved in something beyond the business of financing a movie. He continued on to the old house and went inside.

Sebastian Simms sat in front of the dormant fireplace for a long time. He had always liked Olivia, in spite of her dominating ways. Yet he still felt obligated to bring this situation to his brother's attention. The problem facing Sebastian was that there was no delicate way to broach the subject with Hollis. The younger Simms became so absorbed in this internal debate that he neglected to make his phone calls.

Hollis Simms spent the better part of the next afternoon lounging around Fairhaven's in ground pool. This was a beautiful spring day, which happened to be exactly what the doctor needed. The workload generated by his recent fame had him feeling somewhat frayed at the edges.

Yesterday had been a particularly hectic day. One of his long time patients, Henry Evans, insisted on seeing him on an emergency basis.

Hollis was dubious about the legitimacy of his crisis, but not to the point of refusing to see him.

"So what do you want to talk about today?" Hollis began their session after his patient assumed a recumbent position on the couch.

"It's closing in on me, doctor. I mean I can't be everything to everyone all of the time. My wife and kids are getting more demanding every day. The job is crazy. They think I'm some kind of indentured servant or something."

Hollis had learned over the years that Henry would never reveal what was troubling him for at least thirty minutes after the session began. He would start with his usual laundry list of complaints about every person he had ever known before telling the doctor what had actually caused his most recent anxiety attack. The psychiatrist listened patiently.

"And my mother-in-law, God she's an unforgiving bitch. I think she was sent straight from Hollis."

"Straight from Hollis?"

"What?"

"You said she was sent straight from Hollis."

"I said straight from hell."

The doctor looked at him and smiled.

"So what have I done to offend you?"

Henry sat up. He looked at the psychiatrist squarely in the eye.

"You cancelled Tuesday's session. I don't understand why. We've been meeting on every Tuesday for I don't know how many years. I can't function without that session."

Hollis had recognized how dependent this particular patient had become on him. He had been hoping to find a way to begin reversing the process. *The Robin Wainscot Show* had provided a perfect excuse.

"I have another commitment," he told him.

"You have the damn t.v. show. Now you're too big to care about your old patients."

"I believe you're strong enough to tolerate a change in our routine. This is a sign of the progress you've made."

"Bullshit! Do you know how tough it is to get back into the grind after the weekend? I have to start sucking up to the morons I work for again. I need to deal with the frustration caused by that degrading chore here with you. I can't do it on my own."

"Then change jobs, if you feel so strongly about it."

"That's easy for you to say. You're probably banging Robin Wainscot. All doors open for you now. I'm just surviving, doctor."

Henry continued on in the same vein for thirty more minutes. Hollis was eventually able to persuade him that the change in routine was something he could adjust to.

"Can I have your autograph?"

Hollis looked behind him. Paul Nustad was standing there.

"I can't seem to get away from my fans," Hollis replied with a laugh.

"Well, it's not really for me. It's for my daughter."

"And what might her name be?"

"Paul. It's an odd choice for a girl's name, but one that makes her hard to forget."

After shaking the psychiatrist's hand the historian sat down in the lounge chair next to him.

"So what brings you to New York?"

"I'm speaking at a seminar in the city. So I thought I'd pay you a visit. I've seen the show. You seem very much at ease on television."

"I'm more so now than I was at the beginning. But I still suffer from stage fright before every appearance. Would you like something to drink?"

"Today is a perfect day for a gin and tonic. You wouldn't happen to have one handy, would you?"

"I'll take a look around."

Hollis went inside and made the drinks. He then tracked down the maid to ask that another place be set for dinner. Hollis was about to call Sebastian to see if he wanted to join them when his younger brother walked through the door.

"I was just about to call you. Paul Nustad is here. Why don't you come over for dinner?"

"I actually came by to see if you were interested in a game of tennis. I didn't know you had company."

"Have a drink with us instead. We're sitting by the pool."

They joined Paul outside. The brilliant sunshine illuminated the deep green spring foliage all around them. The three men did not fail to notice this living collage. Their conversation remained very casual until Nustad mentioned Angie.

"By the way, I have some more information about the woman who wrote the diary," Paul told him.

Hollis suddenly became very intense. Sebastian looked away. He had to resist the temptation to tell Paul about Fairhaven's ghost.

"Did I say something wrong?" he asked them.

"No, of course not," Hollis assured him. "I was going to talk to you about her later on, but Sebastian can hardly contain himself at the moment. So I'll do it now. I've had several encounters with the ghost of Angie Barton."

Paul stared at him, saying nothing for a long time. He knew that Hollis was not above fabricating a story in order to enjoy a laugh at someone else's expense. The historian had been his victim on more than one occasion. Yet he could not detect any evidence of guile in the expression his host now wore. Paul ran his hands through his bushy gray hair several times before responding.

"You're telling me you've actually seen a ghost?"

"I have."

"Where?"

"In that garden." Hollis pointed to it.

Paul stood up to observe the array of plants inside the wrought iron gate. He thought it was a pretty spot, especially on this lovely day. Still that was not enough to explain why a supernatural being would be drawn there. In any case the historian was a skeptic when it came to the paranormal. Though he had heard many stories about people encountering spirits, including tales of long dead presidents appearing in the White House, he personally did not believe that those who had departed this world could revisit it.

"You don't believe in ghosts," Hollis observed.

"That's correct," Paul replied as he turned around and sat down again. "Has anyone else seen her?"

Hollis was reluctant to speak for Sebastian, though in this instance it turned out to be completely unnecessary. His brother not only acknowledged seeing Angie, but also produced a photograph of her.

"I was going to show this to you before," he told Hollis. "But then you told me that Paul was here, so I decided to wait until later. I took this several nights ago."

Hollis and Paul looked at the photograph. Sebastian had taken it from a considerable distance, due to his brother's admonishment about not startling his patient. Despite the small image that was produced by the camera, it was possible to discern a solitary figure standing in the garden. There was an unnatural radiance surrounding her. Hollis could be seen sitting on the large rock outside of the fence.

Paul Nustad examined the picture. Then he looked at his friend incredulously. For his part Hollis was not only intrigued by the photograph, but also appreciated the vindication it provided for him.

"There is certainly something there," Paul conceded. "Though the photograph is of such a poor quality that I can't hazard a guess as to who, or what, it is."

"Don't blame me," Sebastian told him. "Hollis won't let me get any closer to the garden when he's with his patient."

"Patient?" The historian questioned the doctor.

"Yes. The person I met in the garden was too reserved to be the brave woman who challenged the Oregon Trail, in my opinion. Then there is the question as to how she became a domestic servant on Long Island. Even if her father went broke, I believe Angie would have been doing something much more interesting. The only explanation is that she suffered some kind of trauma during her journey."

Paul sat back to think about what his host had told him. Hollis had always been the first to question the validity of any unusual claim or story. Now he seemed to have accepted the existence of this ghost at face value. Apparently the woman from the nineteenth century was not the only one who had changed.

"I am a skeptic, as you correctly pointed out. The first question that occurs to me is why would the spirit of someone who died over a hundred years ago appear to you? And why would she come here? This could not have been where she had the most memorable experiences of her life."

"That's true," Hollis agreed. "But it is the place where her diary was buried. She may have been visiting the garden for many years before I found it. I think that by reliving the experiences described in the diary, Angie is able to reclaim the spirit she's been lacking. After it disappeared she probably kept coming back in the hope of finding her journal. I just happened to be looking towards the garden during one of Angie's appearances."

"But you dug it up years ago. And you happened to see her only now?'

"Maybe she's been looking for the diary all along, but chose not to reveal herself to anyone until now. Angie may have reached the point where she decided to seek someone's help. And perhaps Angie's seeking help not only in locating the diary, but also wants to share her experiences with someone, so that she can finally find peace."

"If that's true then it's very convenient for her to have a psychiatrist living here," Paul responded in a doubtful tone. "What has she told you so far?"

Hollis hesitated for a moment. He was very concerned about infringing on doctor-patient confidentiality. The he realized the historian would probably discover much of the information Angie had provided on his own.

"As you know, Angie's lover, Tom Shanahan left Boston because of William Conner's death. He was shot during a scuffle between the two men. Angie followed him. Her friend Cassia was going west with her fiancée. Angie went with them to find Tom."

"That's not entirely correct," Paul told him. "I've learned more about the death of Conners. He did not die of a gunshot wound. He died after hitting his head on a rock near the Charles River."

"How did you find that out?" Hollis questioned him.

"I read the official records concerning the incident. The authorities considered his death an accident. He fell during an altercation with Shanahan. So your *patient* has given you the wrong information."

"She did say it was an accident, though Shanahan didn't think the police would believe that if he turned himself in. The public outrage over Conner's death, and Reginald Barton's desire to keep Angie from becoming involved with a common seaman, would force them to charge Shanahan with murder. Reginald had a lot of influence in Boston. As for the manner of his death, it's possible I misunderstood Angie. As I think back she never said Conners was shot. Angie just said the gun went off, and then the two men fell to the ground. Tom got up and realized Conners was dead. Her description would fit if the man died from hitting his head on a stone."

"That makes sense," Paul conceded. "You should ask her about it, though, if she appears again."

"Angie has started describing her journey west. I wouldn't want to spend any time rehashing the events that led to her departure."

"Don't you think this situation cries out for a scientific investigation?" Paul asked him.

"I do not intend to have a bunch of college kids with ectoplasm detectors or a team of writers from *The Enquirer* harassing my patient," Hollis replied firmly.

"There are many reputable scientists in the field of paranormal research," Paul countered. "Ed Barnes from the University of Minnesota is one. He's not with *The Enquirer*. You could really get to the bottom of this. If she really is genuine, then this event is too important not to be investigated."

Hollis looked away. He could not deny the validity of his friend's logic, but his relationship with Angie was too precious to be put in jeopardy. Fortunately for the doctor, he did not have to respond at that very moment due to his wife's intervention.

"Gentleman, dinner is served," Olivia called to them from the house.

The three men joined Annabelle and her mother at the dining room table. Paul was always taken aback by the way Olivia managed to maintain a youthful glow about her. He did not know if cosmetic surgery had played any part in this, but his appreciation of Olivia Simms would not have been diminished if it had.

"You should take advantage of Paul being here, Annabelle. You could use some help with your history studies," she chided her daughter.

"Oh, please, mother," Annabelle answered in an exasperated tone. "I just can't get excited about studying dead people."

"Some people find dead people to be very interesting," Sebastian said while grinning at Hollis.

His brother did not seem to appreciate the remark. Olivia and Annabelle were puzzled by it, while Paul was mildly amused.

"If we don't learn from history, we are doomed to repeat it," Olivia pointed out.

"And people never learn from it," Annabelle replied. "And that means there's no point in reading about what happened before, because it's going to happen again anyway. Then I'll be able to watch it on the news."

"You mean people like you never learn from it," Hollis told her with a smile.

"I did very well in the rest of my subjects, thank you," Annabelle retorted.

"I know it's hard to believe that the events of hundreds, even thousands of years ago have any relevance to the present," Paul conceded. "But you can encounter some of the most interesting, and often courageous people while studying the past."

Nustad pointed to the large tapestry on the dining room wall.

"The scene depicted there is the signing of the Magna Carta. Some would say it was the moment when freedom became a possibility instead of just a dream. We might not be living in a democracy if not for that document."

Annabelle was unimpressed. She quickly finished her meal and then took advantage of her own freedom by leaving the table in the same fashion. The adults remained behind for coffee and desert.

"So what brings you to New York, Paul?" Olivia asked him.

"I attended a lecture at Queens College. They discovered the remains of some slaves at a construction site. The find dates back to the early 19th century."

"You always were consumed by your work," Olivia observed. "And Hollis is becoming as bad. He spends far too much time mulling over his patients. I barely have a moment with him anymore."

"You exaggerate, darling," Hollis responded.

"Well, I'm going to Becky's for a game of bridge. It was good to see you again, Paul. Don't be a stranger."

The three of them sat on the veranda after she left. They could see the garden in the fading light.

"So why are you so resistant to having this ghost of yours investigated?" Paul asked him.

"I want to help her."

"What do you think caused her problem?"

"He won't discuss that with you," Sebastian said before Hollis could answer. "It would violate the doctor-patient relationship. Though I don't know how a ghost would go about bringing charges against her psychiatrist even if he did violate it."

"What is your belief regarding an afterlife?" Hollis asked Paul while ignoring his brother's remark.

"I'm not convinced there is one. But you obviously are."

"I believe we evolve into a more advanced form of life. Just as all the complex organisms evolved from simpler ones. Death is just evolution."

"But when a more complex life form evolves from a simpler one the simpler one usually becomes extinct. They don't continue on as more complex creatures."

"That's the flaw in my theory," Hollis conceded. "So I still have to work on it. But for the sake of our discussion, I'll still use it in regard to Angie. I believe she's afraid to take that step. Something has made it impossible for her to move on to the next level of existence. I want to remove the obstacle that is preventing Angie from doing so. I want her to find peace."

The phone rang. Hollis went inside to answer it.

"So what do you think?" Sebastian asked Paul.

"It's not what I would expect of Hollis. He always questions everything. I would have thought he'd be trying to verify the reality of this ghost. Instead he's only interested in treating her. What do you make of it?"

Sebastian thought his brother's behavior might be attributed to Olivia's apparent defection. Still this was only conjecture about a very private subject that he would not discuss with Paul. Sebastian instead offered another possible explanation.

"Hollis has been putting in a lot of extra hours since he started doing the show. So maybe he's too tired to be bothered with the scientific approach. There's also his concern about Alec Collins. They're both candidates to head the Psychiatry Department at the hospital. If word got out that Hollis was seeing a ghost Alec would win easily. But I have to say that on the one occasion I got close to her, his ghost looked very real to me, too. So it could be that Hollis just believes in her."

"And do you believe in her?"

"I'd like to talk to her. Then I'd know for sure."

"Have you looked around the garden for anything unusual?"

"Yes. I've done that several times. There's nothing out of the ordinary there."

"There's a scientist I know who investigates this phenomenon. But I think Hollis would be furious if he showed up unexpectedly."

"You've got that right."

"Let's see if we can stake out the garden tonight. I'll tell him I'm leaving for the hotel. You can say that you're retiring for the evening. We may see something."

"That's a good idea."

They had to wait for another 30 minutes before Hollis finished his phone call. He apologized to them, offering to compensate for his absence with brandy. They both declined.

"Someone has to make the bagels in the morning," Sebastian told him.

"And I have an early flight. But I'll call you soon. I want to hear more about this unusual patient of yours," Paul said as he shook his hand.

"I look forward to it," Hollis replied. "Have a safe trip."

The historian got into his car but drove only as far as the old house. He slowly shut the door after getting out of his car, sitting down under the large tree near the garden. Sebastian joined him. The night was utterly still, which served to heighten their anticipation. Ultimately their vigil was for naught, however. There was no sign of the visitor they anxiously waited to see.

As he sat there Sebastian decided not to leave Fairhaven unless the questions regarding Angelica Barton, and Olivia Simms, were answered. He could not be sure if his brother's welfare was the only factor influencing his decision. The younger Simms acknowledged that he might possess an unconscious aversion to reentering the business world. In any case Sebastian was committed to being here to watch over Hollis, no matter what the reason.

They remained there for two more hours without observing any signs of the specter.

"Here's my number at the college," Paul said as he handed him his card before leaving. "Let me know what happens."

"I will."

Hollis observed the garden from his office window that night. He was also disappointed by the woman he was trying to save.

CHAPTER SEVEN

Angie did not appear for three weeks. Hollis lay awake at night, wondering if he would ever see his most interesting patient again. Being of flesh and blood the doctor could not even imagine where the specter had gone. Hollis was now more determined than ever to learn how Angie had come to be a servant at Fairhaven. He hoped the lure of recovering the diary would be enough to insure her return.

Hollis was momentarily distracted from his concern about her by another patient. Despite the enthusiasm he displayed at their previous meeting, Gregory Hill had left the office without scheduling another appointment. Several days later he called the receptionist to do so, but Hollis was less than certain that the detective would show.

On this afternoon Doctor Simms was involved with another patient from the talk show. Perry Albright had called in with a behavioral problem that was jeopardizing his ability to earn a living. He was a clerical office worker with the annoying habit of thinking aloud. The endless soliloquies Perry gave while processing his paperwork had begun to drive his co-workers to the brink of revolt. The office manager informed Perry that he was to cease the endless chatter or *be gone in very short order*. Hollis's office happened to be next to a health club offering scuba diving lessons in their Olympic-size pool. The doctor suggested to Albright that he participate in the classes. The patient was to sit on the bottom of the pool with a board scuba divers use to communicate with each other while underwater. Instead of writing messages as the divers do, Perry Albright was to write numbers in order to mimic a typical day's work in the office. As there was no way to talk aloud under those circumstances, Hollis believed it would teach his patient to work silently.

"I didn't expect you to wear the scuba suit while walking around town," Hollis said to him when he walked into his office dressed to dive.

"I just wanted to show you my outfit. I'm having a blast."

"And how are things going at work?"

Perry nervously shuffled his flippers.

"Not too good. Ben, my boss, says I'm still driving everyone nuts. If I could only wear this stuff in the office, I'd be able to keep my job. Could you write a note for me saying that it's medically necessary?"

"You really need to learn how to work quietly," Hollis responded.

Albright's shoulders sagged. The doctor reconsidered his position.

"I could write a note saying that you needed to wear the regulator. That would only cover your mouth. But even so, you'll be subject to a lot of ridicule, I'm sure."

"I don't care. As long as I'm quiet, they can't do anything to me."

"I'll send the note to human resources. Good luck."

His newest patient arrived at the doctor's office. Hill started to sit down next to Albright's wife Alma in the waiting room. She gave the detective a disapproving look.

"You're sitting on my friend Eric," she protested.

"Eric? I don't see anyone there."

"He's invisible," Perry's wife explained.

Gregory stood up and looked for another place to sit. Alma suddenly laughed hysterically.

"I was only joking. I'm just waiting for my husband. There's nothing wrong with me."

Hill thought about beginning a debate with her on the subject, but then decided against it. Perry Albright walked out of the doctor's door, dressed in his diving attire. Greg eyed him curiously when he walked by. Alma and her husband left for the health club.

"Do you give diving lessons, too, doc?" he asked Hollis when the doctor walked over to shake his hand.

"I really can't discuss my other patients."

Hollis escorted him into his office. He shut the door behind them, and then motioned for him to sit in a chair. Gregory handed him the drawings he had made and sat down.

"I thought you would make me lay down on the couch, doc," Gregory said as he sat down.

"Today will be a continuation of our get acquainted session," Hollis replied. "As for future sessions, I let my patients decide if they want to lie on the couch or sit in a chair. I will say that over the years my experience has been this: most people find it easier to relate their thoughts and feelings to me when they're lying down. But it's up to you. I see you're originally from Brooklyn."

"Once you're from Brooklyn, you're always from Brooklyn," Gregory said with a smile. "I only live in Manhattan now because it's where I'm assigned. I need to be there twenty-four seven. You pick up a lot just listening to the people in the neighborhood. But every Sunday I go home. I usually make mass at St. Catherine's. You ever see the churches in Brooklyn, doc? They're beautiful. Most of them have been around for a 100 years or more. And then there's the food. I'll take you to Mama Rosetta's sometime. You haven't eaten pasta till you've had a plate of it there. Of course, the old neighborhood isn't what it used to be. When I grew up there it was a tight knit community. You couldn't mess with any of us without the whole damn place coming down on you. But things change."

"That they do. I appreciate your letting me read your personal file. You've given twenty years of exemplary service to the NYPD. It's no wonder your superiors are so anxious for you to begin your duties as chief of detectives."

"I'm just doing my job," Gregory said as he shifted his position in the chair.

"Why did you decide to become a policeman?"

"I was going with a girl named Joann Confessore in high school. Her old man owned a deli on Greenpoint Avenue. One day a couple of animals robbed the place. They popped him on the side of his head with a tire iron. Jo's dad survived, but I saw how it affected the old man and the rest of his family. Those lowlifes were never caught, so there was no justice for the Confessores. And I don't think he ever went to his store again without wondering if he'd be dead before the day was over. So I decided to do what I could to help people like them."

"That's a very noble reason. Tell me, do you feel you've been able to help the victims? You've certainly solved a large number of cases, and brought the criminals who committed those crimes to justice. But at the end of the day, do you feel your efforts have really helped the people who have been robbed, or worse?"

Gregory put his hands behind his head and looked up towards the ceiling. He stared at it for several moments before he replied.

"I guess you could say that about some of the cases. If it's just a matter of getting someone's jewelry back, it's possible to make things right for the victim. But I've also handled rape cases and homicides. That's when you can't ever make it right for the victim or their family. The best you can do is to get the scum bucket off the street. Then let them rot in jail."

"And how does that make you feel?"

"I'll bet it's pretty much like you feel, doc. You do what you can, and it's really all you can do. I'd be bonkers in a week if I let the people who never get justice haunt me. So I don't. And I'll bet you're the same way about the patients you can't cure."

Hollis ignored his patient's remarks regarding his feelings. Their discussions had to remain relevant to Gregory Hill alone.

"You're 40-years-old and still single. Why do you think you've never married?"

"I guess partly because I'm in love with my work. A good detective gets too caught up in the job to have much of a social life. If the right girl had come along I probably would have changed for her, though. But she never did, so I never did."

"Is there any particular issue that you're having trouble coping with at the moment?"

"Do you mean like hating my mother or father? Or maybe wanting to sleep with my sister?"

"You tell me," Hollis replied.

"My parents are both gone, God rest them. I get along fine with my brothers and sisters. Of course I don't see them very much, which is probably why we get along. No, I don't have those kinds of problems. In fact, I don't have any problems."

"Your superior thinks you do," Hollis pointed out.

"That's because of my project," Gregory said with a smile.

"Your project?"

"Yeah, or you could call it a plan. See Avalor has a lot of information about what's going to happen tomorrow, and the day after, and for as far into the future as you can imagine. She can tell us all we need to know to prevent crimes that haven't happened yet."

"I understand. This woman can access the records pertaining to our time when she goes home. Then she'll tell you about crimes that are going to be committed before they occur."

"Right. I just have to convince her to do it for me. And she will, I know she will."

"Have you ever wondered why Avalor contacted you?"

Gregory was at a loss for words. He had apparently never considered the question before.

"I can see you at the same time next week. Think about my question before we meet again."

"I'll be here, doc."

They shook hands before Gregory left the office. Hollis sat at his desk for some time after and began to plan the treatment of Detective Hill. The patient's unshakable belief in his delusion would be difficult to overcome. Gregory was not here because somewhere on the deepest psychological level he had come to the conclusion a doctor's help was required. Hollis began to develop a strategy as he looked through the detective's drawings.

Two days later Doctor Simms left for a psychiatric conference in San Diego, though his concerns about Angie made him a reluctant traveler. He had desperately searched for a legitimate reason to cancel his plans. Ordinarily finding one would not have been very difficult for him to do, but in this instance Olivia and Annabelle were to accompany him. They would be extremely displeased to learn that he had decided not to attend.

"Who is this patient?" Olivia asked him after Hollis hinted he might have to stay home because of a particularly difficult case.

"She's someone with a deeply troubled past," he replied. "She needs my help, and we are at a very significant juncture in her therapy."

"All your patients need your help, Hollis. That's why they're your patients. If they didn't need your skills as a doctor then you'd never know these people. Just tell her to take a sedative and watch a rerun of you on *Robin Wainscot*."

Doctor Simms gave his wife a stern look. He never tolerated any humor that came at the expense of his patients.

"Come on, Dad. You're becoming a workaholic," Annabelle, who had overheard their conversation, said as she entered the room.

"I suppose there's no harm in leaving for several days," Hollis finally conceded in a very unconvincing tone of voice. "I'll pack my duds and be ready to leave when you are."

He walked over to the old house to visit Sam. His brother offered him a beer and Hollis accepted it. They sat in lawn chairs under a large weeping willow tree. Springtime at Fairhaven always made a deep impression on the psychiatrist. The fresh scent of the newly emerged flowerage struck a cord within him that no other living things could reach. Hollis drew a deep breath so as to enjoy the sweet aroma of life renewing itself.

"I was thinking of painting the place while you're gone," Sebastian interrupted his thoughts.

"That's nice of you. But it's completely unnecessary. We'll have Frank see to it."

"You've done enough for me already. I'd like to do something for you and Olivia."

"We appreciate it. But you'd help us if we hit a bump in the road."

"You've got that right," Sebastian replied. "I'll keep an eye on the garden for you. If the ghost reappears, I'll give her your apologies."

Doctor Simms gave his brother a strange look. Sebastian thought the expression on his face indicated jealously, as if Hollis believed that his brother was interested in a woman he loved. The doctor regained his usual continence before he spoke.

"I thought you didn't believe in Angie," Hollis said.

"I don't believe in ghosts, per say. But I will admit there's something strange going on here."

"Ain't nothing but a bugaboo," Frank said with a laugh as he walked up behind them. "My grandma knew how to get rid of them. She'd mix some garlic and rotten apples in a pot. Then she'd heat it up over a big fire."

"That got rid of the ghosts?" Sebastian asked him.

"We never knew, because it sure as shit got rid of us. That stuff smelled something awful."

"Would you like a cocktail?" Sebastian asked.

"I'll take a rain check on that. I just wanted to ask Mr. …I mean Hollis if he wanted me to weed the garden."

Hollis displayed the peculiar expression once more. Sebastian thought Frank's suggestion was a good one. A closer examination of the garden might reveal something important about the unusual visitor. He wondered if that was the explanation for Hollis's reaction.

"By all means, attend to it," the doctor finally said as he stood up. "I have some work to do, gentlemen. I'll see you later."

Hollis walked to the house.

They flew to the West Coast on a magnificently clear day. The plane passed over the state of Nebraska. Hollis saw a river flowing lazily across the plain and assumed it was the Platte. Simms wondered if the spirits of the Crawford Party were still continuing their journey across the new frontier. If so, his patient might be among them.

The hotel the three were staying in was not lacking in any of the most desirable amenities. Still Olivia managed to find fault with the robes provided; they were too short for her liking. The other two members of the family had no complaints. Annabelle emerged from her room a half-hour after they arrived and knocked on her parents' door.

"Daddy, what are you doing on the bed?" she asked after Olivia let her in.

"It's generally referred to as taking a nap." He then smiled without opening his eyes.

"We're supposed to be playing tennis," his daughter pointed out.

Hollis opened them and looked at her.

"You do seem to be dressed for the occasion," Hollis observed.

"And you are not," Olivia pointed out as she playfully struck him with a pillow.

"I would imagine any attempt to postpone the game until tomorrow would be futile. Just remember that if I lose, it will be because of jet lag."

The two of them walked onto the sun-drenched courts and began their game. His daughter was a very competent player, returning his volleys in a manner that often left Hollis struggling to catch his breath. Her long pony tail swayed back and forth as Belle moved from side to side. Despite the doctor's labors he still managed to notice how his opponent attracted the stares of the young boys playing on the other courts. Belle was becoming a young woman. Like any father he was proud of his rapidly maturing daughter: yet at the same time Hollis felt a twinge of melancholy when he thought about her becoming an adult.

"I knew the fatigue from flying cross-country would do me in," Hollis told her as they enjoyed a cool drink after the match.

"I took the same flight. It had nothing to do with it. I just waxed your tail," Annabelle corrected him with a self-satisfied grin.

"What do you think you'll do after high school?" Hollis, who had been meaning to broach that subject with Belle for some time, asked her.

"I don't know. Maybe I'll join the Peace Corp. Or I could do some volunteer work in Africa or someplace like that."

"You're not thinking of attending college? You should be considering all your options, sweetheart. You'll be graduating in two years."

"Yeah, I know. It's just that when I look around at the people who did all the right things I see a bunch of clones. It's nothing personal, Dad. But I want to find my own way, not someone else's."

"There's nothing wrong with that. But just don't do something different simply for the sake of being different. It would be worse than being a clone."

Hollis gave Annabelle a kiss on the forehead before she went back to her room. John Block joined him soon after.

"Welcome to San Diego," Block greeted him.

"Thank you, Doctor Block. This is a beautiful place."

"Don't let that distract you from your speech tomorrow," he warned while occupying the seat next to Hollis. "You had better be ready to match wits with Alec."

"I may have an unfair advantage. If he begins to insist that human beings are no more than the sum of their biological processes, I'll be able to present some very compelling evidence to refute his claim."

"And what is this evidence?"

"Human beings do have a soul. I know, because I've met the spirit of a woman who lived over 100 years ago."

John Block looked at his friend carefully. He took a long sip of his drink before speaking.

"Are you saying you've seen a ghost?"

"I've haven't just seen one, I've had some very long conversations with her."

"Where and when did this happen?"

"I met her several months ago in the garden at Fairhaven. Her name is Angie Barton. She lived in the 1800s, and wrote a diary that I found many years ago."

"So what's the punch line?" John asked him with a smile.

"If you mean is this some kind of joke, well, it isn't. I'm currently listening to her account of her experiences on the Oregon Trail. I think something traumatic happened to her there. Angie worked as a servant at Fairhaven after her journey, so she survived the trip west. But something must have changed her in a profound way during it, or she would have never become a domestic servant on Long Island. I'm hoping she'll tell me what it was. I'll probably write a paper about Angie when we've finished."

"Does she contact you regularly?" Block asked in a skeptical tone.

"I look out my window at the garden every night. There's a strange glow around Angie when she first appears. I can see it from my office. That's how I know she's there. You don't believe me, do you?"

"Hollis, I've known you for a long time. I've never doubted anything you've told me before, because I know you're a level-headed person. And I think you're a consummate professional, no matter what other people are saying about your television appearances. But this is something that would stretch anyone's credulity. Has anyone else seen her?"

"Yes. My brother Sebastian has, and possibly the groundskeeper. Sebastian even took a picture, though it's from far away. "

"You should have another doctor verify this. I'd be happy to come over to see for myself."

"But I'm currently treating her. I can't risk the presence of someone else chasing Angie away. When I feel that I've discovered the reason for her trauma, then you can meet her. I'll even ask Alec to come by."

John looked at him intently.

"You don't want to do that. Not until it's proven beyond any shadow of a doubt that this ghost of yours is real. Someone could be putting you on, you know. Or perhaps it's from overworking."

"I must admit that after being cooped up in an office all day it's refreshing to imagine myself traveling across the wide open prairies of that era," Hollis replied with a smile. "There is something exhilarating about hearing her describe life in the wilderness. They had to police themselves. The settlers dealt with thievery and other transgressions person to person. These courageous people had to rely on their wits to cope with the environment. That's especially refreshing for someone who lives in a time when people have electric naval lint removers."

"I prefer the more scientific name. Electric belly-button lint removers," Block said with a laugh. "I guess challenging nature is a very romantic thing to do when you're not the one suffering from the hardships and depravations."

"That's true," Hollis conceded. "I'm not imagining this, Doctor Block. As I said before, my brother saw her too."

"I understand that Sebastian has been under a lot of pressure lately."

"I'm not the first professional to encounter a spirit. Remember the professors at Gettysburg College? They were working late one night and got in the elevator to go to the ground floor. Instead it took them to the basement, where they saw Civil War doctors treating the wounded from the Battle of Gettysburg. One of the professors was an alumnus of mine."

Block took another sip of his drink. He then hesitated for several moments before speaking.

"The staff at the hospital will listen to what I have to say when they decide who my replacement will be. I don't mind telling you, Doctor Simms, that I believe you're the best man for the job. And they'll most likely agree, since they believe the Psychiatric Department needs new thinking. And you certainly can't be accused of being a chip off the old block. But remember the same could be said about Alec. He desperately wants to be named as my replacement, especially since it would be at your expense. Doctor Collins would love to see you taken down a peg or two. So don't give him any ammunition. He's never really forgiven you for finishing ahead of him in college."

"Well, I deserved to. I paid damn good money for the answers to the final exam."

"This is serious, Hollis. No more talk about writing a paper on this *Angie* until we know what she is. You might consider letting your brother take a better picture of this *spirit*. If you prove she's real, then you can present her case to your colleagues."

"So there you are," Olivia said as she walked up to their table. "I've been looking all over for you. You boys look like you're having an intense discussion."

"I'm just trying to be sure that he doesn't make a fool of himself," John said as he stood up.

He had tried to sound flippant, but Olivia could see how concerned he was.

"Did you challenge John to a game of cribbage again, Hollis? After the last beating you took I should think you'd know better."

"I'll see you two later," Block told them as he walked away.

"What was all that about?" Olivia asked her husband.

"We were just talking about one of my new patients. The doctor gave me some sound advice."

"It didn't seem like you wanted to take it."

"Don't worry, my love. Let's get ready for dinner."

Doctor and Mrs. Simms joined some of his colleagues for dinner. Annabelle begged off, citing an aversion to listening to a group of psychiatrists talking about their profession while she was eating. They drove to Weston's, an upscale restaurant on the Pacific Shore. They took in the breathtaking San Diego sunset along the way. John Block met them there, along with Dick Knowles, who practiced in Los Angeles. His wife Terri accompanied him.

The last to arrive was Alec Collins with a very attractive woman named Cynthia Ryan. Doctor Collins believed that the human race consisted of advanced biological units whose emotions were nothing more than the result of complex chemical reactions. As a result, he saw nothing unique in the make-up of any given individual. Yet Alec Collins believed that he was *sui generis*, even to the point of being able to make a receding hairline look fashionable.

The seven of them sat at a table providing a panoramic view of the broad blue ocean. Several people approached Hollis to ask for his autograph. The doctor obliged them, despite his discomfort at being singled out in a social situation. Alec and Dick reacted as if his celebrity amused them, though in the former case Hollis knew there was jealousy involved. He had not spoken with Doctor Knowles since his appearances on the show began. Hollis did not know how his associate felt about it, though he did not have to wait long to find out.

"So how does it feel to be a television star, Hollis?" he asked.

"Strange. I can't get used to having people I've never met act as though they know me."

"I'm sure you'll be getting a lot of feedback about it at the conference," Dick told him. "There are many people who think you're guilty of making snap diagnoses."

Alec smiled at Hollis. He had made the same criticism.

"I don't recall doing that," Hollis said defensively.

"I happened to catch you on the tube a couple of weeks ago," Dick replied. "You advised a young woman from Topeka about her phobia concerning supermarkets."

The woman who referred to herself as Wren had called in for advice about her irrational fear of being in large grocery stores. For the last five years the woman had been unable to step inside one without becoming disoriented. Wren had been ashamed to discuss the problem with anyone she knew. Hollis had encountered a patient with a similar problem years before, though in that case the person could not ride in a bus. After many sessions he discovered that long before the man had been riding on one next to a passenger who was listening to a newscast on the radio. This was how he had learned that the company he worked for was going out of business. The patient did not consciously remember the incident, yet it remained a traumatic memory in his subconscious. Doctor Simms suspected Wren had a similar problem. He was correct. Ten years before Wren had been shopping in a supermarket when a neighbor came running up to her. This was how she learned her father had died.

"I had a patient just like her a while back," Hollis told him. "Besides, I spoke with the woman for a couple of hours on the phone before we hit on the cause of her problem. There was nothing *snap* about it. They only played a short part of our conversation when the show aired."

"That's the problem," Alec interjected. "A layman watching the show would be led to believe it only takes a short time to diagnose a patient."

"I think Hollis makes it clear that only a small percentage of patients can be treated so expeditiously," John Block said.

"I don't agree," Doctor Knowles retorted. "Your appearances on the show will do irreparable harm to our profession."

"Gentlemen, the women at the table are becoming bored," Olivia told them. "We did not come to this lovely restaurant so the four of you could talk shop. You'll have all day tomorrow to do that."

Dick smiled at her.

"I apologize. Let's talk about something that's far more important. My golf game."

"You have a great deal of courage, my friend," Alec said. "The last I heard your game had gone south for the winter, never to be seen again."

"You'll find out if that's true soon enough," Dick replied.

For the rest of the meal the conversation remained casual. There was the usual news and reminiscences about old friends interlaced with selected commentary on the state of the world today. They returned to the hotel at a reasonable hour. The conference began the next morning. Doctor Simms and Doctor Collins were each to give a lecture on the prevalence of drugs in psychiatric treatment.

Alec Collins was the first speaker. He was short in stature with a well honed sneer made so from repeated use. His speech was entitled *Acknowledging What We Are*. Doctor Collins cleared his throat before he began.

"Good morning. I don't know why they always hold these conferences in such beautiful locales. I'm sure the last place you want to be is inside listening to me on such a wonderful day in San Diego. But then again if they didn't have it here no one would come."

There was scattered laughter. Alec paused for a moment before continuing.

"My friends and colleagues, I believe that the time has come for those of us in this profession to take stock of our beliefs and methods. We spend a great deal of our time, and our patients' time as well, in attempting to dig deep into the minds of those we treat for the cause of their emotional problems. Then many of us will spend hours and hours analyzing the traumatic events that appear to have created the patients' difficulties after they've been identified. Even those who have adopted behavior therapy are going the long way around. We must acknowledge, once and for all, that the brain is like any other organ of the body. It functions through chemicals, and when it is not functioning properly, the best way to address the problem is through chemicals as well. We can cure patients quickly, efficiently, and completely with drugs."

Alec paused to allow his audience to think about what he had said. The expressions on his colleagues' faces indicated his speech had contained no surprises so far.

"I believe some of our traditional methods are not only inefficient, but detrimental as well. Stress Debriefing, for instance, is used to help a patient suffering from post traumatic stress disorder deal with the feelings that were caused by some terrible experience. Yet in having a patient relive the experience one runs the risk of compounding the negative emotions. If the patient couldn't deal with them the first time, why we do we assume the person will be able to do so in therapy? I believe this is a dangerous approach to use for treating the patient's problem. Medication would be far more effective without subjecting the person to more negative emotions."

Some of the doctors nodded. Hollis made a mental note to respond to the speaker's point in his speech.

"I know there are some of you who would dispute this. In fact, I believe one of those people is speaking after me." Alec smiled at Hollis. "You would tell me that our emotions are more than just a series of incredibly intricate chemical reactions. You believe man occupies some special place in the universe, and has been endowed with a soul that separates us from the rest of the animal kingdom."

Now Doctor Collins had their attention.

"I thought about that point of view while observing my 6-year-old nephew, Willie, the other day. He's a fine boy, mind you, yet like any child that age Willie has much to learn about the social graces. The child is also in the process of learning right from wrong. Now if we are truly more than just the sum of our parts, with something incorporated into our being making man more than just a very complex life form, why wouldn't

Willie know about right and wrong, as well as good and evil without being told? I submit to you that any child must learn it, just as a cheetah on the Serengeti Plains must be taught which animals to hunt. There is no metaphysical organ within a human to guide them. Studies have shown that children are inherently prejudiced against those who are less fortunate than themselves. Benevolence is something they learn from adults. This is accomplished by the chemical processes in the brain. When the process goes awry, drugs are the most effective way to correct the problem."

Alec's speech elicited a strong reaction from his audience. The consensus was that though his basic premise might have merit, his way of expressing the idea left something to be desired. The whispered comments of his peers were loud enough to reach his ears. Alec Collins was quite pleased with himself, for he had been trying to strike a nerve with his discourse. He continued on for some time in the same vein before yielding the floor to Hollis.

Doctor Simms entitled his speech *Taking the Easy Way Out*. He would have been the champion of many in the audience on that day if not for his decision to become a television celebrity. As it was, the people sitting before him begrudgingly hoped he would trump the previous speaker.

"I have also observed many children," he began. "And I've also read about some new studies done on them. I would recommend reviewing the results of one that was conducted in Uganda. It clearly indicates that altruism is not just a learned behavior. Experiments with infants have shown that the tendency to help others is present on an instinctive level."

Collins silently cursed the organizers of the conference for having him speak first.

"But in any case, to compare the functions of a child's brain with that of their kidneys or stomach is absurd. While they all are vital to the health and well-being of an individual, the brain is extraordinarily special. It lets us understand the world around us, which includes all the beautiful and terrible things that make life so rich. And unfortunately in some instances, that which makes life so tragic. We can, due to our mastery of certain chemical substances, dampen the mind's reaction to stimuli. This is a very good thing, in many circumstances. I have gratefully prescribed medication for those who need immediate relief. And those who, unfortunately, cannot improve their condition by any other means.

But I believe there are just as many emotional and behavioral problems which can be addressed by using the patient's ability to reason. This kind of a solution will ultimately make for a much more contented, fulfilled human being. We should not fall into the trap of always using something expedient, such as prescription drugs, to treat our patients. I will readily concede that some therapies can be dangerous. But there are also some surgical procedures that entail certain risks. No one is suggesting that we abandon surgery as a means to a cure. As always it is up to the physician to weigh the potential benefits against the risk, and only then to advise our patients on the most promising course of action. "

Hollis's remarks received enthusiastic applause. Doctor Simms paused until they subsided. He started wondering how his audience would react if he told them about Angie Barton. The subject would certainly be appropriate, given Alec's mentioning a patient's soul. John Block stared at his former pupil with a concerned expression on his face. His apprehension was unnecessary, however. Hollis knew the doctors would laugh him off the podium, so he did not refer to the lady from Boston. Instead Doctor Simms cited several examples from his experiences as a psychiatrist to prove the value of Stress Debriefing and other therapeutic methods.

"I cannot prove that there is more behind our thoughts and feelings than chemicals," he said sometime later at the conclusion of his speech. "Yet I cannot bring myself to eliminate the possibility that there is. Our science has not given humans the ability to know everything at this juncture in time. I will reserve judgment until we do, if I happen to still be alive at that moment."

Hollis hesitated, and then smiled as he said, "In one form or another, that is."

The audience responded with generous applause.

There were several more speakers that morning. The three doctors met for drinks by the pool after the session ended. Hollis and Alec politely acknowledged each other's efforts. John Block tried to remain neutral; though it was clear his sentiments were with Doctor Simms.

"Drugs are a very important part of treatment in some cases," he said after Alec coaxed him into declaring his beliefs. "But I also think that we are more than just a series of nerve endings that fire or misfire. The human element cannot be disregarded."

"We have got to start to think like mechanics, gentlemen. There is no evidence of our feelings and emotions being anything more than the result of some well-defined chemical processes. I urge you to get in step with the times. Now if you'll excuse me, my hormones are urging me to find my Cynthia. I'll see you later."

Hollis watched him walk away.

"I've never known you to hold your tongue before," he remarked. "But in this case I'm glad you did. Let me know how things turn out."

"I will," Hollis replied.

Hollis went back to his room and picked up the phone to call Sebastian.

"Hello Sam. How are things back east?"

"All's quiet here. How's your trip going?"

"I've attended lots of conferences and have had a beneficial exchange of ideas with my fellow psychiatrists."

"That's good to hear. Now tell me the truth. How many rounds of golf have you gotten in?"

"I resent your implication. This is hard work," Hollis replied with a laugh. "I was calling to see if my friend has appeared."

"No. I haven't seen her, and Frank hasn't mentioned anything about a bugaboo."

There was silence on the other end of the phone.

"Are you worried about her?" Sebastian asked him.

"Yes. Angie was upset when we ended our last conversation. I'll see you in a couple of days."

"Enjoy the rest of the convention."

Sebastian hung up the phone. All thoughts about his brother quickly disappeared from his mind. The younger Simms was on his way to see Clare. They were meeting ostensibly so he could sign the papers that were required to sell an investment the two of them had made together. Sebastian hoped their conversation would expand to include other subjects. The returning exile had a spectacular view of Manhattan as he drove over the Brooklyn Bridge. After arriving at Clare's building he parked his car and walked up the staircase to her apartment.

"Hi there," she greeted him pleasantly. "Thanks for coming. How have you been?"

"Fine," Sebastian replied. "I hope you can say the same."

"Things couldn't be better. Would you like a drink?"

"I'll have the usual."

Clare knew he meant scotch and soda, though she was tempted to reply *what's the usual? It's been so long I've forgotten.* She refrained from doing so. Instead his estranged lover made the drink and handed it to Sebastian. Then she showed him the papers he had to sign in order to sell the stock. He hesitated for a moment. This was to be their children's college fund. After a long pause Sebastian signed the document.

"So I heard that you're working in a bagel shop," Clare said with disbelief in her voice.

"Well, yes, but only temporarily. In fact I met a guy there about a month ago that I knew from the street. We talked about a couple of openings at his firm."

"So what happened? Did you go on an interview?" Clare, whose interest was now piqued, asked him.

"I told him that I'd have to wait a while before resuming my career, because there are family considerations involved."

"What family considerations? Is everyone all right?"

"Well, I think Olivia is having an affair. And it might be more than Hollis can handle at the moment."

Clare sat down on the sofa next to Sebastian.

"I'm sorry to hear that. But Hollis is certainly capable of dealing with it. I can't believe you want to stay at Fairhaven because of your brother's marital problems."

"There's more to it than his marriage. You have to keep what I'm about to tell you now very confidential. You can't tell another soul."

"All right."

"Hollis has seen, on a number of occasions, a ghost."

"A ghost? Are you putting me on?"

"No. And I've seen her too, though from a distance. I even took a picture."

Sebastian showed her his photograph. Clare was unimpressed.

"I can't tell what that is," she said. "I also can't imagine Hollis believing in such a thing. I would have said the same about you too, until recently."

"You don't believe there's something waiting for us after we die?"

"Yes. They're called worms. Who is this *ghost* supposed to be?"

Sebastian found being interrogated by a skeptic to be a very unpleasant experience. He never would have broached the subject if he had known that Clare was a non-believer. This was not how Sebastian Simms had envisioned their evening together. He suddenly noticed the glow from her unblemished complexion. Sebastian wanted to run his hands through her long blonde hair, and share a passionate embrace with Clare. Instead he answered her question.

"Hollis found the diary of a woman from the 19th century when he was a teenager. Apparently this woman is the author of the diary."

"She came back to get it?"

"Yes. Look, I'm not a hundred percent sure about this either."

"Have you spoken with the ghost?"

"No. Hollis insists that I keep far away from the two of them when he meets with her. He acts like she's one of his patients. I think Hollis is using it as a diversion to forget about his problems with Olivia."

"You're practicing psychology now? My, but you do have a busy life. Why don't you just stop the bullshit, Sebastian? This is just another excuse for you to avoid going back to work. I don't know what's going on with your brother. I hope it's nothing serious. But you have your own problems. And using his to avoid dealing with your own future is just absurd. You could go back to Wall Street and still live at Fairhaven. Or is spying on your brother a full-time job? Have a good night."

Clare stood up and ran into the bedroom. A dejected Sebastian drove back to Fairhaven.

That was a wasted evening Sebastian thought with a sigh. *I guess I'm going to have to find a ghost of my own.*

CHAPTER EIGHT

O livia Simms walked down the long, winding staircase of Fairhaven. Her progress was halted just before the lady of the mansion reached the first floor. Two servants, each dressed in jeans and a tee shirt, were standing on the steps discussing the activities that had been planned for that day. Olivia asked their pardon, and then continued on as they stepped aside.

In her childhood home there were never any servants to be seen on the main staircase. There had been a separate set of stairs used by the household help to access their quarters. This lack of decorum was a concession by Olivia to the man she had married. While Fairhaven also had another staircase on the opposite side of the mansion for the servants to use, Hollis could never see the point in making them walk the extra distance to reach their rooms.

This bright summer day also saw another tradition that would not have been acceptable in her parents' estate. Hollis had organized an annual softball game in which the entire staff and their families participated. Doctor Simms played in the game along with his daughter: both of them enjoyed themselves immensely. In deference to his wife, Hollis made sure the field was situated so there was no chance of a batted ball damaging the limestone facade of the mansion. There was a barbecue after the game, the smell of pork being roasted over an open pit now reminding the players of what was to come after the athletic competition.

Olivia walked over to the large open section of the lawn that had been converted into a softball field. Belle was speaking with the son of a house servant. The young man had participated in several of these events, and had developed quite a crush on the young Miss Simms. He was pointing out the fragrant qualities of one particular plant that could be found on the grounds of the estate to her. The young suitor brushed one of its leaves against his face.

"You just rub it against your cheek, Annabelle. The aroma is amazing."

She followed his instructions, and smiled when the sweet smell was released. Frank was standing nearby. He picked a leaf off one of the plants with a grin, and proceeded to follow the young man's instructions, though his interpretation was somewhat different than Belle's.

"That wasn't the cheek he was referring to," Olivia said while trying to suppress her laughter as she walked by. "He didn't mean your ass, Frank."

The game began, with Hollis, Sebastian and Frank taking their positions in the outfield. Belle was the first batter. She hit a hard ground ball to David the cook at second base. He bobbled it, giving the runner a chance to reach first safely. Harold the butler was playing first, and he did not position himself properly to take the late throw. As a result Annabelle ran into him when she reached the bag. The domestic servant went down in a heap. Hollis and the others came to his aid.

"Are you alright?" the doctor asked.

"Yes, sir."

"I'm sorry," Belle told him.

"This is a softball game, not a rugby match," Hollis reminded her with a grin.

"No harm done, young Miss," Harold said as he stood up. "But do be careful. Your mother would never forgive you if you were to break her butler."

Play resumed, and the future botanist stepped up to the plate. The young man promptly hit a long line drive over Frank's head. The ball rolled into Angie's garden. Frank would have normally reached it before the other two outfielders. In this case he was not eager to pass through the gate, however. For all his ridiculing the idea of a ghost visiting Fairhaven, the groundskeeper was actually afraid of them.

Sebastian should have been the first Simms to reach the garden, given his relative youth. Yet he was not, for Hollis inexplicably regained the vigor of his youth when he saw the other two running towards the garden. He managed to beat both of them to the ball. His brother looked at him with a startled expression on his face.

"I've been working out," Hollis, who was now gasping for air, explained.

"Just let me know what vitamins you're taking," Sebastian replied. "I want to be 20-years-old again, too."

Olivia observed her husband's spirited pursuit of the ball. She then turned away and went back inside.

The next evening was balmy and Hollis decided to take advantage of the summer weather. He took his walking stick out of the closet and began a long walk around the estate. The doctor intentionally chose a path that would bring him to the garden. Though Hollis had all but given up hope of seeing his most intriguing patient again, he still looked for her every night.

On this occasion his desideratum appeared. There was a mist around the garden even though the night was clear. Angie was standing near the wrought iron fence, looking out over the varied trees growing on the estate. To Hollis's surprise her appearance had changed dramatically. This leaner specter exhibited the effects of the arduous journey across the plains. She was no longer dressed in servant's garb, but instead wore a dark green dress that had been smart for its time. Angie's cadaverous white skin made her head appear as though a cameo against the dark night. Hollis's joy at seeing her was plainly visible on the usually inscrutable face he presented to his patients.

"Mr. Simms," she greeted him with a barely discernable smile of her own.

"You were to call me Hollis, Angie."

Angie suddenly noticed the wolf's head on the walking stick. Once again she recoiled from some distant memory that the silver handle evoked.

"This was a birthday present," Hollis told her.

"They are formidable creatures," Angie said with bitterness in her voice. Then in a lighter tone, "Have you managed to retrieve my diary?"

"No. My friend has returned from Europe, but he lives in Boston, ironically. And I've been very busy with my patients, so I haven't had the chance to see him. You needn't worry, though. I won't forget about it."

Angie was obviously disappointed.

"The last time we spoke you were telling me why you left Boston. I'd be interested in hearing about your journey west."

"You are very clever, Hollis. You hope to escape my wrath at your failure to return my diary by enticing me to talk about my travels. I can't help but oblige you, though."

Angie recalled how the lights of Boston slowly faded behind her as the carriage she rode in made its way down the road leading out of the city. She felt a tinge of guilt about departing without saying goodbye to her father, yet realized there was no other way to leave. Reginald Barton would have used his considerable resources to prevent his daughter from going to San Francisco.

Their first stop was the tiny town of Maple Grove, Ohio. There Wyatt and Cassia became man and wife. They were married at the home of Roger McGrew, the groom's cousin. As Angie watched her friend marry the lanky New Englander she could envision standing next to Tom at her own ceremony. Her happiness for Cassia produced a tear that slowly rolled down her cheek. Angie's anticipation of her own wedding day was responsible for the one following it.

The three immigrants then traveled to the town of Independence, Missouri where the Oregon Trail began. This frontier town was a wild place, with several lively saloons to lure the people from the camps that had sprung up all around it. Cassia was appalled by the conditions at their campsite. There were no outhouses, and the resulting stench from so many using makeshift privies was very difficult for her to endure. Angie simply regarded it as one more obstacle to overcome before she could be reunited with Tom.

Wyatt, with Angie's financial backing, purchased the food and other supplies needed for the journey. He also bought a covered wagon that was commonly known as a *Prairie Schooner*. Wyatt then purchased a team of oxen to pull it, at the suggestion of Silas Crawford, the man he had hired to be their guide.

"The oxen can eat the grass along the way," Silas told him. "But you'll need some real expensive grain to feed a mule."

On the night before her journey was to begin, Angie Barton ventured into Independence alone. This would be the last opportunity to enjoy the varied forms of entertainment one could only find in a town, albeit a very small one in this case. Angie quickly discovered that the saloons here were as loud as those on Ann Street in Boston. She stepped into one of them and recognized several faces from the camp.

"Why Miss Barton," one of the men greeted her. "I'd never figure to see you in this place."

"When in Rome, do as the Romans due, Mr. Clever," she answered with a grin.

Angie bought a glass of whiskey, sipping from it as she watched the crowd. These people were about to face hardships they could not even imagine now. The urgency in which they enjoyed the music and spirits could only be found among those on the edge of the frontier. Angie danced with several of the men. Their complete lack of self-consciousness more than compensated for these awkward dancers' lack of grace. Her spirits soared as she moved across the floor.

As the evening wore on, one man became increasingly bold. Until this moment Angie had managed to put off his unwanted advances in a good-natured manner, but Tim Nash had now reached the point where alcohol holds sway over reason. He managed to maneuver Angie into a small corridor that led to the supply room. He put his arms around her and kissed her hard on the mouth. Angie pushed him away.

"You are not yourself. Leave me alone, or I will have to call for assistance."

Angie spoke loudly, but the din of the crowd was too great for anyone to hear her. Nash hesitated for a moment, but when no one came, he resumed his aggressive behavior.

"Come on, darling. Shoot, this is why you came here tonight."

He took a step towards her, and then suddenly fell to the ground in excruciating pain. Angie had prevailed with a well-placed knee in his groin.

Another man arrived just as the assailant hit the floor. He escorted Angie away from the drunken Nash.

"I guess you don't need my help," the tall stranger said to her as they rejoined the crowd.

"No, but thank you, anyway," Angie, who was still somewhat shaken, said to him.

"My name is Ted Sanders. I work for Silas Crawford."

"Oh, yes, he's our guide. My name is Angie Barton."

"You're with Wyatt. I saw you buying supplies with him. Can I buy you a drink?"

"Actually, I could use some fresh air."

"That sounds about right. Let's go."

They stepped outside, strolling along the dirt road that was the main street of Independence. Angie took out her silver flask of whiskey and offered some to Ted. He accepted. There was a full moon rising above the level plain that began at the edge of town. Angie wondered what was waiting for her beyond the horizon.

"Do you know where I could buy a knife?" Angie asked him.

"After tonight, I don't blame you for asking. I have a few in my tent that I bought to trade with the Indians. I can spare one."

"How much do you want for it?"

"It cost me a dollar. But I bought it with the money you gave Silas, so I'm not gonna charge you twice."

They walked back to the camp. Ted gave her the knife, though the expression on his face revealed his lack of faith in her ability to use it. The two then bade each other good night. Angie went into her tent and received a visit from Cassia shortly after. She showed the visitor her weapon.

"You got a knife? Why?"

"A man tried to force himself on me tonight."

"Are you alright?" Cassia asked as she put a hand on her shoulder.

"Yes. I barely managed to overcome him. But I wouldn't want to be caught defenseless again."

"Have you ever used a knife to defend yourself before?'

"No I haven't. But I expect to learn how to do many things on this trip. I probably won't be the same after it's over."

Angie had a faraway look in her eyes.

"I never thought about that. But you're right. I guess we'll all be different people at the end. I'll see you tomorrow."

A bugle awoke Angie before first light. Like the others in her group she would come to despise that sound over the coming months. The immigrants arose, and then sleepily prepared their breakfast. The animals were hooked up to the wagons as the dawn illuminated the sky. Silas Crawford addressed the people before they began their long trek. He had assembled the group that was now known as the Crawford Party next to a large fire near their wagons. In this way the guide could look each of them in the eye as he spoke.

"I just want to give you some good advice before we leave. Don't think you've seen the worst, or had your toughest day, until you've reached wherever it is you're going to. Some of you are gonna find the traveling too rough about halfway there. Those folks will just settle down at the first decent place they find. And I know there are some of you who will see the elephant before we even travel sixty miles. If you're one of them, then do yourself a big favor, and the rest of the folks, too. Go home now. Because this ain't no Sunday buggy ride, folks. Your feet will be hurting more than they ever have in your life, and your bones will be aching before we're two days from here. And if that's the worse that happens to you, then you're one of the lucky ones."

His weather-beaten face lent credence to the words of their guide.

"If you want to go all the way, you'd best listen to what I tell you. Now let's get going," he said in conclusion.

Silas had looked directly at Angie when he mentioned *seeing the elephant*. Though she did not know what that expression meant, the woman from Boston sensed her courage was being questioned. As a result Angie now believed she had something to prove.

"What does *see the elephant* mean?" Cassia asked her husband as the three of them walked back to their wagon.

"It's when someone knows the trip west is just too tough for them to handle," Wyatt explained. "Those are the ones that turn back."

"Fortunately I've never seen an elephant," Angie pointed out. "So I won't recognize one if I ever do."

Angie stood on the shore of an endless sea of grass, watching the sun peek over the horizon. She knew being with Tom was worth any hardship, yet for just a moment her feet would not move. The speech Silas had given made the privileged woman from Boston reluctant to begin the journey. Then Angie focused on Tom Shanahan, and all her uncertainty faded away in the early morning light.

Hollis observed how the recounting of her journey had revitalized Angelica Barton. There was a grim determination displayed in the specter's cool green eyes. Though narrow, her shoulders seemed capable of sustaining the hardships and perils associated with the Oregon Trail. This was the woman who had written the diary.

Angie and Cassia received the first of many unpleasant surprises just before Crawford gave the order for the party to move. Only Cassia's husband was to ride in the wagon, as he was the driver. The two women had to walk alongside, as was the case with the other schooners traveling in their group. This was done to ease the burden on the animals. Even had this consideration been put aside, there was no room in the wagon for passengers. The settler's possessions and supplies occupied all the available space.

"My feet are killing me," Cassia complained after a half day of walking. "Just wait until I get Wyatt alone. He never told me about this."

"He probably never thought about it," Angie pointed out. "So you can't blame him for not telling us."

"I sure can. And I sure will."

At dusk the wagons stopped for the night and Angie set up her tent next to the one occupied by the newlyweds. This was another unexpected circumstance. She had anticipated sleeping in the wagon, but there was not enough room inside to allow for that either. Angie smiled as she thought about the earful Wyatt must be receiving from his new bride. She was tempted to listen to their conversation, but could not bring herself to be so gauche.

Instead Angie crawled into her tent, settling in for the evening to read *Irish Eloquence* by candlelight. The book contained the speeches of noted Irish orators Charles Phillips, John Curran and Henry Grattan. Angie had left the flap of her tent open to eliminate its musty smell. After reading only a few pages she noticed a pair of curious eyes peering inside from the darkness. She nonchalantly located her knife.

"Who's there?" Angie asked.

There was no answer so she asked again. Suddenly a nine-year-old boy poked his head inside her tent.

"I'm sorry, ma'am. We were just walking around the camp when I saw your light. I didn't mean to bother you."

"Who's with you?"

"My sister. Pa said we were making him antsy, so we thought we'd best be somewhere else fast."

"Come inside," Angie replied pleasantly. "My name is Angie Barton."

Benjamin Aston entered the tent with his sister Clara in tow. Angie took an instant liking to the well-mannered youngsters, though she could see that they were wound up from the events of the long day. Angie easily understood why their father would find their restlessness distracting. She thought reading to the children might relax them. *Irish Eloquence* did not seem suited to this audience, so she took out her copy of *David Copperfield* instead.

"'To begin at the beginning'," Angie began the story. Clara and Benjamin listened eagerly to Dickens's description of the English boy's life. Angie read to them for an hour before escorting the children back to the Aston's wagon.

"You never mentioned the children in your writing," Hollis interrupted her narrative.

"There were so many things to describe. I couldn't include them all."

The next morning the settlers were again woken by the sound of the bugle. They crawled out of their respective tents, gingerly standing up on their aching feet. Angie took some bacon out of the wagon for breakfast. The cooking fire Cassia had started illuminated the meat, revealing that it had turned green. Upon closer inspection Angie discovered that the bacon was also infested with maggots.

Angie dropped it on the ground. She ran away from the wagon, falling to her knees before vomiting. The Boston immigrant's recovery was hastened by the sound of footsteps coming from behind her.

"Are you all right, Miss Barton?" Crawford asked her.

"Yes, I am."

There was a self-satisfied expression on the face of their guide. He was apparently thinking that his initial evaluation of her had been proven correct. The big man turned and started to walk away.

"I won't become one of the turnarounds," Angie called after him. "I will travel all the way to California."

Silas stopped in his tracks. He turned to face her.

"There's no shame in going home, Miss Barton. You're someone who's used to living high on the hog. And that makes it twice as tough when some scurvy butcher in Independence sells you bad bacon."

Silas walked away. Angie finished making breakfast.

Angie continued to read nightly installments of *David Copperfield* to the children. For Angie these sessions entailed a significant sacrifice. The other adults in the wagon train spent their evenings dancing to the fiddler's bow. The immigrants moved to the lively music as though they did not have a care in the world.

"I don't want to cause any trouble, Miss Angie," Benjamin said as they walked back to the Aston wagon one night. "But there's something I have to tell you. Miss Patty Henderson, she, well she borrowed Miss Cassia's broach."

"Borrowed?"

"Well, she took it, Miss Angie. I just thought you should know."

Angie gave Benjamin a hug.

"Thank you for telling me about this. Good night."

There had been several incidents whereby a settler inexplicably lost a valued possession. Patty Henderson, who was traveling with a sinister looking man who was not her husband, was often mentioned as a possible suspect. Angie remembered the broach Benjamin had referred to. Cassia had received it from her late mother. Up to this point she had not been aware the jewelry was gone. Angie was pleased to see that Patty and her companion were still dancing with the others when she arrived at their wagon. Cassia's friend searched the schooner, discovering the broach in a large wooden chest. She waited in the shadows until the pair returned. When they arrived, Angie grabbed Patty from behind, throwing her up against the wagon. The knife in her hand was enough to prevent the man from reaching for his powder horn pistol.

"You take one more thing from anyone in this camp, and I'll see to it that you're both left behind for the pleasure of the Indians!"

Angie knocked her to the ground before leaving.

"Why didn't you mention the thief in your diary?" asked Hollis, who was impressed by the apparition's actions.

"I'm not one for casting aspersions, even if they are true. I thought someone might read my diary one day. And as you know, I was right."

"As I remember you stopped writing in the diary after reaching the Devil's Gate. Why?"

Angie stared at him with her brilliant green eyes. Hollis noticed that she wrung her hands before speaking.

"Cassia was badly hurt before we reached Fort Bridger."

"I'm so sorry, Angie. What happened?"

The apparition was swayed by the doctor's sincerity. After considering the matter for a moment Angie decided to continue, in light of Hollis's genuine concern about her friend.

The Devil's Gate was a canyon formed by two imposing rock formations through which the Sweetwater River ran in what would later become the state of Wyoming. The rocky walls on either side of it were over 400 feet high. Many who explored the canyon came out of it feeling as though they had been somewhere where time had stood still. The name of this place made some of the settlers uneasy, so the Crawford Party did not linger for long.

"We can't go through it," Silas informed the settlers. "The drop off on the other side is too much for the animals to manage. We'll go around it."

After the party reached the other side they encountered a series of deep ravines. Suddenly an uneasy murmur spread throughout the party.

"Look, on the rocks," Cassia said with both amazement and fear in her voice.

Angie observed a countless number of rattlesnakes sunning themselves on the rocky outcrops along the side of the trail. She had never been afraid of snakes, yet these insolent looking rattlers were enough to start her heart racing.

"This land is evil," one frightened settler remarked.

"I'm surprised you didn't turn around," Hollis said. "I can't imagine a more intimidating place to travel through."

"I'll admit I thought about it for a minute," she conceded. "But I said I wouldn't quit, and I didn't."

Angie continued her story. Jake Anderson, another member of the Crawford Party, had come walking up beside them with his rifle in hand.

"Don't worry, ladies," he assured them. "They won't bother you if you don't bother them."

"That truly was the Devil's Gate," Angie remarked. "His serpents are all gathering before it to serve their master."

Cassia said a quick prayer. Wyatt chuckled to himself on the buckboard.

"Come on, Cass," he said with a smile. "There are more snakes then that in Ohio. And they're bigger, too."

"But most of those are the two legged kind, dear husband," she replied with a grin.

After the wagons stopped for the night Angie began to make a batch of Johny Cakes. This popular fare was made from milk, corn meal and flour. Just as she was about to place her concoction on the fire a swarm of hungry insects arrived. Though Angie shooed many of them away, an even greater number landed in the batter. The woman who had set out from Boston two months before would have never tolerated such conditions while preparing food. Yet the now hardened traveler ignored this unintended ingredient and placed the cakes over the fire without hesitation. One of Crawford's men happened by at that moment, giving her a look of approval.

"You do what you've gotta do," he remarked before walking on.

After finishing her chore Angie went to her tent. She was repairing a tear in the sleeve of her dress when Cassia interrupted her. Her friend gratefully accepted the whiskey Angie offered to her.

"I've done my share, right?" Cassia asked her.

"You certainly have. Did someone say otherwise?"

"And I haven't been complaining. Well, not that much anyway. I just mean I haven't been worse than anyone else, right?"

"You've been fine, my dear friend. What's the matter, Cass?"

"I've just been feeling a little different since we saw the Devil's Gate. Like I've got something coming after me, you know? So if anything happens, I just want you to remember how I was."

A concerned expression came over Angie's face as she embraced her friend.

"You're just tired, Cass. We're all feeling the same way. Jake told me that we've traveled over 900 miles since leaving Independence. Things will look a lot brighter in the morning."

"Good night," Cassia responded. She left without concurring.

Angie found it difficult to sleep after their conversation so she joined the men and woman who were dancing to the music of the bow. The stars above them shone with an intensity she would remember for the rest of her life. Angie did not return to her tent until late that night.

"We are truly in the hands of God," she said aloud before finally falling asleep.

The next morning Silas Crawford spotted several Indians on the trail some distance ahead of the party. He ordered the wagons to halt. Ted Sanders rode up beside him and questioned whether the delay was justified.

"There's not very many of them," he observed. "They won't have much to trade with."

"It seems that way to me, too. But you can't always go by what you see. I'm going to talk with them."

"I'll be right next to you, boss."

"No. I want you here to lead the wagons, just in case those bastards are up to something."

Silas carefully approached the Indians. He quickly satisfied himself that they had no untoward intentions. They were hunters, with an ample supply of freshly killed buffalo. He traded some cloth for several pieces of fresh meat. As a result the two cattle the settlers had with them were spared. Silas had intended to butcher the animals that evening, but it would not be necessary now.

The Crawford party continued on. They were little more than a half days journey from Fort Bridger when darkness fell. The settlers put their hardships aside for the evening to enjoy a hearty meal. The fiddle players began to play and their vibrant music inspired the people to dance with more enthusiasm then should have been possible at the end of a hard day. Cassia squealed with laughter as Wyatt twirled her around. A lace on one of her shoes was broken in the process.

"That's what I get for acting like a school girl," she said with a laugh. "I'll fix this and be back directly."

She walked to their wagon.

A lookout stood guard over the animals. He was envious of the laughter that was coming from the center of the wagons. Yet his job was too important to allow it to be a distraction. Suddenly a pair of glowing eyes became visible in the night. A wolf had taken notice of the cattle and oxen. The lookout carefully walked around the perimeter of the wagons. He saw the predator in silhouette against the rising moon. The man fired his gun.

The wolf fled, while the rest of the animals nervously bellowed. One of the cattle, however, was sent into a panic by the sound of the rifle being discharged. Stampeding through the settlers, it barely missed several of them. Cassia had just reached the wagon when the rampaging bull ran by. The frightened animal made contact with her hip, slamming the petite woman into the side of the schooner. She screamed in pain, which momentarily froze her companions. The music stopped as her anguished cries tore through the night.

Angie was the first to reach her. Cassia's left arm was hideous to behold, the shattered bone having broken through the skin. Angie Barton felt nauseous, but could not let her friend see that. She fought off the urge to vomit.

"It's broken, Cass. But we'll get it fixed for you," she calmly said.

Wyatt fought his way through the crowd then knelt down beside his wife. He was not as adept at hiding his repulsion as Angie was, but it no longer mattered. Cassia took no notice of those around her now. The pain was too excruciating. She let out a hideous wail when the settlers carried her into the wagon. Donald Fletcher, who was the only settler who had any medical experience to speak of, examined Cassia. He spoke with Wyatt outside the wagon afterwards. Angie stood by them.

"It's bad," he told them. "I've given her some opium for the pain. In a while I'll clean it up as best I can. I learned doctoring from my pa on our farm. I ain't never gone to school for it. There might be someone at Bridger who's a real doctor. But I do know that if it gets infected…"

He did not have to finish his sentence. Angie and Wyatt knew that an infection would most likely result in the death of Cassia.

"I'll give her a Sappington pill, just in case she gets a fever. I'll do the best I can."

"We know you will," Wyatt said softly.

Angie looked at Hollis with a pained expression on her face. The torment she was feeling was to a greater degree than Hollis had ever witnessed in any of his other patients.

"Did Cassia live?" he asked her.

"I don't know," Angie said while bowing her head. "I left soon after she was hurt."

"But can't you see her now?"

"I can't go where she is, or where the children are. I am not fit to stand in their presence, or his presence."

Angie turned and floated towards the back of the garden.

"Don't leave. I can help you."

His words fell on deaf ears. After the now familiar flash of brilliant white light, Angie faded into the night. Hollis waited for several moments before going inside. Olivia was still awake.

"That was a very long walk," she said suspiciously. "What on earth were you doing?"

"Just organizing my thoughts," he replied. "I lost track of the time."

"You should start carrying your cell phone with you constantly," she suggested. "That way I can keep track of the time for you."

"You're too kind, my love."

Hollis kissed Olivia, suddenly becoming aroused by the shapely woman in the light blue chemise. He exposed her breasts and manipulated them with an unrestrained fervor. As Hollis entered her he suddenly thought of the woman who had challenged the plains. As a psychiatrist Doctor Simms knew all about the psychological phenomenon of transference. Hollis tried to tell himself this was not the case, yet he could not drive the image of Angie from his mind. Even as he satisfied his wife, Simms wondered if his passionate thrusts were really intended for Angelica Barton. This was the guiltiest pleasure Hollis Simms had ever experienced.

For her part Olivia sensed the turmoil within her husband. At first she found it to be an unwelcome distraction, but soon discovered that the movements of a conflicted lover could be both unpredictable and extremely satisfying. She thoroughly enjoyed making love with the stranger in her bed.

As his wife enjoyed a contented slumber, Doctor Simms lay awake for the rest of the night. Hollis felt as though he had betrayed Olivia. He managed to extradite himself from this emotional morass by focusing on Angie Barton as his patient instead of as his first love.

Angie knows she's dead, he thought to himself. *She just can't face the children or Cassia. Or him, for that matter, with him being Tom Shanahan, I would assume. But why? Something must have happened between the Devil's Gate and San Francisco to traumatize Angie.*

Hollis intended to find out what it was.

CHAPTER NINE

ollis sat on the set of *The Robin Wainscot Show* and stared at the empty seats in front of the stage. In a couple of hours they would be filled by an enthusiastic crowd of people, most of whom were more excited by the prospect of appearing on television than by anything that was said during the show. Hollis wondered why anyone would want their personal problems laid bare before such an audience. Yet the callers were certainly anxious to reveal their deepest feelings; if that was not true, he would not be here.

One such person whose story would be discussed on that day's show was a man from Baltimore. He was a young and aggressive salesman who had quickly developed an impressive clientele. This individual, who called himself Roger, had only one thing standing in the way of his continued success. For some reason, soon after his career had started to take off, he developed a strong fear of flying. Roger's anxiety attacks began hours before the plane was due to leave. On his last trip he barely made it to his destination.

"I can't go on this way, Dr. Simms. I have a great wife. We want to start a family, and this is the only way I can support one. I have to fly."

Hollis noticed something in the inflection of his voice. The doctor suddenly knew what was troubling this man.

"Do you really want to be a salesman?" he asked him.

"Why, of course. I'm a natural at it. I could sell a drowning man a bucket of water."

The audience chuckled at his remark.

"You probably could. But would you want to? Isn't it possible that you'd really rather do something else? As a salesman you often have to coax people into buying things they might not really have any use for. Could that be bothering you?"

Hollis could hear Alec complaining about a *snap diagnosis*. The doctor was confident about his analysis of this patient, however.

"When did you first start to have trouble flying?" Hollis asked him after receiving no reply.

"About a year ago," Roger replied.

"Did anything significant happen to you around that time?"

"Sure. I got married."

"And as a result you suddenly felt the pressure which comes with being the breadwinner in a family. You believed there was no other option at this point in your life. You were suddenly locked in to being a salesman."

Once again there was silence on the other end of the line.

"You could be right, I guess," Roger finally responded. "So what should I do now? Should I quit my job?"

"I can't answer your question. Only you can decide that. But I think you're not really panicking because of your impending flight. I believe it's because you're feeling trapped by your new responsibilities. Your mind is interpreting the cause of your anxiety as a fear of flying so you won't have to deal with the real issue. That's just my opinion, of course. If you find that my interpretation doesn't help you, by all means see someone else."

"Thank you Doctor Simms. You've given me a lot to think about."

Hollis believed he had really helped the caller. Now as he sat on the stage, his thoughts turned to Angie Barton. She still had not reappeared in the garden. Hollis feared that the most fascinating individual in his life had slipped away from him.

"A penny for your thoughts, doctor?" Robin asked as she sat down next to him.

"I charge much more than that, actually," he replied with a smile.

"You know, I don't have your ability to analyze other people's thoughts and feelings. In fact, I have enough trouble doing it with my own most of the time. But in my line of work, I talk with a great many people. I've developed a good sense of what's going on in their heads. I think you're having woman trouble, Doctor Simms."

"You could say that. I'm concerned about one of my female patients."

"Just tell me if I'm out of line. I think you have a thing for this patient. I know you're a married man, and that it's none of my business. But I also know the look on your face very well."

Hollis felt embarrassed, as if he were standing in front of the talk show host naked. As a teenage boy he had fallen in love with the woman who had challenged the plains. Yet surely as a man Hollis had grown out of that infatuation, or so he had assumed.

This isn't a romantic relationship Hollis told himself. *I just want to help her.*

"I'm sure you've learned a great deal about people over the years, Robin," Hollis said as he stood up. "But in this case you're wrong. I could not possibly be romantically interested in this patient."

Hollis went to his dressing room. He later emerged for his appearance on the show, and the crowd responded well to Roger's story. Hollis then drove back to Fairhaven. The phone rang just as he walked through the front door.

"So how was your trip to the West Coast?" Paul Nustad asked him. "I hear San Diego is a beautiful place."

"I wouldn't know. The conference kept me so busy I didn't have any time to take in the scenery."

"I'm sorry to hear that," Paul replied with a laugh. "I also don't believe it for a moment, of course. I have some interesting information about your ghost. It seems that Angelica Barton's father paid Thomas Shanahan to leave New England."

"How did you find that out?"

"We managed to locate some letters written by people who were friends of the Bartons. Apparently Reginald found out about his daughter's relationship with Shanahan. He offered a significant sum of money to him if he would leave his daughter alone. There was also the matter of William Conner's death. Barton threatened to pin it on Shanahan if he refused to leave. And with his clout among the authorities in Boston Reginald might have been able to pull it off."

"I wonder if Angie knew about it. She said Tom mentioned that her father would be glad to hang him. But there was never any mention of an agreement between the two."

"I haven't found any evidence indicating she did know. You could ask her though."

"I thought you didn't believe in my ghost," Hollis pointed out.

"I'm still not convinced she's real. But this would be a good test to see if the woman you've been seeing knows all the facts about Angelica's life."

Hollis hesitated. He was as curious as his friend was about the origin of the specter that appeared to him on certain nights. Yet to challenge her authenticity could cost him the most compelling relationship Doctor Simms had ever known.

"I hold it in abeyance," he finally replied. "I'm at a very delicate point with Angie. If she ever does appear again, I want her to continue telling me about the events on the Oregon Trail. That way I can learn how she came to be a house servant on Long Island."

Paul thought his friend was avoiding the issue. Still he chose not to press Hollis on that point.

"I'll continue to look for information about Angelica," he said. "I'll talk to you soon."

"Take care," Hollis said as he hung up the phone.

He sat down on the sofa, staring out the large window dominating the living room. Hollis was deep in thought when Annabelle arrived home. He did not even notice her walking into the room.

"Have you seen any good plays, lately?" she asked him.

Hollis looked at his daughter with a guilty expression on his face. He had intended to see her perform the role of Shakespeare's Juliet yesterday afternoon. Then two emergency phone calls suddenly changed the doctor's priorities. Hollis had asked Olivia to apologize for him since he did not arrive home until very late that night. She had tried, but apparently failed to appease their daughter. Hollis motioned for Annabelle to join him on the couch. She reluctantly obliged him.

"I'm sorry, Belle. You know I would have given anything to be there. But there were two patients who desperately needed my help yesterday. I couldn't make it."

"There's always something keeping you away from us now," she responded. "Between the t.v. show and your patients you're never here anymore, Dad."

"I thought you approved of my becoming a celebrity," Hollis pointed out.

"I think it's great, yeah. But I didn't know you would just disappear. And even when you're here your mind is a million miles away. It's like when I walked in the room before. You had that weird expression on your face. It's really creepy."

Hollis was embarrassed. He almost felt as though his daughter had caught him with another woman. The doctor put his arm around Annabelle.

"I know I've been preoccupied," he conceded. "But I've not only taken on *The Robin Wainscot Show*, I also have a new patient who is very unusual. It's the kind of case that comes along once in a lifetime. So bear with me Belle. I'll always be here for you. Promise."

She returned his embrace and stood up.

"Aunt Nora and Aunt Wilimina called yesterday," Annabelle told him. "They want you to call them back."

"Will do. There's nothing wrong with them, I hope."

"No, they're fine. But I did mention how stressed you've been lately. Sorry Dad, I was upset because you missed my play."

"Not to worry, my love. But I'm sure the two of them will insist on coming here to check me out for themselves. And since you instigated their visit, it's only fair that you entertain the itty old bittys."

She was startled. Annabelle didn't know Hollis was aware of how she referred to the two elderly women. He smiled at her, and his daughter responded in kind. Then she left the room.

After dinner Hollis and Olivia sat on the veranda sipping their coffee. The lush trees and well-kept lawn were pleasing to the eye. On these occasions Hollis often wondered why fate had been so kind to him. Then the doctor's gaze found the setting sun as he wondered if Angie would visit him tonight. Olivia took notice of the detached expression on his face. As with Annabelle, Hollis felt as though he had been caught with his mistress.

"Would you like me to go inside? I seem to be competing with something or someone else for your attention. And I'm losing. I hate to lose, love."

"Not at all, darling. I was just thinking about how fortunate I've been. To live on this beautiful estate with you for my wife and Belle for my daughter is more than I ever could have hoped for."

Hollis kissed her hand. Olivia believed him, yet she knew there was more on her husband's mind than just his good fortune.

"The feeling is mutual, dear. But I've known you too long for you to keep anything from me. Now what has you so distracted these days?"

"I've taken on a quite extraordinary case. The patient exhibits all the signs of having repressed memories. But I haven't had enough time with her to find out what those memories entail. And due to some very unusual circumstances I don't anticipate having the opportunity to spend enough time with her to accomplish that. I'm concerned she might never reveal the cause of her trauma to me."

Olivia was extremely surprised, and very pleased. This was the first time she could ever remember receiving a detailed response to such a question.

"And the television show doesn't help, I'm sure," she said. "That's my fault. I talked you into that."

"Yes, I had to be dragged into the studio kicking and screaming," Hollis said with a smile. "You know what a retiring creature I am."

They shared a long laugh at his response.

"But seriously, you're spreading yourself too thin, Hollis. You're in your office until all hours of the night to compensate for the time you spend with Robin. I think you should take a hiatus from the show."

He was tempted to explain that those long nights in his Fairhaven office were due to his watching the garden for Angie's glow. Yet he knew Olivia was a skeptic when it came to the paranormal. Not only would she dismiss the idea of a visitor from the spirit world, his wife might very well have him committed.

"Things will calm down shortly. My patients are finally becoming acclimated to my new office hours, so I should have fewer emergencies to deal with in the future. I'll be able to spend more time focusing on the two women in my life."

"Speaking of focusing on our home…"

"Actually I said I wanted to focus on the two women in my life," Hollis corrected her.

"I know. But I had another matter on my mind. You know I love your brother."

"Do you? I can't ever remember hearing you say that."

"It's such a deep feeling words cannot be used to describe it."

Hollis smiled at her.

"I just think that Sebastian should be getting on with his life," she continued. "How long is he going to stay in the old house? I intended to have it commemorated as the birthplace of Hollis Simms. We could even turn it into a museum."

"That's perfect. Sebastian can be the tour guide."

Olivia playfully put her arm around Hollis's neck as if to strangle him.

"I mean he can't live here forever. I think you should ask him what his intentions are."

"I already know what they are. He intends to work in the bagel shop until the dual trauma of losing his job, and the woman he intended to marry, has passed. Then he'll get on with his life."

"Has he told you that?"

"He doesn't have to. You forget that I make a living at interpreting people's behavior."

"Or more precisely, making excuses for their behavior."

Then Olivia smiled at her husband. The warm summer air and the gray shades of the twilight suddenly made all thoughts of continuing the debate disappear. They sat hand in hand for quite some time without uttering a word. Eventually Hollis stood up and kissed her.

"I do have to review some cases for tomorrow," he told her. "But I don't think it will be a late night."

"I'll wait up for you, darling."

Olivia watched him walk away before resuming her appreciation of the summer evening.

Hollis went up to his office and reacquainted himself with the patients he would see the next day. One was a woman who had developed a severe case of kleptomania. Hollis did not feel he was even close to discovering the cause of her behavior. Another patient had developed a nervous tick. Hollis was sure it was due to some traumatic event from his past that had resurfaced because of some trigger suddenly appearing in the present. He suspected it was related to a blonde woman who had just become employed at the man's workplace.

He read through the files and then looked out the window of his office. The garden was now invisible in the darkness. Hollis anxiously awaited the eerie glow that always surrounded Angie Barton when she first appeared. He was interrupted by a shout from downstairs.

"Dad, you have a phone call," Annabelle bellowed. She possessed a surprisingly loud voice and often used it to avoid walking up the stairs. He picked up the phone.

"Hollis? This is Clare."

"Well, this is a pleasant surprise. How have you been Miss Johnson?"

"I'm doing all right. I've seen your show. You're really terrific on it. Everyone I know says the same thing."

"Thank you. I appreciate the compliment. But just remember that it's Robin's show. I'm only an occasional guest. She wouldn't appreciate your forgetting that. So how goes the advertising game?"

"It's a grind, but I still like it."

"Sebastian is doing well, too."

Hollis was not inclined to pry into the affairs of others. That was with the exception of his patients, of course. Yet in this instance he could not resist the temptation to find out how she felt about his brother. Hollis still believed Sebastian and Clare would make a fine couple.

"I know. I saw him recently. That's why I called. He told me something, well, that I found a little strange. Sebastian said you were communicating with a ghost."

Hollis looked out towards the old house. His brother had revealed his secret.

"Well, yes, I have to admit it's true. At least that's what she appears to be."

"I usually mind my own business, but in this case I just had to talk to you about it. Are you feeling okay?"

Clare was genuinely concerned about the doctor. She also believed that if Hollis Simms could become delusional, then there was little hope for anyone else.

"Maybe one of the other doctors at the hospital could help you," Clare continued.

Hollis chuckled to himself. He could understand why his claim to have met with one of the dead would elicit such a response.

"I appreciate your concern," Hollis told her. "And to be honest you're not the only one who thinks that I might be in trouble. But Sebastian has seen her as well, though from a considerable distance for the most part. Did he tell you that?"

"Yes."

Hollis received the distinct impression that his brother lacked credibility in her eyes.

"Do you believe in an afterlife, Clare?

"Not really. I take it you do, though."

"I've always believed there's something for us after we die. But I never thought a person could come back from the great beyond until now. This has been the most incredible experience of my life."

"You have a gift for understatement."

"I'm not just interested in her because she's a spiritual entity. I want to help her deal with the trauma she experienced on the way to California."

"Is this person real, or are you just imagining her? You would know if you needed help, right? I'm only asking because I've always considered you a friend, Hollis. I don't want anything to happen to you."

Hollis paused for a moment.

"The feeling's mutual, Clare. I can assure you that my mind is as sound as it's ever been. Which, come to think of it, isn't saying all that much."

"I have to get up early tomorrow to sell the people in America all the things they could really live without," Clare said after she stopped laughing. "Keep in touch, Hollis."

"We'll get together for lunch. Sleep well."

Hollis hung up the phone and went to see Sebastian. He found his brother watching a baseball game with Frank.

"What the hell are you swinging at!" Frank yelled after a Met player struck out. "The damn ball is ten feet over your ass!"

"Your guys just can't lay off the high heat," Sebastian observed.

"Because my guys are a bunch of damn fools! They got no more sense than a chicken with its head stuffed up its ass."

"Hello, gentleman," Hollis said in greeting.

"Can I get you something to drink?" Sebastian asked him.

"A beer will do. I'll get it myself."

Hollis took one from the refrigerator and then took a seat next to the groundskeeper.

"It seems strange to be watching television in this room again," he said.

"Remember the 1986 series?" Sebastian reminisced. "I'll never forget the look on your face when that ball went between Buckner's legs. I thought you were going to weep for joy."

"I watched it, too. That's when I became a Met fan," Frank told them. "I saw that game in Virginia before we moved up here."

"I'll never forget that night," Hollis said.

"Of course you won't. Met championships are few and far between," Sebastian, who was an avid Yankee fan, pointed out.

"That's only because my team doesn't buy a pennant every year," Hollis retorted.

"As a Yankee fan it's very difficult to watch you poor Met fans experience such frustration from being losers so much of the time. Maybe we'll loan you a couple of bucks next year so you can get out of last place."

"Shit, you spend all that money and your asses are still getting beat to hell," Frank said. "You should spend some money to get someone who can throw the damn ball."

The conversation continued in the same vein for the remainder of the game. Sebastian came out on the short end of the debate that evening as the Mets rallied to win three to one. Frank said good night and went back to the groundskeeper's house.

"I received an unexpected phone call this evening," Hollis said after he left. "Clare called to check up on my state of mind."

Sebastian was at a loss for words.

"I hope you're not making Angie a general topic of conversation, Sam."

"Oh, no, of course not. I only mentioned it to Clare because she asked me what my plans were. I said that there was something very strange going on here, and that I was curious to see how it turns out. I wouldn't embarrass you."

Hollis stood up and walked over to the window. He gazed in the direction of the garden for several moments.

"I'm not embarrassed by anything I've done," Hollis finally said. "I just don't want this to turn into some kind of media circus. If word gets out that a ghost is visiting Doctor Simms, then Fairhaven will be overrun by reporters. And talk show hosts as well, including Robin Wainscot."

"Clare knows how to be discreet. Even though she is in advertising."

Hollis sat down on the couch once more.

"So that's why you haven't looked into returning to Wall Street. You want to see what happens with Angie."

"Yes. I'd like a chance to speak with her. And the only way that will happen is if I'm here."

"I can't blame you for that. Talking with Angie reminds me of listening to broadcasts of the Cleveland Indians' games in the room upstairs when I was a boy. On certain summer nights, you could get a radio station from Ohio on Long Island."

"Do you know why? It's because radio signals are absorbed by the ionosphere during the day. When night comes the upper atmosphere cools off, so the signals bounce off of it instead. That's why you can receive stations from so far away."

"How do you know that?'

"I actually attended a few of my science classes when I was in college."

"I'm impressed. But whatever the reason, there was something magical, and a little eerie about being able to hear something you shouldn't be able to hear. At least as far as I knew at the time, though thanks to you I now know better."

"Speaking with Angie has to be a really amazing experience. For you it must be a little like hearing the siren's song."

"That's true. But as far as your speaking with her, it might never happen, you know. I can't risk having someone else distract her when she appears. Angie rarely visits the garden, so I need to use every one of those occasions for treating her. And as things stand now she might never appear again, anyway. So you should think about your career instead of waiting around here for a chance to communicate with her."

"Did Clare say that?"

"No, I said that. I also said you're welcome to stay here for as long as you want, and I meant it. But there could be serious consequences if you don't find a job in the brokerage business soon. You might not be able to get back in if you wait too long."

Sebastian could not deny the validity of his brother's statement. Yet he still could not put aside his desire to speak with the apparition. If he had been honest with himself, there was also his strong inclination to avoid the world of corporate politics that prevented the younger Simms from leaving Fairhaven.

"I understand that," he told Hollis. "But I need some more time to decide what I really want to do. If Olivia is complaining, I can stay somewhere else."

"As Frank told you when you first came here she loves to complain," Hollis said with a laugh. "If you're not the reason de jour then our groundskeeper and his verbal abuse of the plants will be. So don't concern yourself about it."

"So how is Clare doing?" Sebastian asked him.

"She's fine, but misses you terribly."

"Did she tell you that?"

"No. But I'm a psychiatrist. I know these things. Although come to think of it she is Irish, and Freud said the Irish can't be analyzed. So I could be mistaken."

"Clare sure doesn't act like she misses me," Sebastian said in a despondent tone.

"You really didn't expect her to support your decision to work in the bagel shop, did you Sam?" Hollis asked with kindness in his voice.

"I guess we believe what we want to believe. I thought Clare would stick by me, even when I hit a rough spot in my life."

"I don't think she's given up on you. Courage, my friend."

Hollis walked by the garden on his way back to the main house. The summer stars twinkled contentedly overhead. He stepped inside the garden to look for some trace of his most unpredictable patient. There was none to be found.

A dejected Doctor Simms went inside the house.

CHAPTER TEN

S ebastian walked out of the old house one morning and opened the door to his car. He breathed in the autumn air, pausing to admire the myriad colors displayed by the trees. The bagel shop manager started to get in when the movement of someone on the veranda caught his attention. Harley Fox was visiting Fairhaven once more. As always, he had arrived at the time of day when Hollis was not home.

Sebastian sat in his car for several moments before driving away. He watched as Olivia brought out breakfast for the two of them. They appeared to be enjoying each other's company immensely, though he could not hear their conversation. Simms was about to leave when Frank happened by. He gestured for him to get into the car.

"Are you having trouble?" Frank asked as he sat beside him. "I can give you a ride if you need it."

"No, I'm not. Do you see who's sitting on the porch with Olivia?"

"Oh, yeah, he's the movie guy. He's been here lots of times."

"Do you know what Harley's doing here?"

"Do I know? Who do you think I am? I'm just here to do a job. I mind my own damn business."

Frank looked at Sebastian carefully, and then let out a sigh.

"Now don't tell me you think Mrs. Simms is fooling around."

"I don't know," Sebastian replied. "I know he wants her to finance his movie, but this guy spends enough time here to get the financing for five movies. I think something is going on."

"And what if it is? Are you dumb enough to tell Hollis? Man, that don't ever make anyone happy. You just gonna knock him on his ass, and probably break up his marriage. And what's gonna happen to that snotty little girl of theirs? She'll be hurt worse than anybody else. Stop thinking with your butt and use your brains."

Hollis's brother thought about the groundkeeper's admonitions for a moment.

"You're right. I should just go to work and mind my own business."

Sebastian arrived at the bagel shop and quickly put Olivia out of his mind. The breakfast crowd kept the workers behind the counter very busy. As a result he had to service some customers in order to keep the long line moving. The morning was gone in an instant.

Later Sebastian sat down at one of the tables to take a break. He was about to start thumbing through the newspaper when Harley Fox walked into the shop. Sebastian Simms watched him with barely concealed disdain as he ordered a bagel with cream cheese. The aspiring director saw him sitting there after walking away from the counter. He sat down at his table.

"You're the brother-in-law, right?" Harley asked. "I don't know if you remember me from Hollis's birthday party. But we did have a brief conversation."

"I remember," he replied with little enthusiasm.

"Didn't you say that you worked on Wall Street?"

"I said that I used to work there."

Harley took a bite of his bagel while giving Sebastian a disapproving look.

"And now you're doing this," said Harley after swallowing. "Man, this has to be some comedown for you."

"I just wanted a change, for a little while at least. So how long will you have to badger Olivia to get the money for your film?"

"Who says I'm badgering her?" he replied with a coy expression on his face.

"Why else would you be spending so much time at Fairhaven?"

"Do you spy on her for Hollis?" Harley asked him with a nasty grin as he brushed back his unfashionably long hair. "Let me tell you about the entertainment business, ah, what's your name again?"

"Tom Cruise," Sebastian replied.

"That's good. I happen to know him. But anyway, you can't do anything these days without the proper financial backing. And money is tight right now."

"I keep hearing about movies with budgets of two hundred million or more. How tight could it be?"

"It's tighter than a mouse's asshole. And that's because you have to spend so much money to make a decent film these days the investors want a sure thing before they'll put up the cash."

"And you haven't been able to convince anyone that yours will produce a profit. Maybe you should wait until you have a really good idea for a movie."

Harley did not respond. He quickly finished his bagel and then stood up to leave.

"I'll put in a good word with Olivia for you the next time I see her," Harley told him with a wry smile on his face. "It might help you freeload for a little longer."

Sebastian silently watched him walk out the door.

Hollis Simms sat at his desk impatiently tapping his fingers on the top of it. Paul had left a message on his answering machine. He had more information about Angelica Barton, and was to call Hollis that evening. The psychiatrist sat there for two hours before the phone finally rang.

"Hello Hollis."

"Paul, it's good to hear from you. I hope the summer treated you well."

"Better than I deserve, I'm sure. How are Olivia and Annabelle?"

"They're doing fine," Hollis replied, while managing to mask his growing anxiousness. "So what have you found out about my night visitor?"

"It seems that her father paid someone to find Angelica after she left Boston. He was to bring her back home in exchange for a very respectable sum. As far as I know he had no success in locating Reginald's daughter, though."

"Did Angie know about this?"

"I can't say for sure. We found out about their deal from an old gentleman who is a distant relation of the Bartons. The story had been passed down through the generations."

Hollis ran his hand through his hair.

"Is that all you found out?"

"No. It seems that Angelica Barton had a cousin named Penny Nolan. She tried to rally the women in the state of Massachusetts to fight for the right to vote. Penny did so long before the officially acknowledged start of the woman's suffrage movement. I found it…."

"Look, Paul, I appreciate your looking into this for me," Hollis cut him off. The doctor was squeezing the phone so hard he thought it would break in two at any moment. "And while that's an interesting bit of information it hardly addresses the salient point. I need to know what happened to her on the Oregon Trail. Can you find some distant relation who can tell me about that?"

"I don't know of anyone who can provide those details at the moment."

"I want to know what happened to Angie. So don't give me some story that you heard from a man in his twilight years about what her cousin did for women's suffrage. Tell me what I need to know or stop wasting my time, damn it!"

Hollis slammed the phone down. He instantly regretted that gesture, and was about to call Paul back, when he noticed Annabelle standing in front of his desk. She had never seen Hollis display his temper in such a fashion. His daughter quickly recovered, however.

"Homework!" she exclaimed.

"Excuse me?"

"Homework! Homework! Homework! You said you would help me with my math homework."

"Yes, of course. I'll be with you shortly."

"You don't even remember talking to me about it," Annabelle said angrily. "And we just had the conversation during dinner."

Hollis could not deny her allegation. The truth was there for anyone to see in the expression on his face.

"I'm sorry, Belle. I had to wait for an important phone call from one of my patients. But now that I've spoken to him, I can take a look at your math problems."

"Do you always slam the phone down on your patients?" she asked suspiciously. "Besides, your patients always have emergencies, and mother always has to see a friend or meet with someone from the foundation. I guess I'll have to ask Uncle Loser to help me with my homework."

Sebastian walked into the office just as Annabelle uttered those words. Her remark made him cringe.

"We'll talk about this in a little while," Hollis said sternly.

Annabelle quickly left the room without looking at her uncle.

"She's just at a difficult age," Hollis told him. "They forget that other people have feelings."

"I know. I'm not really offended," Sebastian said in an unconvincing manner. "What do you know about this guy Harley Fox?"

"I know that at the moment he's probably more popular than I am," Hollis said with a grin. "He has an idea for a film about the Civil War. Harley wants to produce and direct it, though right now he doesn't have the money to make it. That's where Olivia comes in."

"He seems to spend an awful lot of time around here," Sebastian told him.

"That's not surprising. Olivia is very careful about what she invests in, especially since…. well; let's just say she's very careful. Harley will have a difficult time convincing her to become one of his backers."

"You should keep an eye on him," Sebastian said ominously.

"Have you heard anything untoward about him?"

"No, but he just seems like someone who is not to be trusted."

"I appreciate your concern. But my wife is quite capable of tending to her own affairs. Now if you'll excuse me, I have to help Belle with her homework."

"Sure."

Sebastian wondered at his brother's choice of one particular word as he walked back to the old house.

Hollis Simms went upstairs to Annabelle's room. After a short lecture about the proper respect to be shown for the sensibilities of others, he answered his daughter's questions about the math problems she had been assigned for homework. Then Hollis joined Olivia in the master bedroom. His wife was watching the nightly news. Her husband sat on the edge of the bed as he undressed. The weary doctor tried to alleviate the tightness in his shoulders by stretching them.

"Let me help," Olivia volunteered as she slipped over to his side of their bed.

She gave him a vigorous massage about his neck and shoulders.

"You are tense," Olivia said. "You should take some time off."

"Thanks," Hollis responded. "I feel much better now. It was just a very long day."

They lay down to watch the rest of the news together. The weatherman was predicting that tomorrow would be a gorgeous day. Hollis had intended to call Paul in the morning. He now changed his plan, based on the forecast as well as Olivia's suggestion.

"You know, I think you're right," he told her.

"You are overworked. I think you should be examined by one of your colleagues immediately. The day you start listening to my advice is the day I know you've gone around the bend."

"I always listen to your advice. I don't always follow it, though. But I am going to take some time off. I'm going up to Boston tomorrow to visit Paul. Would you care to join me?"

"I can't. Mr. Fox is coming by to show me a marketing study which proves his film can't miss being a box office smash."

"Do you think he'll convince you?"

"I happen to believe that the words *can't* and *miss* should never be used together. But we'll see."

Hollis kept his morning appointments the next day and then drove to the airport. He was standing at the door to Paul Nustad's office by early afternoon. The history professor was with a student, but he gestured for Hollis to come in anyway.

"I'm sorry, Dana, but I didn't hear your last question," he said as Hollis walked through the door. "Someone slammed a phone down in my ear yesterday. It hasn't been functioning as well as it used to. Why Hollis, this is a surprise."

"Who would be rude enough to hang up on you?" Hollis asked with a quizzical expression on his face.

"Have I answered all your questions?" Paul asked his student.

"Yes, you have. Thanks for helping me out, professor. I'll see you in class." Then to Hollis: "Can I have your autograph, Dr. Simms?"

He obliged, and the student departed.

"One of the young minds that will shape the future," Nustad said after she left. "But you and I Hollis, we're firmly entrenched in the past. Though for you that's a recent development."

"Actually, I've always spent a great deal of time probing my patients' past experiences," Hollis told him as he sat in the chair vacated by the student. "So it's not new to me at all. I'm truly sorry about yesterday. I'm just very eager to find out what happened to Angie. I think she's about to tell me, but I don't know when, or if, I'll see her again."

"My friend, we've known each other too long for anything to come between us. So your apology is unnecessary. But I do wonder about your state of mind. Do you really believe that this woman you've been seeing is the ghost of Angelica Barton?"

"Yes. I know it's incredible, but I'm convinced she has come back. Something happened on her journey that makes Angie want to avoid facing the people she loved. That's why she stayed on Long Island when she came back east. And that's why Angie's spirit remained at Fairhaven after she died."

Paul looked at him carefully for several moments before speaking again.

"But why would she appear to you now? You've had her diary for a long time. Why did Angelica only think to look for it recently?"

"I've thought about that. Do you know that many of the native people couldn't see Columbus's ships when they arrived in the new world? They stood on the shore as the explorers' vessels came into view without acknowledging them. This was because their minds could not conceive of ships that were so large. So their eyes didn't register the image of the three ships as they anchored just off shore. Eventually the medicine men were able to see them, and they convinced the others of their reality."

"I know that story well. I told it to you. I've never completely believed it, though."

"Well, I do. And I think the same concept explains why I haven't seen Angie until now. In my younger days I gave little or no thought to an afterlife. As a young boy, like everyone at that age, I believed I would live forever. But now I'm older, and the thought of an existence after death has entered my consciousness. Therefore, I can see the woman in the garden."

Paul looked at him curiously for several moments.

"So you took today off?" he finally asked his friend.

"I'm playing hooky, actually. I should be choosing a caller for my next appearance on *The Robin Wainscot Show* but I called in sick instead. It can wait until tomorrow."

"You picked the perfect day for it. Dana was my last appointment for today. And I don't have any classes until tomorrow. So I will now show you something more mysterious than anything I've ever encountered in the long history of mankind."

"And what's that?"

"The Boston subway system."

Hollis never would have been able to decipher the subway maps provided by the city. Fortunately Paul was expert when it came to this transit system and they rode the subway train into the center of Boston. Nustad stopped at a liquor store to purchase a bottle of wine, placing it in a small cooler he had brought with him to chill. The two of them walked along the streets of the city as Professor Nustad pointed out the points of interest to his friend.

"This is Park Street," he said as they turned the corner. "Angelica Barton was born here."

"Is the house where she lived still standing?" Hollis asked.

"No. None of the townhouses from that era have survived."

They turned onto Tremont Street and then entered Boston Common. The rich green grass of the park made for a picturesque scene. The two men strolled down the paths with the rest of the crowd for a while before stopping at Frog Pond. Hollis looked around him, trying to imagine what this place looked like more than one hundred years ago.

"She loved to play here as a child," Hollis said after taking a drink of wine.

"I can see why. There's a lot of room for a youngster to run here. There was even more in her day, I'm sure. And it was right across the street from her home."

They continued on, leaving the park through the Beacon Street exit. Beacon Hill now stood in front of them. Hollis found it to be less prominent than he had imagined and the close proximity of the residences did not provide the seclusion the doctor had expected. As he walked through the quiet neighborhood occupying the hill, Hollis Simms entertained the thought of bringing Angie here to see the changes which had transpired over the last century. Then he realized that her movements were beyond his control.

"This is Mount Vernon Street. Angelica lived in a mansion here, which has long since been torn down."

Hollis saw Reginald's estate rise up before him. The lawyer's abode could no longer command the striking view of the city it once did. The skyscrapers of the twentieth century made that impossible.

"Where's the Old North Church?" Hollis asked him.

"It's in that direction." Paul pointed to his right. "We can walk along the river to get there."

The Charles River moved towards the sea at a leisurely pace as they strolled along its banks. Hollis envied the people on the sailboats that were using the brisk breeze to navigate the river. The two men sat down on a bench to have another glass of wine. Hollis carefully observed the landscape around them.

"I don't know where he died," Paul said with a smile.

"You read my mind. I know William Connors met his demise somewhere around here. The records concerning his death didn't pinpoint the location?"

"The references they used to describe the place where it happened don't exist anymore. Maybe you'll meet his ghost one night. Then we'll both find out."

"I wouldn't find him half as intriguing as Angie."

"I've learned how he came to be here that night. Reginald suspected that his daughter was involved with someone else when she rejected Conners' advances. He had a detective follow her, and that was how her father learned about Tom Shanahan. Conners overheard the detective talking about the whaler with Reginald. He followed Angelica and her lover to the river one evening. After she left he confronted Shanahan. A scuffle ensued, and William fell, striking his head on a rock. Reginald threatened to have Tom prosecuted for murder even though he knew it was an accident. And with his influence Barton could have probably made it happen. So Tom Shanahan left Boston. He did so with a substantial amount of money in his pocket from Reginald to sweeten the deal for him."

"I do appreciate your efforts in finding this information."

"It's my pleasure. Do you know I was reading an article in a newspaper from that era and came across the word *computed*? The person writing the article said it had been computed that over a half million people were traveling west in 1845. I never would have expected to see that particular word being used in her time."

Hollis looked at his friend with an eerie expression on his face.

"Angie mentioned that fact to me," Hollis said. "She also used the word computed."

"This is getting interesting," Paul remarked.

They continued on to the Old North Church. Hollis walked behind the historical landmark. He found an old pine tree, and knew that this was the spot where the two lovers met whenever the whaler returned from the sea. He touched it and instantly found himself traveling back in time. Hollis could hear their laughter. He witnessed the couple's warm embrace.

"This is just how she described it," he told Paul. "This must be the place where they met."

"It is possible. But I'm sure that most of the trees from her era have long since disappeared. So you can't really be sure."

"But I can feel it."

"That is a very weak basis on which to validate your claim, doctor," Paul said with a grin.

"But they're all that matter, really. If not for feelings, human beings would be a very uninteresting lot."

They used the subway to reach their next destination. Paul would not tell Hollis where they were going, but the psychiatrist was certain he knew. The train stopped at the Forest Hills station. Paul led his friend off the platform. They walked outside into the sunshine and stood before the entrance to the Forest Hills Cemetery.

"I wonder why you brought me here," Hollis said with a knowing smile.

"Do you really?"

The two men walked through the entrance. The cemetery with its well-tended flora reminded Hollis of a garden. There were some very old headstones with dates that coincided with Angie's time. They walked at a leisurely pace, each taking the time to appreciate the beauty of their surroundings. Paul stopped when they came to the headstone he had been looking for.

Hollis stared at the inscription on it, which read *Angelica Barton, daughter of Reginald, pioneer of the west*. She had died in 1887, 25 years after her journey on the Oregon Trail. Doctor Simms felt as though he was visiting the final resting place of a very dear friend. Though his encounter with Angelica Barton's spirit had forever eliminated the finality of the grave for him, he was still overcome with emotion. Hollis turned away to gather himself.

They read Reginald's headstone, which was next to his daughter's. Hollis knew this arrangement would not please his patient. The two men then walked to the lake that was in the middle of the cemetery. Hollis and Paul sat on a bench near the placid body of water.

"I didn't think this would make you so emotional," Paul remarked.

"I surprised myself, too. But this has been a very unusual experience. So I guess it's to be expected."

Paul looked at him thoughtfully.

"Your response to this phenomenon hasn't been very scientific. Frankly Hollis, I think you've become emotionally involved with this woman. And as I understand it, that's not very healthy for the doctor-patient relationship. Of course I'm not convinced that she really is a patient."

"I do admire her; and perhaps it's something even more than that. But I can't very well refer Angie to another psychiatrist. She trusts me because I know so much about her. I'm the only one who can help her. In addition to that, this is a remarkable opportunity to learn about what happens after we die. What would you have expected? That I'd just dismiss her out of hand? I can't explain what's happening, but that doesn't mean I have to put my head in the sand and ignore it."

"I wouldn't expect you to just walk away from her. But the way you're reacting to this woman makes me wonder if you've lost your perspective. If she were really a patient, you would have proceeded in a much more professional manner."

"You believe I've been unprofessional? How so?" Hollis asked him in an irritated tone.

"You talk about her like she's a long lost love. I'm not referring to what you've said, but how you've said it. And then you become frustrated, and very angry, over my inability to provide the information you requested. That's not like you at all, Hollis."

"As for your first point, she is one, in a way," Hollis grudgingly conceded. "After reading her diary as a teenager I was quite smitten by Angie. Her courage and her willingness to take chances inspired the first romantic feelings I ever had. But that doesn't mean I'm interested in anything but seeing her at peace now. And as for my hanging up the phone, well, I can't be sure when I'll see her again. So I am very anxious to discover the root of Angie's problem so she can be cured."

"Cured of what? You keep saying that something terrible must have happened to her because Angelica Barton would never have become a domestic servant for any other reason. But maybe the journey west cured Angie of her desire for adventure. Could it be that after all the harrowing experiences the woman endured, she just wanted to do something simple with the rest of her life? Did that thought ever occur to you?"

"No, it hasn't. And if you had read her diary like someone who's not a historian it wouldn't occur to you, either. But this debate is really pointless. Because I think she'll tell me about her trip from the fort to San Francisco the next time we meet."

They watched in silence as two swans swam on the lake. The elegant creatures created a perfect picture of contentment. Hollis often wished he could achieve that same state of mind.

"That gentlemen I mentioned on the phone has some more information for me about Angie," Paul said after a while.

"Really?"

"He said that one of his relatives had written a family history of the Bartons. If so, it could give us a wealth of information about your ghost. I'm very curious to see if the document matches Angie's account."

"That sounds interesting," Hollis replied in a strangely unenthusiastic manner.

"I'd also like to know how Angelica came to be buried here if she was living on Long Island."

"Her relatives probably brought back her remains," Hollis suggested.

"That makes sense. I'll keep you informed as to what I learn from the family history. We should start back. Your flight is leaving soon."

"I'm glad one of us is keeping track of the time."

They walked past Angie's grave on their way out of the cemetery. Hollis stopped to stare at it once more.

"It must feel strange to know that you might encounter the occupant of this grave again some day," Paul observed.

Hollis said nothing as they continued on.

Angie's not in this garden anymore, she's in mine he thought to himself.

CHAPTER ELEVEN

etective Gregory Hill sat in one of the comfortable leather chairs in Doctor Simms' office. He had already attended two sessions there, the detective having noticed the neutral nature of the colors featured in his psychiatrist's workplace. Apparently Hollis believed his patient's emotional offerings were not to be induced by their surroundings. They were to be elicited by his talents, not by the stimulation that could be provided by a decorator's scheme.

Hollis said as he entered the room, "How have you been, Gregory?"

"Not too bad, doc. I'm sorry I was so late. I had to testify in a spousal abuse case. The poor woman stayed with this guy until he put her within an inch of death's door. I'll never understand why they do that."

"It's a pattern that's often developed in childhood," Hollis said sadly. "When a person expects to be abused, only their tormentor can put an end to the victim's dreadful anticipation of the next encounter. The act itself actually provides relief since the person knows they won't be attacked again for a little while, at least. In this way the behavior becomes acceptable, even welcomed, to the abused person."

"I guess you're right," Gregory conceded.

"You can remain seated today if you'd like. But I would like to remind you that the couch is available if you want to use it."

Detective Hill had chosen to sit through his sessions with Hollis during his previous visits. He felt more comfortable looking him straight in the eye. The doctor believed that a reclining patient had a better chance to reach a state of complete relaxation. Still he always left it up to their discretion.

"I like this chair," Hill told him.

"Very well. At the end of our last discussion you began to describe your first encounter with Avalor. Why don't you continue?"

Gregory described his initial contact with the mysterious woman. He had just finished working a long shift and decided that a walk in the park was in order. The detective did several laps around the small lake there. He was about to leave for home when a woman sitting on the grass caught his attention.

"It was like looking at a photograph. You know how the colors in a picture always seem brighter than they were when you looked at them with the naked eye. That's what it was like for me. Avalor just stood out that way. Her hair was the softest, shiniest brown I've ever seen. And this was in the middle of a sun shower. The drops of rain sparkled all around her. But it was only coming down where she was sitting. And the rain never seemed to touch her."

"You're describing what many would call love at first sight," Hollis pointed out with a smile. "And you observed her when you had just worked a long shift. Could fatigue have affected your perception of Avalor?"

"I know what you mean. But this was something more. I just knew she didn't belong there. And her eyes just blew me away. They're copper colored."

The detective walked by the strange woman several times. He was undaunted when questioning a suspect yet very shy in social situations. Finally Avalor initiated their first conversation.

"How many times are you going to pass by before you speak to me?" she asked with a pleasant grin.

"You caught me," Hill answered nervously with one of his own. "I just couldn't help notice that blue jump suit you're wearing. It's very nice."

"Why thank you. I like your clothes, too. Why don't you join me?"

"So I walked up to her and introduced myself," the detective continued. "We talked about what a beautiful day it was. I just couldn't understand why everyone in the park wasn't staring at her. Avalor should have attracted a crowd. But they just kept walking by. Then I asked her where she was from. Avalor laughed and said I wouldn't believe her. She told me anyway, though."

"Did you believe her?"

"No, not at first. I've met a lot of dizzy broads and a lot of crazy people in general for that matter. So I'm real careful about believing strangers. But Avalor won me over. She told me people had developed copper colored eyes in the future because the ozone layer was shot to hell."

"Did she use the expression *shot to hell*?"

"Well, no, that's me talking. But anyway the sun's rays are so strong in the future people needed a way to protect their eyes from them. And nature obliged. I guess Darwin was right."

"What else did she say about the future?"

"The people there have found a way to get along. They had to. When the scientists discovered how to travel through time the authorities were able to find out about accidents and violent acts before they ever happened. They set up a special agency to prevent them. So the population grew really fast. And the demand for food grew with it. Every country in the world would have been in a constant state of war over the limited food supply if they didn't work together to solve the problem."

"The demand for energy grew as well, I'm sure," Hollis interjected.

Gregory smiled at Hollis. He had initially felt reluctant to tell him his story. Though he did not expect ridicule from the doctor, Hill feared the psychiatrist would be snickering inside. Yet there was no evidence of that.

"You've got it, doc. You know I thought you'd think I was a flake. But you're really listening to me."

Hollis smiled back.

"As I said at our first session, I don't believe in labels. Did you ask her to take you to the future?"

"Yeah, I did. But Avalor said she couldn't, because then I'd find out how it was done. And the authorities from her time don't want that information to get out. She said that it was a shame, because you can see a million stars at night from where she lives."

Hollis jotted down a note to himself. At some point he would question how someone from a time with a much larger population than the present one could see so many stars. He would expect the atmosphere to have become even more polluted than it was now. Doctor Simms intended to use the damaged ozone layer that the woman from the future had mentioned to support his assumption.

"Did you ask her why she had come back to the past?" Hollis questioned him.

"For the people from her time it's like going to an amusement park. They can visit all kinds of places and meet a lot of different people."

"That was quite a story," Hollis said as he stood up. "We're finished for today. Friday's one o'clock cancelled, so I can see you then if you'd like."

"I'll be here. Have a good one, doc."

Hollis returned home that evening with the intention of planning Gregory's next session. Instead the doctor found himself thinking about Angie's next session as he joined Olivia for coffee in the sitting room. This was not lost on his wife.

"Damn it Hollis, what has gotten into you!" she suddenly exclaimed. "It's like living with a ghost! I can see you, but you're not really here!"

"I'm sorry, love, I was just thinking about a patient."

"You're always thinking about a patient and you're always sorry," Olivia responded in an irritated tone.

"What can I do to make it up to you?"

"You could ask me how my day was. I know you're really not interested, but at least give me the courtesy of pretending to care."

"Of course I care. How was your day?"

"The battery in my car died. I had to call for help. I seem to remember asking you to have it checked out two weeks ago."

Hollis could not believe that two weeks had passed since Olivia had made her request. Doctor Simms realized that his increased workload was beginning to take a toll.

"I've been very inattentive lately," he conceded. "I'm sorry, my love. I kept meaning to have it done, but there have been so many things on my mind."

Her response was interrupted by Annabelle suddenly entering the room. She was holding up the sheet from her bed, displaying the hole in the middle of it to her parents.

"Look. Holy sheet!" she said while barely containing her laughter.

Hollis struggled to do the same, while Olivia gave her daughter a stern look in response to her remark.

"That is not a very nice expression, young lady," she informed Annabelle.

"What do you mean?" Belle replied innocently.

"You know exactly what I mean. I know the vulgar expression you were thinking of. Please have Esmeralda put a new sheet on your bed. And kindly refrain from using such objectionable language in my presence."

Annabelle left the room. Hollis was now the object of Olivia's scorn.

"The least you could have done is support me!"

"She's growing up, love. And I thought it was clever. But I'll have a talk with her if you'd like."

Olivia answered with her eyes. Hollis walked up the long winding staircase to speak with Belle. He then walked through a narrow hallway, which when his daughter was younger, echoed with the sweet laughter peculiar to little girls. The entrance to Belle's room and the doorways of the ones next to it were reached by climbing a narrow staircase with only three steps. A wooden owl, or as she had referred to it years ago *a wise old towl*, sat on the polished oak banister at the end of the stairs. The door to his daughter's room was slightly ajar. He could hear her telephone conversation with Celia.

"It's like they're too involved with their lives to bother with me. Olivia is always hanging around with that creep from Hollywood. I don't know what they're doing together."

Hollis cringed at his daughter's suspicions. That was not something a girl her age should have to deal with. He could not hear her friend's response, yet knew it was probably not very encouraging.

"I know," Belle replied. "And Hollis is in his own little world. He never remembers a thing he tells me. He's become a stranger. They're both forgetting the most important thing in their lives-me! Maybe Uncle Loser will adopt me. You know only my grandparents from Hollis's side stayed together. And they died young. So it looks like I'll either lose my parents through a divorce or an early death. But either way I'll lose them."

Hollis felt as though he had betrayed her. For all his concern about the state of mind of his patients the plight of his own flesh and blood had managed to elude him for a considerable time. Belle was the most precious thing in his life. Hollis would not forget that again. He waited for several moments after her conversation ended before knocking on the door.

"Hello Belle," he said after having been invited in.

"I'm sorry about before."

"Well, between you and me, I didn't think it was so out of line. But do try and consider the feelings of your mother."

"That would make one of us," she replied with a dramatic jerk of her chin. "You're always too busy for mother, or me."

Hollis sat down on the bed next to her.

"Remember when you were my little ragamuffin?" he asked with a sentimental smile.

Annabelle responded in kind at first, for the times she spent as a child romping with her father were very dear to her. Then the realization that she had grown far beyond that little girl made Belle roll her eyes towards the ceiling.

"Your mom is just a little uptight at the moment. She has a lot of things on her mind."

"Like who?"

"If you're implying that Harley Fox is anything but a business matter to her you're sadly mistaken," Hollis said firmly. "I know these things."

Annabelle felt she had reached a line which should not be crossed. She did not broach the subject again.

"And I know I've been distracted," Hollis conceded. "But I'll do better. I know it's hard to be your age."

Annabelle accepted his embrace. No matter how old she became, Hollis's daughter could always be a child once more while in his arms. Of course she would never admit that to her father.

"I want a dog," Annabelle announced after Hollis released her.

"That shouldn't be a problem. You're certainly old enough to be responsible for one."

"I didn't say I wanted to be responsible for it," she replied. "I just want a dog. Whatever happened to the one called Mr. Peepers?"

"You were five years old when we bought you that poodle. As I remember the chef ran out of food one night and served him for dinner."

"Daddy! That's horrible."

"I agree. One should never serve poodle for dinner. Perhaps for breakfast or lunch, but never for dinner."

Hollis hugged his daughter once more.

"I'll be more careful when I'm joking around, Dad," she told him as he walked towards the door.

"And I'll do a better job of paying attention. Did you know there's a hole in the sheet on your bed? I just noticed that."

They shared a laugh before saying goodnight. Hollis walked down the stairs and told his wife about Annabelle's request immediately.

A week passed and Gregory Hill sat in Hollis's office once more. The psychiatrist asked him to resume his story about Avalor. The detective did so enthusiastically. He described her first visit to his apartment.

"This is a very nice place," she remarked after examining the contents of the detective's home.

"You looked at the microwave as though it was an antique," Hill observed.

"I've heard of these before, but I can't remember when or where. What does the microwave do again?"

"It heats up food. What do you people use to do that? Do you have x-ray-vision?"

"No, not quite," Avalor replied with a laugh. "We use an air circulator to cook with."

"What's that?"

"It's a device that excites the molecules in the air until they produce the heat required for the job," she explained.

"What does it look like?"

"I can't go into that. In fact I've said too much already."

Gregory offered her a cup of tea and she accepted. They sat at his kitchen table, talking about their respective lives. Avalor lived with her daughter. Her husband was no longer a part of the family.

"What happened to him?" he asked his guest.

"I'd rather not say. Now you tell me about yourself."

"Well, there really isn't much to talk about. I'm a detective in the New York City Police Department."

"A detective? Yes, I've heard of those, too. What do you do?"

Gregory gave her an incredulous look.

"I investigate crimes. You've heard of those, haven't you?"

Avalor examined her host carefully. She was obviously making a very important decision. After a very long pause she finally spoke.

"I don't know why I'm being so open with you. I just hope it doesn't come back to haunt me. But here it goes. You see, in our time, there's very little use for detectives. There's not much in the way of crime, and the ones that are committed tend to be petty in nature."

"Has everyone suddenly become honest?"

"To a large degree, yes. You see at some point in the future the leaders of the world are going to realize what the most prevalent cause of violence and strife on the earth is. It's poverty. The fact that some have too much while others have too little causes people to behave badly. When they take steps to insure a more equitable distribution of the resources crime will be greatly reduced."

Gregory thought about what he just heard for several moments before responding.

"What you just said makes sense," he finally said. "But there's always some hot head or sleaze ball that's going to hurt someone because they pissed him off. And no matter how much certain people have they'll always want more, and in many cases without working for it."

Avalor nodded at him.

"You're right. But you forget how I came to be here. The people in my time can travel into the past, or the future. And by traveling to the future the authorities can discover who the *sleaze balls* are. They are detained before they have the opportunity to commit their crime."

Detective Hill was impressed.

"So I would be obsolete," he thought out loud.

"You might be as a detective. Like I said, there is a miniscule amount of police work to be done. But I think you would take advantage of the situation. You seem like a bright person. In our time people can be what they want to be. Everyone has the chance to get the necessary education for any occupation they desire."

"So who collects the garbage?"

"Most of those chores are automated. But there are still some distasteful tasks which must be performed. We all take a turn at them, so no one feels exploited."

"I can't picture you driving a garbage truck," he said with a smile.

"You'd be amazed at what I've done. We've also used our time travel capabilities to eliminate the deaths caused by accidents."

"That sounds like quite the utopia," Hollis interrupted his story.

"It's not perfect. There's still disease. And people just wear out like they do now. But I'd still be willing to give it a try."

"But she won't let you."

"No, that's against the rules."

Hollis jotted down a few more notes before speaking again. Gregory eyed him anxiously for he was certain that the doctor would reject his story. Yet Hollis appeared to be intrigued by Avalor.

"Did she just disappear?" he finally asked.

"No, she went back to the park. It was clear to me that Avalor didn't want me to follow. So I didn't. I haven't seen her since."

"Will you see her again?"

"She usually shows up once or twice a month."

Hollis now asked the question that had occurred to him during the previous session.

"If you see her before our next session, ask Avalor how she is able to observe millions of stars in the night sky over her home. If her eyes have developed to block out the sun's rays, then I would assume that the adaptation would limit one's ability to see in the dark. Also, with the increased population, I'd expect there to be increased pollution, which would limit visibility."

Hollis watched his patient's reaction carefully. He saw just a brief flicker of uncertainty in the detective's eyes.

"I can see why you're so enthused about the project," the doctor continued. "You should put together a proposal for your superiors. They might agree to meet with Avalor. Of course, she'll have to agree to meet with them. Let me see it before you show it to them, though."

"I will, doc. That's a great idea. Then I'll really be doing something."

"You're not doing anything now?"

"Well, I do, but it's always after the fact. I come into the picture after someone's been hurt. There are times when I'd rather be one of those bureaucrats who pass laws to protect people. Like the one that makes traffic stop for a school bus when the kids are getting on or off of it. That really accomplishes something. It stops a kid from being hurt."

"We'll meet again next week," Hollis said as he stood up.

"That sounds good, doc," Gregory replied as he shook his hand.

He turned and walked towards the door.

"Oh, by the way, did you ever find out what happened to her husband?" Hollis asked before he left.

"Yeah. He was one of the sleaze balls the authorities eliminated."

John Block joined Hollis in the hospital cafeteria the next day. They arrived well after the majority of the doctors and visitors had finished eating lunch. The two psychiatrists went to a deserted corner of the eatery and sat down.

"So, how have you been?" John asked him. "It's been a while since I last saw you."

"Very well, thank you. How are things with you?"

"I can't complain about anything except this chicken. I think this bird was a reject from McDonalds."

"And it's such a swanky place. I'm so disappointed," Hollis said with a laugh.

"Are you aware that Alec is wining and dining everyone on the staff? He's trying to buy their vote."

"I hope he's taking them to a better place than this," responded Simms with a grin. "But as for me, I'm not interested in campaigning."

"You want to win on merit. Bully for you! I just hope you don't live to regret it, though."

"I'm working on a very interesting case," said Hollis in an attempt to change the subject. "It involves a man who called me on the show. I thought his problem required a more traditional approach, so I've been seeing him in my office for the last two months."

"What's his story?"

"He believes that a woman from the future is visiting him."

Block stopped eating and stared at Hollis for a moment.

"You're not putting me on, are you?" he finally asked.

"Not at all."

"You see the irony, don't you?"

"What do you mean?" Hollis replied.

"This man thinks that a woman from the future is visiting him. And you believe a woman from the past is visiting you. Do you two ever swap stories?"

The expression on Hollis's face revealed that the similarities between the unusual woman in his life and the one in his patient's had not occurred to him.

"Do you think it's a delusion?" Block asked him.

"Which one?" Hollis asked with a grin.

"You know I don't think you're delusional. I meant your patient."

Doctor Simms thought for a moment before answering.

"I think it's a defense mechanism. He's in law enforcement, so the man has to deal with the dregs of humanity on a daily basis. This woman claims that the authorities in the future have used their ability to travel through time to prevent crimes before they happen. He's hoping that she will help him do the same."

"So what's your approach going to be?"

"The man absolutely believes in Avalor. That's the woman's name. I've decided to convince him I believe in her as well. By doing so, I can demonstrate the absurdity of his belief to him."

"That's a good plan."

"I suppose."

"What's the matter?"

"I just wonder if it's really necessary to spoil this man's illusion. I mean, my patient believes that with Avalor's help he can prevent the pain and suffering of a countless number of people. Taking her away from him is going to be like telling Don Quixote that he can't be a knight."

"But the man holds a responsible position. Your patient can't very well do his job if he's distracted by a fantasy. Some might say he's even psychotic. He certainly appears to lose touch with reality when she visits him."

"I think it's no more harmful than daydreaming. I've checked his record. He's had an outstanding career. That includes the period after he claims to have met Avalor. He only came to me for help because his superior found some drawings he made of her world. My patient was forced to get help or risk losing his career."

"I think you know what has to be done here, my friend. And I also think you're sympathetic towards this man because of your own visitor. You're feeling guilty. By the way, have you seen her lately?"

"No, I haven't. But that has nothing to do with this. Though I must say my time with Angie has rejuvenated me. My cases had started to seem mundane before I met her. But as for the patient who sees Avalor, I've just been very impressed with the way this man has used his relief valve, if you would. He's found a way to remain optimistic about the future even though the man must deal with depravity on a regular basis."

"I can't remember hearing you speak so impractically," John observed. "If a person feels they need a fantasy to enable them to make it through the day, then they are heading for serious trouble."

"You're probably right," Hollis reluctantly admitted.

"Probably?"

"If you met my patient, you'd understand. But I'll do the right thing. You know the last time I saw Angie she had begun to physically manifest the hardships of her journey."

"A ghost reliving her past. How ironic," Block observed.

"I hadn't thought of that. And the strange thing is, she's more beautiful now then when I first met her."

"You seem to be dealing with your patient on a visceral level, doctor."

"She was the first love of my life. But I can still function in a professional manner."

"And speaking of physical manifestations, you look very tired to me. Are you sleeping at night?"

"Yes. I just have a lot on my plate at the moment. I'll be fine."

Block stood up to leave. He looked down at Hollis with a concerned expression on his face. "Take care of yourself, my friend."

Before their next session Hollis made some discreet inquiries about Detective Gregory Hill. He called a friend who was an administrator for the New York City Police Department. Doctor Simms asked him to see if the name Avalor was related to any of the cases that Hill had been involved with. There was no record of any suspect or victim with a name like that of the woman from the future.

Then he thumbed through the detective's personnel file once more. Doctor Simms found the answer.

Detective Hill arrived on time for his next appointment. Hollis greeted him affably and they took their respective seats.

"The last time we met, I asked you about Avalor's claim that she could see a million stars in the night sky. I wonder about that, given the adaptation that humans developed in the years between our time and hers. Then there is the matter of the increased population, and the resulting increase in pollution. Did you ask Avalor about my concerns?"

"No, I haven't seen her since we last spoke," Gregory answered while shifting ever so slightly in his chair.

"I had the opportunity to look at the drawings you made based on her description of the buildings from the future. They are beautiful. Are they made of glass?"

"No. It's a kind of plastic, only much stronger than anything we have now. They can put up a huge building for next to nothing."

"It would seem that the clear walls would make people uncomfortable. There wouldn't be any privacy at all."

Gregory did not respond.

"I've also been thinking about the authorities using their time traveling capability to avoid accidents and other undesirable events, including crime. Of course it's a wonderful idea, and I can certainly see the benefit to society, but I'm concerned about the law of unintended consequences coming into play."

"What?"

"Suppose, for example, that you're out walking in the wilderness and you come across a man hanging from the edge of a cliff. Your first impulse is to help him. But what if you save this man's life and two years later he kills your wife during a robbery? How would you feel?"

Gregory was becoming agitated. During the previous sessions Doctor Simms had been an enthusiastic listener. Now he seemed intent on questioning every aspect of the detective's story. Hill stood up and walked over to the doctor's desk.

"The louse would be stopped before he could ever do it!" he exclaimed. "Don't you see, Simms? They would know about it before it ever happened!"

The patient picked up a small wooden figurine and slammed it down on the deck for emphasis. Hollis silently applauded his decision not to have any easily breakable objects in the room. He then continued with his plan.

"Did you ever wonder why she chose you as a contact? Wouldn't the United States President or the Secretary of the UN have been able to take better advantage of the information Avalor has to offer? They could see to it that all the murderers in this country, and the world, were stopped before they ever hurt anyone. And they could get the drunk drivers off the road as well."

Hollis had noticed that the emergency contact listed in the personnel folder of Detective Hill was changed several years before. He called Hill's superior and discovered that the original name listed on the form was that of Gregory's sister, Rachel Hill Avallone. Further research indicated that she had been killed several years ago by a drunk driver. As Hill had been on vacation at the time, no one in the department was aware of his loss. Doctor Simms now watched his patient erupt.

"But they weren't walking in the God damn park that day, were they, hot shit? You think you know everything! She chose me because I'm the only one who really knows what goes on out there! The fucking higher-ups don't have a freaking clue! And neither do you! You never saw your best friend lying in the morgue because some asshole got behind the wheel after drinking a bottle of scotch! You didn't know Rachel! You're just a high brow stuck up son of a bitch, Simms!"

The patient broke down. Hollis listened to his sobs for what seemed like an eternity.

"I couldn't help Rachel!" Hill exclaimed as he slammed his fist down on the desk.

"No, but you put away the man who caused her death," Hollis said softly. "He won't hurt anyone like Rachel ever again."

The detective walked out of the door without looking back. Doctor Simms contacted his superior the next day. In his professional opinion, Gregory Hill was cured.

After reluctantly slaying Don Quixote, Hollis would now try to give his visitor from the past a chance to find peace.

CHAPTER TWELVE

ollis came down with a severe case of the flu several weeks after his breakthrough with Gregory. As always, his immediate concern was for his patients. Olivia kept reminding him that he had now become one of them. The only way to resume his sessions, she repeated over and over again, was to get well again. Hollis initially resisted her advice, but then became so ill the effort required by his wife to convince him that he needed rest was minimal. He did not leave their bed for two days.

Hollis managed to sit at his desk on the third day. He was still weak but was determined to keep a vigil for the patient who constantly occupied his thoughts. The psychiatrist's effort was rewarded when he saw the soft iridescent glow that could always be seen in the garden just before she appeared. Angie had visited him three times in the last month, but on each of those occasions refused to continue her story. Doctor Simms had decided to use the only leverage he had over the stubborn spirit to force her into revealing the undisclosed details of her journey. The psychiatrist picked up her diary, putting it in the pocket of his coat. Then he walked outside. Angie was pacing back and forth as usual. She smiled when the doctor said hello.

"I recently made a trip to Boston," he told her. "I walked through the Boston Common, and along the Charles River."

Hollis suddenly felt very unsteady on his feet. He sat down on the rock before his rubbery legs gave way.

"Did you, indeed," Angie replied with a heartfelt smile. "I especially remember the Boston Common from my childhood days. We used to run around for hours at a time there. I've never felt quite as free since then."

"I visited a friend of mine while I was there. He gave me this."

Hollis took out the diary. Angie stared at it with an intensity the doctor had seldom witnessed in the eyes of another human being, living or dead.

"You brought it back for me. That was very kind of you, Hollis. Bring my diary to me, please."

Angie had always been reticent to leave the confines of the garden. Hollis wondered if he could manage to walk the distance between himself and the apparition. Yet that was an academic question at the moment, given his plan. The doctor had decided to bribe his patient.

"I did so with an ulterior motive," he told her. "I want to make a bargain with you. If you'll tell me about the rest of your trip to San Francisco, I'll return your diary to you."

Angie glared at him for a moment. The menacing expression on her face made Hollis suddenly realize that this specter might possess the power to take the journal by force. He feared for his safety, but did not reveal this to the woman from Boston. To his relief a faint smile suddenly appeared on her lips.

"You are a rare scoundrel, Mr. Simms. You're bargaining with something that is not yours. Why is hearing about the rest of my journey so important to you?"

"You've told me about most of it. So now I feel like someone who had to leave the theater before the play was finished. I'm anxious to know what happened after you left the fort."

Angie paced for a few moments before answering. Hollis was on tether hooks. Her diary was the only thing that might entice the entity to tell her tale. Angie looked up at him with weary eyes. Hollis knew this expression. He had seen it countless times on patients who had decided to unburden themselves to him.

"I'll tell you about it," she somberly said. "Even though I know you'll think less of me when my story is finished. I decided to take a shortcut."

Angie began her narrative with the Crawford Party arriving at Fort Bridger. The majority of the settlers looked forward to the brief respite from their travels, while those who were traveling with Cassia only thought of getting better care for her. There was a doctor at Fort Bridger, yet he could do little more than Fletcher had done. Still he did try to be encouraging.

"She seems to be recovering," he told them. "But only time will really tell. When do you leave for California?"

"Sanders says we have to go in four days," Wyatt told him. "He wants to cross the mountains before the snows come."

"You'll be taking a mighty big chance if you let her travel in this condition," the doctor told him.

"How long does she need?"

"Two weeks, at least. I'll check in on her later."

Cassia had fallen asleep so Wyatt and Angie stepped outside. They walked through the gate in the wall that protected the fort. The rugged landscape looked intimidating enough to these two healthy individuals. Neither one of them could envision someone in Cassia's condition traveling on the unforgiving terrain.

"I guess we'll be here for a while," Wyatt told her. "We might even settle here if the two of us get the notion. There's good farm land and plenty of people."

"I can stay here until the spring," Angie told him. "That would give Cass plenty of time to get well. Then I'll go to San Francisco."

Wyatt looked at Angie without speaking for some time. Then he smiled and took her hand in his own.

"You're truly the best friend anyone could have," he told her. "But if I let you wait around for my wife to get better she'd never forgive me. You've got to find Tom Shanahan, Angie. I can take care of my Cassia."

"I can't leave her," Angie said as tears began to run down her cheeks. "After all the three of us have been through I have to make sure Cass gets well."

Wyatt hugged her. Angie knew he was right, though her loyalty to Cassia still argued against his reasoning.

"She won't think less of you for doing what you've got to do," Wyatt said softly. "You have to leave for California now."

Angie met Ed Black later that day. He was what the people of her time referred to as a mountain man. Black lived off the land while traveling throughout the west. A big, burly individual, he projected a fearlessness few people possessed.

"Ed says that we can reach California much faster if we ride over the salt plains," Jake said after introducing them.

"You can't ever be sure about snow in the Sierras," Black told her. "The mountain passes might be closed by the time you reach them if you take the Hastings Cutoff. You could get trapped in the mountains. If you go over the salt plains you'll be there with time to spare, ma'am."

"What does Mr. Sanders think about that?"

"Who?" Black asked her.

"Sanders works for Crawford," Jake explained. "He's leading the people who are going to California, while his boss goes with the people who are settling in Oregon."

"I'm sure he's a good man," Ed said. "But he's just going to do whatever Silas Crawford tells him to do. And Crawford only knows one way to get to California. There's another way."

Black squatted down to draw a map in the dirt. Angie watched attentively as he did so. She could clearly see that his proposed route would require traveling a shorter distance, yet the drawing did little to help her decide. Angie did not know what the terrain would be like on either route, and this was the issue foremost in her mind.

"I have to see about getting mules for you and Knowles," Ed said to Jake. "Let me know if the woman wants one."

Ed Black lumbered off leaving the two alone.

"You're going on mules?" Angie questioned him.

"Yep. I always thought people looked better on horses, but these salt flats are supposed to be mighty rough."

"But do you think it's worth the risk?"

"The way I look at it there ain't any easy way to get to California. So if Black's shortcut turns out to be a little tougher, what the hell? At least it will be over sooner."

"It's difficult for me to make a decision now," Angie told him. "I'm so concerned about Cassia."

"I know, but you're gonna have to decide real quick, Angie. Ed means to leave in three days. Like I said, it's a mighty unforgiving way to go. But we'll get there faster."

"I suppose seeing Tom sooner would be worth taking a more difficult route," she said to Jake. "I'll see you at supper. I'll have a firm decision by then."

Angie went back to the cabin where Cassia lay. The doctor was still administering opium to her friend. As a result no conversation passed between the two of them. Cassia would occasionally blurt out something, but it was obvious she thought herself to be in another place and time. Angie fretted over her, spending little time considering the path she would choose to reach her lover. She was fixing Cassia's hair when Wyatt came in.

"How's my wife?" he asked her.

"She seems comfortable. Did you get some sleep?"

"A little, but not much. Thanks for watching over her."

"I need no thanks. She's the best friend I've ever had."

"So you're going with Black?"

"I think so. How did you know?"

"Crawford was mouthing off about it," Wyatt said with a grin. "He thinks a lot more of you than I thought he did. Silas is madder than hell because you're thinking of going another way. I guess you've convinced him that you're worth something since we left Missouri."

"It wouldn't take much for him to have raised his opinion of me," Angie replied with a laugh. "Mr. Crawford thought I was little more than worthless when we began."

"But he could be right about the shortcut," Wyatt said with a concerned expression on his face.

"I know. But as Jake said there isn't any easy way to reach California. And it will be worth the harder road if I see Tom even a little bit sooner."

After dinner Angie walked over to the stables. Ed Black was there with Jake Anderson and his friend Richard Knowles. There was also another man, whom Angie recognized instantly. She gave him a cold stare in greeting. He answered with a very contrite expression of his own. This was the man who had tried to force himself upon Angie in Independence.

"This is Tim Nash," Black told them after making note of Angie's reaction to him. "He just arrived yesterday. Nash has decided to head for California instead of Oregon. He'd like to take the flats with us. Are there any objections?"

He looked at Angie when asking that question. Her bright green eyes had lost some of their intensity, yet still smoldered as she considered the newest member of their party.

"I lost my family on the trail," Nash explained in an almost pleading voice. "There's no reason for me to start a farm in Oregon now."

The devastating loss Tim Nash had experienced was plainly visible in his sorrowful eyes and defeated posture. Angie felt compassion stirring within her breast. Their encounter in Missouri seemed like it had occurred in another lifetime now, and in any case, the people traveling on the trail could not afford to waste the energy required to sustain their anger at a fellow immigrant. She would not deny this dejected soul a chance to start his life anew.

"I don't mind at all," she finally said in a casual manner.

She stayed by Cassia's side for every moment until the time came to leave Fort Bridger, even though the two women could not engage in any meaningful conversation. The doctor had continued to administer opium, and Cassia's speech was incoherent as a result. That circumstance changed on the day Angie had to say farewell. Wyatt had instructed the doctor to let his wife regain her senses if at all possible. The two friends were forever grateful for his thoughtfulness in that regard.

"Well, you can't use me as an excuse to avoid the trail anymore," Cassia told her with a weak smile. "I'm doing fine now."

Angie knelt beside the bed and smiled at her friend. The patient was still in a great deal of pain but forced herself to appear cheerful in order to convince Angie of her improving health. In spite of Cassia's efforts her dearest friend was not fooled. Angie still feared for the life of her confidante, though there was not even a hint of concern in her manner of saying goodbye.

"You could have helped me out, Cass," Angie replied with mock disappointment. "But you look so good I'll have to go now."

"Remember Ann Street?" Cassia asked her. "I never had as much fun as I did there. I probably won't ever have that much fun again. Tell Mr. Shanahan I said hello."

"I will. I'll see you in California, Cass."

Angie carefully embraced her, and then left the room. She departed Fort Bridger with fear in her heart, as Cassia still looked too weak for her liking. Angie said a tearful goodbye to Wyatt before starting her journey to San Francisco.

The next morning five people set out from Fort Bridger on mules. Angie said a silent prayer for the friend she was leaving behind. The woman from Boston managed to hold back the tears which struggled to emerge from the corners of her eyes.

They saw the Great Salt Lake two days later. The plain they rode across consisted of bluish clay that exhibited a countless number of small ridges with a white saline substance on top. Angie was reminded of a snow covered mountain range in miniature. In between these were bands of sandy earth with an ashen shade. The mules often sank up to their knees in this fine powder.

"Shit, this is just about impossible!" Jake exclaimed later that day. He was frustrated from constantly having to coax his mule to move on. "Not only is it hot, but the damn animal can't go no more than three feet in an hour."

"It might be better if we traveled at night," Richard suggested. "At least it will be cooler."

"Yeah, it will be cooler, all right," Ed said with a sardonic grin.

After the sunset they rode for only a short distance before the meaning of Ed's remark became clear. The initial relief Angie and her companions had felt when the blazing orb sank below the horizon disappeared very quickly. The unbearable heat was now replaced by an intolerable cold. Everyone but Black was astonished by how quickly the temperature went from one extreme to the other.

"What in the hell kind of place is this?" Richard shouted to be heard above the wind that now assaulted them.

"I think you answered your own question," Jake shouted back.

"We'll travel for another hour or so and then make camp," Ed told them.

Jake was sure the bitter cold would be the death of him. He tried to embrace the mule as he rode in the hope of gleaning some heat from the beast of burden. Angie kept her head down, for every time she lifted it her eyes were blinded by tears. When they finally stopped for the night she could not set up her tent. The wind made that impossible: it also prevented the others from using their shelters. Ed built a fire with wood he had packed in his saddlebag. Starting the campfire was hard work, as was maintaining it. Tim took his bedroll off the mule, spreading it out on the ground near the flames. Jake and Richard lay down next to the wildly flickering source of precious warmth. Angie wrapped a blanket around her and then lay in between them.

"I hope you don't mind, gentleman," she said with shivering lips.

"Not at all," Richard replied. "This is why I came on this trip. Under normal circumstances, a beautiful young woman such as yourself wouldn't come near me."

Angie smiled at him, though the frozen muscles on her face made it difficult. Jake pushed up against her, and did feel somewhat warmer. Though still extremely cold, Angie's friend now believed he would see another dawn.

"Let's get moving," Ed cajoled them the next morning. "We still have a long ways to go before we're off the flats."

"I just managed to get to sleep," Jake complained.

"You can sleep on your mule. Just don't fall off, cause we're not turning back to get you. Eat fast and let's go."

They ate a quick breakfast of cold biscuits with jam. The image of the rising sun was reflected on the briny water of the lake. Their appreciation of the picturesque scene was tempered by the knowledge that the air would soon become insufferably hot once more.

"I wonder why the good lord would put all that water there if it's not of any use to anyone," Angie thought aloud as they rode away.

"I didn't know you were the religious kind," Jake remarked.

"I just don't wear it on my sleeve. But I do know all of this, for good or ill, had to come from somewhere."

"You should just worry about getting over the flats, and not bother yourself about where they came from, ma'am," Ed Black told her.

"I can do both, Mr. Black," Angie said defiantly.

They stopped for a drink of water at midday. The mules were given some of the precious liquid as well. No one ate lunch, as the blistering sun had taken away all semblance of an appetite from them. Even Black refrained from taking nourishment. Richard looked the worst of the five.

"Did you ever think of rejoining the people who were using the Hastings Cutoff?" Hollis interrupted her narrative.

"There were times when that occurred to me," the ghost conceded. "But then I remembered Tom's stories of his facing physical deprivations while at sea. I became determined to match his strength."

She resumed the telling of her story.

"We're not close to the end of this yet," Ed told them as they made camp for the night.

"But you said it would take two days," Jake pointed out.

"I didn't think the mules would have so much trouble getting over the plains," he conceded. "We have enough water to make it, though."

"I wonder if this man really knows what he's doing," Richard mumbled as they huddled around the fire.

"Wondering about it won't do us any good right now," Jake whispered back. "Let's just see this thing through."

"That's straight talk," Tim agreed.

Angie acquiesced with a nod.

They made good progress the next morning before stopping for a midday drink. Richard was becoming emaciated. Jake had to lift him onto his mule when they resumed their journey. He watched his friend carefully, yet there was little that could be done for him. Their supply of water was now precariously low.

"Damn, there isn't a cloud in the sky," Richard muttered at one point.

"There isn't likely to be one, either," Black said in a matter of fact tone. "Talking about it ain't going to make a damn bit of difference. So just watch the ground in front of you."

"Do we need your permission to speak, Mr. Black?" Angie asked indignantly.

Their guide gave her a stern look but said nothing. For the rest of the day they struggled against the elements without a word to each other. After spending most of the next one riding under the sweltering sun, they reached the end of the salt flats. The country around them now had vegetation, sparse though it was. There was a watering hole shimmering in the sunlight just ahead of them. Angie rubbed her eyes before looking at it again to be sure this was not a mirage.

"Hold on there!" Ed Black yelled as the other four dismounted and staggered towards the water.

Given their wretched state, the settlers at first thought he was trying to reach the precious liquid before them. Then they discovered his true intention. The veteran of the wilderness studied the area around the hole to be sure there was no evidence of the water being unfit to drink. After satisfying himself on that point Ed stepped aside, allowing the others to quench their thirst first.

"I've seen a couple of people die from bad water," he remarked after the five of them had drank their fill. "You can't be too careful."

"That's good thinking," Jake conceded. "Can we stay here for a day? Richard could use the rest."

Jake's friend had fallen fast asleep. Ed looked at him carefully, and then shook his head.

"We've already lost two days crossing the salt plains. I don't want to lose anymore."

As the mountains rose up before them Angie and her companions from the Crawford Party suddenly understood that the most difficult part of their peregrination could well lie before them. Though they had conquered the blazing heat of the salt plains, the migrants knew the cool air of the Sierras brought the possibility of inclement weather. Still the green vegetation now encompassing their path was infinitely preferable to a barren wasteland.

"That's the bluest water I've ever seen!" Angie exclaimed as they came upon Lake Tahoe.

"That it is, ma'am," Ed agreed.

"We have to stop here for the night," Jake insisted. "I need a good long swim."

Ed ran his fingers through his beard, a gesture he had begun to make with greater regularity.

"Sounds right to me," Richard agreed.

Tim nodded.

"I'd like to take a swim as well," Angie added.

"Okay, we'll camp here. I don't guess that a few hours will make a difference," Ed reluctantly agreed.

Angie dove into the water naked after finding a secluded cove. She shivered at first, then managed to acclimate herself to the temperature of the cool mountain lake. The air was as pure as that which one would breathe in a primeval land. Angie heard some wild creature stir in the trees next to the water. She was frightened for a moment, but whatever it was apparently had no desire to harm her and moved on. Angie finished her swim in peace, and then joined the others.

"That water is god damn cold," Jake observed as he put on his shirt.

"But it is refreshing," Angie said as she sat on a log near the fire. Then she noticed that Richard was still dry. "Didn't you take a swim?"

"No, I just want to sit here and take a good look. This is the prettiest place I can ever remember seeing."

"He's just too lazy to go in the water," Jake chided him with a smile. Then he looked at Angie with a concerned expression on his face.

Suddenly a shot rang out in the forest. Angie and Jake each grabbed a gun, while Richard simply looked in the direction from which the sound had originated. Tim came running out of the lake. They heard someone cursing and realized it was Ed Black. He emerged from the trees several moments later.

"Damn it all to hell!" he roared. "I had a bear in my sights but missed him. We could have had some fine vittles tonight, and for a lot of nights to come."

"Maybe you'll get another shot at him," Jake said optimistically.

Black rolled his eyes and responded.

"The reason they call them *bears* instead of *stupids* is because they ain't. He won't show his face around here again."

The five rode off the next morning at dawn. Their mules covered thirty miles that day, which had them feeling very confident as they sat around the fire after nightfall. Angie managed to convince them that a chorus of *Skip to the Lou* was in order. Though he did not join in the chorus, Ed Black refrained from giving her his usual *what is this nonsense* look. Those singing the song recalled the journey in their prairie schooners with a strong sense of accomplishment. Then Angie's thoughts turned to Cassia.

"I'll be going to sleep now," she said softly.

"Good night, Angie," said Jake. "I just want to look at the stars for a while longer."

"Good night, ma'am," Ed muttered as he prepared to keep watch.

Richard had fallen asleep next to the fire. Tim was already in his tent.

Angie awoke before dawn. She sleepily stepped outside only to discover that the stars had disappeared. Then something wet and cold landed on her shoulder. Angie took it in her hand, realizing that snow had begun to fall. She was wide-awake in an instant, and quickly joined her companions.

"I think we should turn back," Jake was saying to Ed as he packed his mule.

"We'll wait until daylight and see what the weather looks like," Ed told him.

"I thought it wasn't supposed to begin snowing for several more weeks. Are you out of your reckoning?" Angie asked him.

"No, but I just might be out of my mind if I have to answer any more fool questions," Ed responded impatiently. "The damn snow comes when it comes. Now just hush."

Angie did not appreciate his tone, yet she knew this was not the time to start an argument. The daylight revealed an ominous looking sky above them. Ed now ran his fingers through his scruffy beard incessantly. Then he addressed his companions.

"We can go back, if you'd like," he began. "But from what I can see the storm seems to be moving from west to east. Which means it will trap us, since we can't outrun it. If we go ahead, and the storm keeps moving on, we might come to some clear weather. That's what I'd think we oughta do."

The four of them looked at each other, saying nothing for a long while. Then Angie spoke.

"As for me, I want to go ahead. I've come all this way to see Tom, and I feel like he's just over the next mountain now. If we go back, I'll have to wait until spring to see him."

"I have nothing to go back to," Tim said solemnly.

Jake looked at Richard with an expression that asked *can you make it though the snow?* His friend nodded weakly.

"I guess we'll go on," Jake said in a hesitant voice. "But I just hope we're not taking a fool's chance because we're so close to California."

"Don't work that way," Ed said with authority in his voice. "I don't want nobody coming up to me two days from now saying they knew we where heading for trouble. You either want to go ahead or you want to go back. It's one or the other, Anderson."

"I'll go ahead," Jake replied.

The snow became deeper as they proceeded along the mountain trail. Large flakes had fallen in the morning, now smaller ones began to descend in the afternoon. Angie and the others winced as the cold white granules stung their faces. She placed a bonnet on her head; it provided some relief, though her scalp itched incessantly. Later in the day, when the light started to diminish, Ed stopped his mule in front of a group of large trees.

"We'll spend the night here," he told them.

"Shouldn't we keep going?" asked Jake.

"No, we could fall into a ravine or ride off a cliff in the dark," Ed responded. "We'll stay here for the night. Hopefully the storm will be over in the morning."

Ed tied the mules to a tree before distributing a small ration of food to his companions. He had hoped to supplement their provisions by hunting, but that would only be possible now if the snow abated. Angie and the others ate their meal in silence. No one in the party discussed the implications of the early snow, but all were aware of them. They finished eating and then wrapped themselves in whatever was available to them. Ed stood watch while the others huddled under the pines.

Jake relieved him later that night. The bitter cold made it difficult for him to stay awake. He tried to remain alert by continuously cursing the falling snow. Jake had started to feel woozy when he heard a noise in the woods nearby. Sitting in the cold had slowed his reactions, and as a result Jake did not respond to the potential threat until one of the mules voiced a loud protest. Then he saw three barely discernable figures untying the animals from the tree. Jake tried to fire his rifle, but his hands were too stiff from the numbing cold to operate the weapon. A shot did ring out just as the mules ran off. That was fired by Ed, whose pursuit of the thieves and the animals was to no avail.

Jake lowered his head. He had let his companions down, and his inaction could quite possibly put their very lives in jeopardy. Ed returned and looked at the others carefully. Much to Jake's surprise, the mountain man did not comment on his performance during the watch. Ed Black instead focused on the task ahead of them.

"Folks, we're up against it now. We've got a lot of walking to do. And we don't have much food left. Most of what we had was on the mules. So get as much rest as you can."

"I'm sorry. I just couldn't get my hands to work fast enough," Jake said to him before retiring.

"There ain't nothing to be done about it now," Ed replied without turning to face him. "Just get some rest."

The next day brought no relief from the snow. They struggled through drifts that were waist deep. Richard Knowles was having the most difficulty, as he had never completely recovered from the salt flats. Angie, Tim and Jake helped him as much as they could, though their efforts were only barely sufficient to keep Richard with them. Their friend was about to suggest leaving him behind when Ed spotted a cabin in the distance. The small wooden structure was situated in the far end of a majestic canyon.

"We'll stay there tonight," Ed informed them.

The cabin was much farther away then it initially appeared. The five of them struggled against the roaring wind that swirled around the horseshoe shaped canyon. They used every last bit of their strength to cross the icy white terrain and reached the shelter of the abandoned home as darkness fell. There was some dry firewood next to the fireplace inside, and the travelers gratefully took advantage of it. Then Ed distributed the evening meal. As he did so the guide received some incredulous looks from the others.

"What little we have has to last a long time," he reminded them. "Unless the snow lets up soon we could be trapped here for a while."

"But you said that we're just staying here for the night," Angie pointed out.

"We ain't going to get anywhere unless the weather changes," Ed told her. "So we'd best just wait it out in here."

Angie started to object, but then realized he was right. She also knew their supplies were precariously low, and that they would not last much longer without replenishing them.

"Yep, it's a rock and a hard place," Ed said after observing the expression on Angie's face. Then to Jake "I'm getting some sleep. I'll relieve you about midnight."

The snow continued for two more days. When it finally stopped, they went outside and attempted to walk out of the canyon. The desperate quintet discovered that the fine white powder was now a foot deeper. After covering less than a quarter mile in an hour, Ed had them return to the cabin.

"We've got to wait it out probably until the spring," he said after they were inside.

"And what in hell are we going to eat?" Jake exclaimed. "We ran out of food yesterday."

"I know that," Ed replied. "There ain't nothing for it right now. I'll stay outside and watch out for any game that might come by. But don't count on it."

Tim went with him.

Angie took a sip from her silver flask as they walked out the door. Jake joined her, though he was reluctant to do so with an empty stomach. Richard weakly declined her offer. He was in a piteous state.

"I never thought you'd turn down whiskey," Angie said with a smile.

Knowles weakly nodded his head to indicate that he too was surprised by his own behavior.

"I put us in this fix," Jake said bitterly.

"That's not true," Angie corrected him. "We wouldn't have gotten much farther with the mules."

"At least we could have eaten them."

"You were cold, and it was dark. Stop blaming yourself, Jake. We'll find a way out of this."

By the next morning, Richard Knowles was dead. Jake gently shut his eyes before taking his remains outside. Angie gave him some time alone before following, while Ed and Tim stayed in the cabin. Jake sadly covered up Richards's remains. As there was no way to give him a proper burial the corpse would remain on the porch of the cabin.

"I guess Richard found a way out," Jake said to Angie with a sardonic grin.

"He's at peace now," she replied.

"We'll all be with him real soon if we don't find some grub."

Angie suddenly noticed how frail her friend had become. His sunken eyes ached with the ravages of hunger. She knew that her own appearance must have also been deteriorating rapidly as well. Yet her determination to see Tom again would not allow Angie to despair for long.

"You can't lose hope, Jake. I don't know how we'll get out of this, but we will."

The increasing intensity of the wind finally drove the two back inside the cabin.

"I'm going to try to find some food," Ed informed them. "We're never going to last until spring unless we get something to eat."

"But you said the snow is too deep for hunting," Angie reminded him.

"It is, but there ain't no choice. If I don't come back, you'll have to try too. It's the only way, ma'am."

He opened the door before turning to face them once more.

"I'm sorry about your friend," he said.

Ed struggled to reach the end of the canyon. The others watched him from the porch. Though they believed he was doomed, no one would express their opinion aloud. After he disappeared they went back inside to stand in front of the fire. Wood and water were the only things they still had left. The original occupant of the cabin had left behind more firewood than was required. The snow provided all the water they could drink. That would not prevent the three settlers from starving to death, however.

"You can make it," Jake said to Angie one morning a week after Black had left them.

She looked at him and knew he would soon be gone. Jake could no longer manage to stand up. His emaciated body barely had the strength left to take another breath. Angie put her head down to hide her tears.

"You've got to make it to San Francisco. Use me when I'm gone, do what you have to do. Tom is waiting for you Angie."

She knelt down, taking his head in her hands. Jake managed to raise one of his bony appendages and let it rest on her shoulder.

"Do what you have to do," he said with his last breath.

Tim held her as she cried. Then the two struggled to drag his emaciated body onto the porch. Though Angie and Tim were barely alive, they could not bring themselves to take advantage of Jake's offer. She watched over the next two days as her last companion approached his final hours. On the third morning he motioned for her to come over to his bed.

"I'm sorry for what I did in the saloon," Tim said as tears slid down his cheeks. "I'm not a bad man."

"It was the whiskey, Tim, not you. Try to hang on. The spring is almost here."

"You can make it," he said before dying.

For two days she sat in the cabin reliving her life. Angie thought about her father, bitterly castigating him when she thought about Tom's leaving Boston because, as he said, *they'll hang me for sure and your father will provide the rope.* Then, in the next instant, his starving daughter regretted leaving Boston without saying goodbye to him. This bereft woman could no longer find fault with those she had loved. Angie Barton could hear Cassia's laughter as she danced a jig with one of the men in an Ann Street saloon. Angie was dancing next to her, in the strong arms of the Nantucket whaler.

"I've given up everything for you," she said aloud to no one. "I have to see my love."

Angie took out her knife just as death was about to take her. She had purchased it after a drunken Tim Nash almost violated her dignity. The woman from Boston used it now to commit an act that defiled her soul. Angie availed herself of Nash's remains.

Hollis suddenly let out a groan. He held onto his stomach and bent over. Angie looked at him with understanding.

"I don't blame you. You know now why I couldn't face Tom. I don't blame you for being sickened by my conduct."

"It has nothing to do with you," Hollis assured her. "I've been very ill. I understand why you did it, Angie. It was the only way you could survive."

"Understand!" she exclaimed bitterly. "Then tell me, was it for my life or my revenge! I don't even know anymore."

"You told me that you forgave Nash," Hollis pointed out.

A bolt of lightening suddenly crackled across the sky. Hollis managed to sit upright once more. His patient was in a very agitated state.

"I was a child of God!" Angie exclaimed as the heavens erupted above her. The specter's long, elegant fingers were intertwined as she wrung her hands in despair.

Another bolt of lightening illuminated the tortured spirit against the dark silhouette of the grand old man. The thunder that followed shook the ground around them, just as it had over 100 years ago on the plains. Hollis tried to speak, but his voice was hoarse and could not be heard above the wind.

"I ate human flesh!" the specter shouted in anguish. "I'm no better than one of the wolves on the trail! How could I ever face the man I love, or anyone I had known again? I walked out of the canyon when spring came. Another party going to San Francisco was kind enough to take me with them. I sailed to New York and worked on the Ellsworth Estate because no one knew me there. They would never suspect that I had lost my soul."

Hollis watched as her eyes welled up with tears. He wanted to console Angie by pointing out that a person in her condition no longer possesses the ability to make moral judgments. Yet he could not, because at that moment Hollis began to feel dizzy. As the drenching rain began to fall, the psychiatrist sat down heavily on the rock.

"How could anyone love me again?" Angie questioned him while frantically grasping her long black locks. For a moment Hollis thought she would pull out her hair. "Could you love me?"

"Yes,' Hollis weakly replied. "And so could your friends. I'm sure Tom never stopped loving you either."

The last image Hollis remembered was of Angie standing in the rain, though it could not touch her. She found kindness in the sincere eyes of Hollis Simms, though they were clouded with fever. While still haunted by her past, Angie now seemed to believe she had managed to retain her soul. The tranquility in the specter's sparkling green eyes communicated this to Hollis. She would know peace once more. The objective of his sessions with Angie Barton had been put at rest. A warm feeling permeated through him as Hollis observed the relief evident on her lovely face. The psychiatrist knew his patient had experienced a catharsis.

Then Hollis fell to the ground.

I'm the first one she's told about this he thought to himself before losing consciousness. *She'll be all right now.*

Sebastian happened by some time later and found Hollis lying there. Angie was gone, and so was the diary.

CHAPTER THIRTEEN

ollis awoke in the hospital, instantly recognizing the antiseptic
surroundings of his private room. The doctor had no idea as to
what day this was. The blinds on the window were closed and
with the door being shut, he could not even garner a clue as to the time
from the volume of traffic in the hall. Hollis was about to press the call
button to summon a nurse when she walked into the room unbidden. He
recognized her immediately.

"Doctor Simms, how are you feeling?" the nurse asked as she took his
pulse with an air of authority. The role reversal was obviously very satisfying
to one who was usually in the position of being his subordinate.

"Not too bad," he replied. "How long have I been here?"

"For about twelve hours. I'll call Doctor Benson."

He saw his watch on a table next to the bed. Hollis picked it up and
discovered that he had slept the day away. This didn't surprise him, given
his state of mind. The psychiatrist always felt fulfilled after a patient was
cured. Rescuing Angie Barton from her emotional impasse had provided
him with his greatest sense of accomplishment.

"Why do I always wind up with jackasses for patients?" Ted Benson
asked as he walked into the room.

"It's probably because you're better suited to being a veterinarian,"
Simms quipped.

"Really, Hollis, how could you go out on a night like that? You're lucky you don't have pneumonia."

"It wasn't raining when I left the house."

"You never should have left your bed. I explicitly told you to rest for several days. If one of your patients so blatantly ignored your instructions, you'd have them committed."

"That's the advantage of being a psychiatrist," Hollis answered with a grin.

"Anyway, you'll be fine. Your wife, who by the way spent the entire day waiting for you to regain consciousness, is on her way up."

The doctor shut the door to the room. He then looked at Hollis carefully before speaking.

"Is something bothering you?" he asked in a sympathetic voice.

"No, not at all. I thought I was well enough to take my usual evening constitutional. The weather simply caught me by surprise."

"We go back a long ways. I find it hard to understand how you could let something like this happen. You wouldn't be keeping anything from me, would you, Hollis?"

"Only the payment of your bill if you pad it by wasting time on foolish questions," Hollis responded with a laugh.

"I won't risk that," the doctor answered with a grin indicating that he had decided to abandon his efforts to find an explanation for Hollis's behavior. "So I'll let you entertain your visitors."

Olivia and Annabelle walked through the door just as Benson opened it.

"Darling! I was so worried about you!"

She hugged him so tightly the needle from the intravenous tube became detached from his arm. The doctor quickly stopped his bleeding and then had the nurse setup another one. Olivia was initially frightened by the blood. Then she became embarrassed by her clumsiness after the doctor brought the situation under control.

"I'm so sorry, Hollis."

"Don't be silly, my love. If there was ever a convenient place to have an accident this is it."

"Are you feeling okay, Daddy?" Annabelle asked him.

"Yes, I'm going to be fine," Hollis said as he hugged her. "Now that my girls are with me."

He was both surprised and relieved by his wife's willingness to forgo an explanation of his conduct on the previous night. Olivia instead focused on the present, making certain that all of her husband's needs were met. Annabelle was too grateful for her father's swift recovery to ask any questions about his behavior. The three of them spent a very pleasant hour together before other visitors arrived.

"I would think that someone in your line of work wouldn't be crazy enough to go out in the rain when they're ill," Sebastian said as he walked into the room.

"I was doing some research on why people like to walk in the rain. The spirit was willing but my stomach was not."

"I'm going to get some coffee. Would you like something?" Olivia asked him.

"I'd better wait and ask the doctor. But thanks anyway, my love."

"Nothing for me, thanks," Sebastian declined as well.

Olivia and Annabelle walked out of the room.

"So what happened to you?" Sebastian asked him.

"I was having a conversation with Angie. I started to feel dizzy and then I fainted just as the rain began. But I think she'll be all right now. I know what made her decide to hide in New York. I believe she's at peace with herself now."

Sebastian refrained from asking what her reason was. He knew that his brother would consider the answer to be confidential.

"You were lying near the garden. I didn't think you were breathing at first. Then I found your pulse, and drove you here as fast as I could. I didn't want to wait for an ambulance."

"Many thanks," Hollis said as he hugged his brother. Then he asked "Did you find her diary? I brought it outside with me. I meant to return it to Angie when we were finished."

"No. I'll look for it tonight."

"You can ask Frank as well. He may have found it during the day. But I think that Angie took it back."

"That would be amazing," Sebastian mused. "To have a spirit remove a physical object from this world would be the ultimate proof of their existence. That is if you can prove she took it."

Hollis said nothing. Somewhere in the unseen world, Angie Barton had rejoined her friends. Hollis was certain of that, though he would have liked a confirmation of some kind from his patient.

"I suppose she won't be coming back again," Hollis said somberly.

Olivia returned and began to dote over her husband once more. Hollis appeared to be amused by her concern, yet he said nothing to ridicule his wife. Sebastian glimpsed a heretofore unknown emotion on Olivia's face. Guilt was driving her efforts to make Hollis feel comfortable, which included fluffing his pillow. Her display would have been maudlin if not for the sincerity with which she tended to his needs.

I guess this is all about Harley Sebastian thought.

"Can I have your autograph?" Clare asked as she walked into the room, interrupting the younger Simms' speculation.

"Well, this is a pleasant surprise. I would have fallen ill much sooner if I knew you would visit me," Hollis said with a grin.

"Actually, I'm here because I've been elected president of your fan club. How are you feeling?"

"You can tell all three members that I'll be out of here shortly. I feel fine."

"Now, darling, we can't rush things. That's how you got into trouble in the first place. How are you, Clare?"

"I'm doing well, thank you."

"Would you like a seat?" Sebastian asked her.

"No thank you," she replied with a smile. "I can't stay long."

"So how is the advertising business treating you?" Hollis asked.

"It's hectic as ever. That's why I can't stay. I have to work on a presentation for tomorrow morning. I just wanted to make sure you were okay."

Clare kissed him on the cheek before leaving.

"I'm going down to the cafeteria. Does anyone want anything?" Sebastian asked them.

No one responded. He walked out of the room behind Clare.

"Did this have anything to do with the ghost?" she asked him as they stood in the elevator. "I'm only wondering because I can't remember Hollis ever being sick before."

"He had the flu, and then aggravated his condition by leaving the house to speak with the ghost. I found him lying on the lawn last night. But according to him, it's all over now. He doesn't think she's coming back."

"Did she tell him that?"

"No, but he thinks Angie's cured. It's a long story, and I don't know all the details. Maybe he'll tell me more about it now that it's over."

"So how are things with you?" she asked.

"I'm still working at the bagel shop. I think I'll be looking for a change in the near future, though."

Clare smiled at him as they stepped out of the elevator.

"I guess you were right to be worried about Hollis. I do miss you, Sebastian. You should give me a call sometime."

She gave him a kiss and walked out the front door of the hospital. Sebastian stood there for several moments after she left.

John Block visited Hollis later that evening.

"How are you feeling?" he asked his former pupil with a concerned expression on his face.

"I'll be out of here by tomorrow," the patient said confidently.

"Good. How's that unusual case you told me about going?"

"I believe her emotional conflict has been resolved. I'm thinking of writing a paper about my sessions with her."

John Block gave him a skeptical look.

"You better be thinking about your career instead. Alec is making sure that all the people who work in this hospital know about your condition. You don't want to let them start speculating about whether or not it was caused by your treating a spirit."

"I guess that would give him an advantage over me."

"You'd best publish that paper after you retire. Don't do anything to help Alec."

"Did someone mention me?" Collins asked as he strode into the room.

He shook his head while shaking Hollis's hand.

"You try to do too much, my friend. You should either become a full-time celebrity or a full-time psychiatrist."

"It's just a simple case of the flu. I do greatly appreciate your concern, however. You'll be glad to know that the doctor has given me several medications. He is treating my condition with some of the most advanced chemicals known to man."

"As well he should, though in this case, I would also prescribe behavior modification."

"I never thought I'd live to hear that," John Block remarked.

"So when are we going to play golf?" Hollis asked them.

"He is feeling better," Olivia said as she joined them. "But I'll decide when you're capable of physical exertion."

"You'll have to rescue me from my confinement, gentleman," Hollis pleaded with mock anxiety. "Or else I'll simply waste away."

"I'm not that brave," John said with a laugh.

"He speaks for me as well," Alec agreed. "I fear the wrath of your keeper."

Hollis took her hand into his. He had discovered that being the object of so much affection suited him, at least for the moment.

Simms returned home two days later. Frank came by to see him soon after his arrival.

"First I find your brother on the lawn flat out on his ass. Then you do the same damn thing. How am I gonna keep it green and growing if you two keep using it to flop on?"

"It must be hereditary," Hollis answered with a laugh.

"I'm glad to see you're feeling okay. Let me know if I can get you anything."

"Thanks, Frank."

Gregory Hill stopped by the next day. Hollis was sitting on the long veranda enjoying the crisp autumn air.

"I'm sorry to bother you, doc," the detective said as he walked up the steps. "But I heard you were under the weather, so I thought I'd check you out."

"I'm glad you did. Have a seat. Can I offer you something to drink?"

"No thanks," Gregory replied as he sat down. "So how are you doing?"

"One hundred percent better. How are you?"

"Good. I want to thank you for helping me out. And also to apologize for the way I left your office after our last session. I was pretty surly."

"It's quite understandable."

"I felt embarrassed. How I ever believed in that woman is beyond me."

Hollis gave him an understanding look.

"The human mind is a very tricky thing," he told him. "It lets us believe in the most incredible things, yet will often let us ignore the most obvious ones. What's most perplexing to me is that you haven't developed a million such devices, given your occupation. You see the truly depraved side of humanity on a regular basis."

"I guess you're right. But you must see a lot of that yourself."

"That's true. But I also get to meet some interesting people as well. I once treated a pro quarterback who was having trouble performing on the field. The general manager of the team he played for was convinced the cause of his problem was psychological."

"How did that turn out?"

"After a year of intensive therapy, we discovered the reason for his difficulties. It was because he simply sucked as a football player."

"I bet I lost a ton of money because of that guy. Thanks again for telling my boss that I'm fit for duty."

"I only did so because it's true. You haven't had any problems dealing with your job since Avalor has been gone, have you?"

Hill smiled at Hollis.

"Will you change your mind about me if I tell you that I miss her? Talking with such an unusual person made me feel kind of special. Now every day is pretty much the same for me as it is for everyone else. But I can handle that. I just take things head on, and focus on all the times I've managed to prevent people from being harmed by getting some of the low lives off the street."

"Good. And believe it or not, I do have a strong sense of what you're talking about. I was in a similar situation not too long ago."

"Really? Can you tell me about it?"

"I can't because it involves another patient."

"I understand. I guess I picked the right shrink. Take care, doc."

Hollis also received a message from Perry Albright. He had sent a note to the company Perry worked for, explaining that his patient had to wear the regulator to alleviate the symptoms caused by his allergies. Albright was initially the object of scorn when wearing the device. Then one day he took a deep breath through the regulator. The noise it produced reminded his co-workers of the sounds produced by the character Darth Vader in the movie *Star Wars*. Their laughter in this instance was much kinder, and Perry soon found that he had become a welcome diversion from the mundane tasks his fellow employees performed. The manager was at first concerned that he would be a detriment to his staff's productivity, but then realized that his presence actually improved their morale, and their performance. Albright enjoyed his new role as Darth, and relished the attention it brought him, which was what Doctor Simms suspected he was after all along.

Hollis was making the final entries in Angie's file when John Block walked into his office. He was so absorbed in his work that the presence of his friend went undetected for several moments. Hollis looked up from the paper in front of him to stare out the window. That's when he finally noticed John.

"You certainly haven't lost your ability to concentrate," Block observed.

"I'm just getting some things in order," Hollis replied. "But don't tell Olivia. I'm not supposed to do any work until next week."

"Mums the word, old chum. I came by to see how you were doing, and also to be sure that you didn't make a very big mistake."

"Whatever do you mean?" Hollis asked with a perplexed expression on his face.

"If you ever grow tired of the talk show, you could become a very fine actor. You know I'm talking about the paper you mentioned in the hospital. The one concerning the patient whose file you're working on now."

"You caught me in the act," Hollis sheepishly conceded. "But it is an extraordinary case, you must admit."

"Yes, too extraordinary. I don't doubt that something unusual happened here. But I'm your friend. The rest of your colleagues and people in general will be far more skeptical."

"I heard a recent survey found that a third of the people in this country believe in ghosts."

"It's the other two-thirds you have to worry about. You have a fine reputation. You could be the most famous psychiatrist since Freud, thanks to the television. Why risk all that for a paper that most people won't take seriously anyway?"

Hollis walked over to the window to look at the garden. He felt a compelling need to tell Angie's story to the masses. Yet Doctor Simms could not rebuke the validity of his friend's argument against sharing his experience with the world.

"I suppose you're right," he finally conceded. "But I am going to write it. Maybe I'll leave a provision in my will to have it published after I'm gone."

"Why bother? You could simply come back after you die and tell your story to someone else, just like your patient did."

"That has possibilities, my friend."

"I'd like you to come to the hospital tomorrow, if you're physically up to it."

"I am, but I don't know if my wife will agree with me."

"Just tell her that you are going to be offered my position. I'm sure she'll allow you to come under those circumstances. Congratulations, my friend."

Hollis returned to the set of *The Robin Wainscot Show* several days later. The host warmly embraced him.

"You look great," she remarked after escorting him into her office. "You're skinnier, but still look great. You won't believe what your illness did for our ratings."

"You seem very pleased about my misfortune," Hollis said with mock indignation.

"No, I worried about you day and night. The producer was happy, of course," she replied with a grin. "So what really happened?"

"What really happened?"

"You're still not used to being a public figure, are you? Whenever a celebrity winds up in the hospital, it's always assumed that they aren't being truthful about what put them there. So did you overdose on something?"

"If I did, would that help the ratings as well?"

"It would put them through the roof!"

"Well, I can give you a much more interesting story than the plain old flu. A ghost from the 1800s has visited me on a regular basis over the last year or so. I went out on the night in question, despite having the flu, to see her. A sudden rainstorm caught me by surprise, and I passed out."

For a moment Robin Wainscot thought the doctor was serious. Then a smile crept across his face. The talk show host roared with laughter.

"You have a great imagination, Doctor Simms. Now let's go listen to some phone calls."

Olivia Simms turned 40 a week later. Hollis had thought about giving her a surprise party, but concluded that it would be a futile exercise. He believed nothing could happen at Fairhaven without his wife being aware of it. So instead Hollis threw a party with Olivia's assistance. The people who gathered together that night were essentially the same ones who had attended his party.

"Why, hello, Jacqueline," Hollis greeted his mother-in-law. "What a pleasant surprise."

"I wouldn't miss my little girl's birthday," she replied while pinching the cheek of her daughter. "Is your father here dear?"

"Yes, but he's promised to maintain a distance of at least 50 feet from you at all times," Olivia responded.

"50 miles would have been more appropriate," Jacqueline said. "But you shouldn't have to be reminded about the state of your parents' relationship on your birthday."

"I'm 40 now," Olivia replied with a sardonic grin. "I can handle it."

"I didn't think your parents would ever occupy the same building again," Hollis pointed out after Jacqueline walked away. "Bringing them together is quite a diplomatic coup."

"Do you think we could ever become so estranged?" Olivia asked with a concerned expression on her face.

"We're too compatible to wind up like them, my love," Hollis reassured her. "We'll always enjoy each other's company."

Hollis hugged her. Whatever concern had been playing on his wife's mind in regard to their relationship seemed to dissipate. Then the two went their separate ways and mingled with the crowd.

"Hollis!" a voice called to him from the other side of the room.

"Aunt Nora," he replied while walking over to her. "I'm so glad you could make it. And how are you Aunt Wilimina?"

"With the cooler weather, not too well, frankly. But I couldn't miss your wife's 50th birthday, nephew."

"It's her 40th, actually."

"Oh, I better not make the same mistake in front of Olivia. She'll kick my butt."

Hollis joined in with his aunt's laughter at her remark. Yet he could not conceive of anyone getting the better of this crusty old busybody.

"I'm not one to pry, Hollis, but how on earth could Olivia send you out on a rainy night right after you had been ill?" Nora asked him. "I mean, doesn't she look after you?"

"It was my fault, Aunt Nora. I was just so anxious to get back on my feet that I completely ignored the doctor's, and Olivia's, advice. They both wanted me to rest for a week."

"They didn't replace you on the show, did they dear?" Wilimina asked with a concerned expression on her face.

She enjoyed her nephew's celebrity. Bragging to her friends about it was one of Wilimina's favorite pastimes. She did not want to see him become just another psychiatrist.

"No, of course not. I'll be back on the show this week. Now if you'll excuse me, I have to greet the other guests."

Nora was disappointed. She was about to broach the subject of what was in her opinion Annabelle's far too revealing dress. As Hollis had seen Alec Collins walk into the room, her protest would have to wait. He went over to greet him.

"Alec. How have you been?"

"Can't complain, because no one will listen," he replied with a grin. "I'm glad to see that you're feeling better." He then paused before reluctantly adding "And I want to be one of the first to congratulate you on becoming head of the department. I look forward to working under you."

Collins gave him a firm handshake. Hollis sensed that his words were sincere, even if they were noticeably lacking in enthusiasm.

"Thank you. But we'll be working together, I can assure you. Can I offer you a drink?"

"I'd feel guilty having one if you can't," he said.

"Why don't I really believe that?"

"Because I'm just being polite. Of course I'll have a drink."

"There's really no need to feel guilty, anyway. I'm cleared to drink alcohol again. Not by my doctor, mind you, but I've cleared myself. After narrowly escaping a lecture from my aunts, I've earned a drink."

"I agree. And if you have a relapse I'll drop you off at the hospital on my way home."

They met John Block on their way to the bar. The three of them discussed the latest developments in their chosen profession. As always their conversation developed into a rousing debate, with Hollis and Alec as the chief antagonists. Hollis implied at one point that he had some very compelling evidence supporting his position.

"So why not write a paper about this unusual case you mentioned?" Alec challenged him. "You seem to think it could change my point of view. I'd be anxious to read it."

"I don't think anyone will ever change your point of view," Hollis told him. "But as for a paper…"

John Block shot a very concerned look towards Hollis. He reassured him with his reply.

"The patient has decided not to allow her case to become public," Hollis said. "I'm very disappointed about that, but I must respect her wishes."

"If I didn't know better, Doctor Simms, I'd say you were afraid to publish the paper," Alec said. "Did the results of your treatment disappoint you?"

"I can give an unequivocal *no* in response to your question," he replied. "Maybe I'll reveal some of the details about her at the next conference, if I have to speak first. Now if you'll excuse me, gentlemen, I have to greet another guest."

Elliot Reese stood in a corner of the large ballroom by himself. He kept a constant vigil for his wife, in order that the two of them might avoid having to converse with one another. Hollis walked over to him.

"It's good to see you, Elliot. How's business treating you these days?"

"Not as well as I'd like. You look quite fit, though. I heard you were in the hospital recently."

"It was just a bout of the flu."

"Do women chase you down the street?"

"Pardon?"

"I mean now that you're on television, do you find yourself being pursued by a lot of women?"

"I'm just a psychiatrist, not a rock star. But I do find it difficult to eat in restaurants sometimes. Complete strangers stop by my table to say hello and then insist on receiving my advice. It's very distracting."

"I see. I'm asking because an associate of mine suggested that I appear on a weekly program about investing. He knows the producer. I just don't know if my becoming a celebrity will be worth sacrificing my privacy."

"Better get your running shoes on, old boy," Hollis answered in an amused tone. "The women won't give you a moment's peace if they ever see you on television."

"I've got to freshen my drink," Elliot said shortly before walking away.

Paul Nustad walked up behind Hollis and tapped him on the shoulder. The two men embraced each other.

"You scared the shit out of me!" Paul told him. "I came back from a conference in Vancouver to find a message on my desk saying that you've been rushed you to the hospital. How did it happen?"

"Let's get some air."

The two men sat on the veranda, each with a glass of brandy in his hand. Paul lit up a cigar as he waited for his friend's explanation.

"I had been ill, and was recuperating when Angie appeared in the garden. I went outside to speak with her. I got caught in a sudden rainstorm, and collapsed. I wasn't as strong as I supposed. Sebastian drove me to the hospital."

"Why do doctors always make the worst patients?"

"Because we know that no one should ever listen to a doctor. Anyway, I'm fine now. And I believe Angie is as well. I discovered why she chose to hide on this estate after returning from California. Angie's at peace now because she was able to tell someone about it. I doubt I'll be seeing her again."

Paul took a long drag on his cigar before speaking.

"I'm glad to hear that. I don't suppose there's any chance that you'll tell me what the reason was."

"You know there isn't."

"Well, I'm on the verge of getting some very detailed information about your former patient. The old gentlemen that previously gave us some documents concerning the Bartons has now provided the name of a family member who has correspondence written by Angie's relatives during her lifetime. He says the letters mention Miss Angelica Barton. We should learn a great deal from them. I'll let you know what I find out, if you're still interested, that is."

Hollis hesitated before responding.

"Why of course I am. Let me know what they say."

Sebastian Simms walked up to the house with Clare Johnson. Hollis was glad to see her as always, and even more pleased to see who had escorted her to the party.

"I hope you haven't consumed all the brandy," Sebastian called out to his brother.

"He tried, but I wouldn't let him," Paul told him. "I made him save some for me."

"You're looking much better, Hollis," Clare told him as he kissed her on the cheek.

"I feel that way, too. Let me steal your first dance from Sebastian."

"I was hoping you would," Clare replied playfully.

Hollis and his friends celebrated well into the night. The psychiatrist not only had the recovery of Angie Barton to lift his spirits, but he also reveled in the sight of Clare and Sebastian being reunited. As Hollis danced with Olivia, he wondered at how perfect his life was.

"I don't think I've ever seen you happier," she remarked.

"And it's not even my birthday. I had a break through with a patient of mine. I'm also very glad that my brother has gotten back with Clare."

"Oh, yes. She's a nice girl. Maybe he'll move back to the city now."

Hollis looked at her with a smirk on his face.

"I'm happy for him," she insisted. "I just meant that being in a serious relationship may get Sebastian to apply himself again."

Annabelle came over and the three of them danced together. At that moment, Hollis understood the meaning of the word *contentment*. He could scarcely wait to see what tomorrow might bring.

CHAPTER FOURTEEN

A beardless Sebastian Simms sat on the couch in the old house, silently surveying the various items that constituted all his earthly possessions. The boxes along with the suitcases he had packed did not seem as though they should have been able to hold the contents that one would have expected to accumulate after more than 30 years of living. Yet Sebastian felt as contented as he had at any point in his life. He had just accepted an offer to work on Wall Street again. The younger Simms was also moving back to Manhattan. Most importantly, Clare Johnson was back in his life.

"I guess Frank and I will have to watch the ballgames by ourselves now," Hollis remarked as he walked into the room.

"You guys can come into the city and watch a game with me there, you know."

"That's true. So when do you start work?"

"Monday morning. Would it surprise you to learn that I'm completely petrified?"

"Not at all," Hollis replied as he sat down next to him.

"But at least I have a shot. I'm back on the street again."

"You make it sound as though you're destitute," Hollis pointed out with a laugh.

"Thanks for boosting my confidence," Sebastian replied in the same manner.

"There's nothing to worry about. You have a real talent for investing. So even though it might take a while to get back into the routine, you'll do well in the long run, I'm sure."

Hollis slapped him on the back, much as their father used to do when they were younger.

"Courage, my friend," Hollis added.

"Thanks big brother."

They took his belongings out to his car. Frank was mowing the lawn nearby. He interrupted his work to say good-bye.

"You don't take any shit from those people," he told him. "I'll come over there and kick their fancy asses all over Manhattan if they give you a hard time."

"I appreciate that, Frank."

"You take care now," the groundskeeper added while shaking his hand.

Olivia and Annabelle came out to bid him farewell. His niece had become almost as tall as her mother. This made Sebastian aware of how fast the years were going by. Hollis did not have to be reminded. Annabelle brought that point home to him everyday.

"I'm sorry to see you go, Sebastian," Olivia said with all the sincerity she could muster. She hugged her brother-in-law for good measure. "Good luck with your new position."

"Yeah, I hope it works out for you Uncle Sebastian," Annabelle added as she did the same.

"Thanks so much. I'll talk to you soon."

He embraced his older brother once more before driving away.

In the coming months Sebastian proved that Hollis had been correct when he said his brother had a talent for investing. The rest of the staff soon came around to the same conclusion. Simms could hardly remember what it was like to do anything else for a living.

He was about to leave the office one evening when Ron Anderson, his supervisor, summoned him into his office.

"You've really fit in well here," he told Sebastian. "Do you miss the bagel shop?"

"Only at breakfast," he replied with a smile. "I haven't found anyplace that makes a bagel quite as good."

"What are you doing tonight?"

"I'm having dinner with my girlfriend."

"Does she like Broadway?"

"Yes."

"I have two tickets to *Light up the Dark*. A client gave them to me. But my wife and I have other plans. They're yours. You've made quite an impression on me. Keep up the good work. And have a great time."

Sebastian thanked him and then practically floated home. He certainly appreciated the theater passes, but the compliment meant much more. Sebastian called Clare.

"Guess what? We're not just going to dinner; we're going to dinner on Broadway. Then we're seeing *Light up the Dark,* courtesy of Prism Investments."

"That sounds great," said Clare. "One of the women in the office told me about a fantastic new restaurant down there. I'll make reservations."

Sebastian and Clare savored their meal before filing into the theater. He found the play to be trite. Sebastian was trying not to doze off when the sound of a familiar voice made him sit straight up. An actress who was sitting near the back of the stage caught his attention.

Sebastian stared at her emerald green eyes. This was the woman who had appeared in the garden at Fairhaven. Clare asked him if anything was wrong.

"No, I'm fine," he whispered.

"You don't look fine," she whispered back.

Sebastian smiled at her. That was assurance enough to allow Clare to enjoy the rest of the play. Her date was transfixed on this one actress for the rest of the evening.

The theater emptied quickly after the play ended to rousing applause. Sebastian hustled Clare to the stage entrance door behind the theater.

"Why are we standing here? Do you want someone's autograph?"

"The woman who played Carolyn is the same person who's been in Hollis's garden."

"What?"

"It's her. I'd recognize that woman's voice and face anywhere."

"I thought you never got close enough to get a good look at her."

"No, I said I never got close enough to take a good picture of her. But there was one night when I walked right up to her while she was speaking with Hollis. She ran away and disappeared. My brother would never let me anywhere near her after that."

"According to the program her name is Rachel Robe. Are you sure it's the same person?"

"I know it's her."

"Is she going to walk through the wall?" Clare asked teasingly.

Sebastian replied silently by way of the amused expression on his face.

"I've never staked out a theater before. Should we pretend to be groupies?" she then asked with a grin. "There's never a dull moment with you around, darling."

Sebastian smiled. They stood waiting in the chilly autumn air for an hour. When she did not emerge he reluctantly agreed to go home.

"I'm going to find out where she lives," Sebastian told Clare the next day. "I'm also going to call Paul Nustad. I don't want to confront her alone. She might recognize the family resemblance and shut the door in my face."

"You think Paul will come all the way from Boston for that?"

"Sure. He'll want to find out the truth about her."

Paul did agree to join him, though he could not do so until the following Wednesday. Sebastian was too anxious to stay idle until then, however. The night before he stood near the theater entrance after the play had ended. On this occasion his patience was rewarded. Rachel emerged with two other performers, and Sebastian followed them to a small pub. Fairhaven's ghost left the establishment by herself an hour later with Sebastian following at a discreet distance. She led him to a small apartment building on the East Side of Manhattan. He made note of the address before returning home.

"So we know where she lives," said the historian after hearing Sebastian's account of the night before. "We'll just wait for her to come home tonight and ask this Miss Robe some questions."

"That sounds good to me. I really appreciate your coming down here."

"I didn't mind making the trip because I'm also very anxious to meet her. I'd like to know what this charade is all about. Hollis is going to be devastated, you know."

"I thought of that. But it's better that he knows the truth about her."

"I agree. It's still not going to be easy to tell him, though."

That evening the two men sat on the bus stop bench that was situated across from Rachel's apartment until she appeared. They watched the actress walk up to the building and then followed her inside. She stopped in front of her apartment door. Paul waited for Rachel to unlock it before he spoke.

"Rachel Robe?" he asked her.

"Who are you?"

"My name is Paul Nustad. I'd like to compliment you on your performance tonight."

"Why thank you. It's not really a big part, but I do have some good moments."

"I'd like to discuss the play with you. Can I come inside?"

"Are you a critic?"

"No, I'm an historian, actually. I'd be curious to know how you prepared for the role of a woman from the past."

Rachel looked at him carefully. Letting a stranger into one's apartment was a risky thing to do. The actress's apprehension rose even more when she saw the figure of Sebastian standing some distance behind Paul.

"Is he a historian, too?"

"No, just a friend of mine. His name is Sebastian."

"It's nice to meet you." Simms said without stepping forward. "I also enjoyed your performance tonight."

There was a faint flicker of recognition in Rachel's green eyes, yet it was obvious from her facial expression that she could not place him.

"You can come in for a little while. You'll have to excuse me for having nothing in the way of a beverage to offer. I wasn't planning on entertaining anyone."

The two men entered her sparsely furnished apartment. Rachel left the door open. Paul immediately noticed something of interest on the coffee table. Despite Rachel's attire, which consisted of jeans and a tee shirt, Sebastian recognized her as Angie. Though her dark hair was much shorter now, the woman's piercing green eyes had lost none of their vitality. The actress sat down warily in an overstuffed chair. Her unexpected guests sat on the couch.

"Playing a person who lived 50 years ago isn't all that difficult," the actress began. "I did research the times Carolyn lived in. There were a lot of photographs available from her era."

"But you have also played a character from another century," Paul pointed out. "That must have been quite a challenge."

"You must be confusing me with someone else," she told him.

Then Rachel took a long look at Sebastian.

"You know my brother," Sebastian said to her. "His name is Hollis Simms."

"Oh, right, that's why you look so familiar. I've watched Doctor Simms on television. I can see the resemblance."

"You know Hollis very well," Nustad said as he picked up Angie's diary from the coffee table. "You've spent several evenings speaking with him at Fairhaven."

Rachel had been completely nonchalant up until that point. She had called upon her stage skills when it became apparent that the two men were here for some hidden purpose. Yet now there was no point in denying the truth. The diary would make any attempt to do so a futile one.

"I didn't know he was sick," Rachel said as she rose from the chair to stand before them. "I never would have gone there that night if I'd known. I was so glad to hear he was all right."

"Why did you do it?" Sebastian asked.

She sat down and was silent for several moments before answering.

"Harley Fox asked me to be his ghost. He said it was a gag someone wanted him to play on Doctor Simms. Harley knew the producer of *Light up the Dark* and offered to get me a part in it if I agreed to play Angie Barton. I couldn't turn down the offer."

"How did you make it so convincing?" Paul asked her.

Rachel was about to tell them about all the special effects equipment used by Fox to create Angie Barton. The actress also intended to mention the draconian diet she went on to simulate the toll that was exacted by the tortuous journey on Angie. Then a much simpler explanation occurred to her.

"Harley and I are magicians," she told them.

"How did you know so much about Angelica Barton?" the historian asked.

"I just followed the script Harley gave me."

"Was this Fox's idea, or did someone else put him up to it?" Paul asked her.

"I don't know. Tell Doctor Simms I'm sorry if it made him feel foolish. I just wanted to get my acting career going. I'll apologize in person if he wants. You can have the diary back. Harley was supposed to come by and get it, but he never did. You don't have to worry about me taking this to the press. I wouldn't do anything to embarrass Doctor Simms."

Rachel felt the same sense of relief she had exhibited in the garden after telling Hollis about Angie's behavior in the cabin. She stood up and showed her visitors to the door in a polite yet forceful way. The two men stopped at a nearby diner for some coffee after leaving her apartment.

"I guess we have to tell him," Sebastian said uneasily.

"Of course. But it will be a blow to his pride, I think. Hollis isn't the sort that gets taken very often, if at all. It will be difficult for him to accept. I wonder if anyone put Fox up to this."

"I have an idea, but I'd rather hear Hollis's opinion before I accuse anyone. I don't think it's his ego that's going to be bruised by this. It's his heart. My brother really felt something for Angie. And now we have to tell him she's a fraud."

They finished their coffee in silence.

The two of them walked up to the door of Fairhaven early the next day. They saw John Block standing on the porch. He had just rung the bell, and was waiting for an answer. The men greeted each other, and then Paul Nustad explained the reason for their visit. They went inside after the butler opened the door.

Hollis was reading in his office when they walked in.

"To what do I owe the appearance of this triumvirate?" he asked with a grin.

"I have some news for you," Sebastian said somberly. "That ghost you were seeing is a living person. I saw her in a play on Broadway."

Hollis stood up and walked over to the window. He did not speak for a long while.

"We spoke with her," the historian finally broke the silence. "We found this in her apartment."

He placed the diary on the desk.

"Her real name is Rachel Robe," Sebastian told him.

"What I don't understand is why someone would go to all this trouble to deceive you. It's fortunate you never published the paper about her, Hollis," Block pointed out.

"I wasn't really going to publish the paper, Doctor Block," Hollis responded. "David Copperfield had already warned me against it."

"David Copperfield?" Sebastian questioned him.

"Yes, Angie, or I should say Rachel, told me that she had read that book to the children on the trail. Being a long time Dickens enthusiast, I knew it hadn't been published until after 1849. I realized early on that at least part of her story couldn't be true."

"Then why on earth did you continue to go along with the hoax?" John asked him.

Hollis did not answer his question. He instead asked Paul one of his own.

"Did you get those letters you told me about?"

"Yes, I did," Paul said as he removed them from his coat pocket and handed them to Hollis.

The letters were written by Angie's relatives during her lifetime. The first one mentioned that Reginald Barton had threatened to have Tom Shanahan arrested for murder if he didn't leave Boston, and his daughter. That, along with a considerable sum of money, was enough to convince Shanahan to abandon Angie. He apparently never believed that she would stay with him in any case. Angelica Barton had a reputation for being fickle when it came to men.

The letter also revealed that Angie did travel west with Cassia and Wyatt. There was no mention of her friend being injured, however. The three of them arrived in San Francisco as planned. While they did take a shortcut, Angie and her friends did not need drastic measures to survive. Tom Shanahan was not in San Francisco. Though Angie never heard from him again, she quickly overcame her disappointment.

The second letter was written some 20 years later. The cousin penning it revealed that Angelica had lived a prosperous and exciting life in San

Francisco for two decades. Then she moved back to Boston just before Reginald Barton died. There they made their peace.

"Angie told me that she left the wagon train to take an alternate route to San Francisco," Hollis said after reading the letters. "How did Rachel know that, or anything else about Angie for that matter?" Hollis wondered.

"Harley gave her a script," Sebastian said.

"How did he know anything about her?" Hollis asked.

"I have an idea about that," Paul responded. "I had a graduate student researching the diary after you gave it to me. His name was Terrance Wright. He's now working in the movie business as a producer's assistant. Fox must have gotten him the job in exchange for the diary and other information about Angelica Barton."

Hollis offered the men a glass of brandy. They accepted, and their host poured their drinks with a contemplative expression on his face.

"How did Angie's diary come to be buried at Fairhaven?" Hollis asked Paul. "The letters indicate that she was never here."

"I asked the Boston Historical society to look into that. Here's their reply. You'll find this interesting too, Sebastian."

Paul handed them the correspondence he had received. The society's research had revealed that Angie's diary had been lost during her journey on the Oregon Trail. Another immigrant found it. Long after Angie's death, a man named Thomas P. Owens bought it through an antique collector. Owens was also the owner of Fairhaven at the time he acquired the diary. A wealthy friend and rival from Connecticut, Albert Montgomery, had also been interested in acquiring it. He offered a substantial sum to a man named Herman Barns, who was the groundskeeper at Fairhaven, to steal her journal for him. Barns stole it from the mansion, but Montgomery decided to reduce the amount he would pay, so the thief refused to deliver it. Barns buried the diary in the garden until he could return it in secret to the study. The groundskeeper was fired before had the chance to do so because Owens had always suspected his employee was the culprit. A man named John Simms was hired to replace him.

"*Dad*," Sebastian said with a smile after he finished reading. Then he said to Hollis; "And now it's your turn to answer a question. How did

Harley Fox even know about the diary? Do you know who put him up to this?"

Hollis thought for a moment before responding. The others in the room quickly surmised that their host knew the answer. His expression communicated not only the knowledge of, but also a grudging respect for the person responsible. Hollis was merely debating whether or not to tell the others what he knew.

"That's two questions," he finally said. "But they both have the same answer. Olivia."

"But why?" John asked him.

Hollis knew the answer to that question. Three years ago, a man named Al Borne ran an investment scam which resulted in the loss of millions of dollars to his victims. He read about it in the paper one morning at breakfast, and made an off hand remark about a *sucker being born every minute*. Hollis didn't realize it at the time, but Olivia had been one of Al Borne's victims. She was furious, but never expressed those feelings outwardly. Instead, Olivia let them simmer. Then Harley came along, giving her an opportunity to make a fool of her husband. Olivia took advantage of it. Hollis decided to keep her reason to himself.

"That's a private matter," he said.

"Why did you go along with it?" Sebastian asked.

"I was inclined to believe in her because Angie was my first love, gentlemen. Although I initially doubted that the apparition was real, my eagerness to meet this woman from the past caused me to cast aside all my doubts. If an individual accepts the fact that spirits walk the earth, then indeed they do, my friends."

"So you suspended your disbelief," John said with understanding.

Hollis smiled.

"Gentlemen, I feel as though I've not only met Angelica Barton, but that I've also traveled over the plains and mountains of the frontier with the brave people who were in the Crawford Party. Reality is actually a very subjective concept. And you have to admit that if one's experiences were restricted to only the tangible, there wouldn't be much to life at all. Harley Fox created a very memorable experience for me."

"You should call the man and thank him," Paul suggested with a smile.

"He's received thanks enough. Olivia is financing his film."

"And that doesn't bother you?" Sebastian asked him. "I mean, this guy tried to make a fool out of you."

Block answered for his colleague. "Hollis wasn't truly deceived by him, and yet he had the pleasure of meeting Miss Barton. This is what is commonly referred to as a *win win* situation."

Hollis smiled and glanced out the window.

"I did invest a good deal of emotion in the experience," he said. "So I did sacrifice something."

Olivia tentatively walked into his office after they left.

"Maybe I was afraid you were becoming bored," she said softly.

"That's why you tried to make a fool out of me?" Hollis responded angrily.

"I'm sorry, Hollis," she said with genuine remorse. "I told Harley about the diary because I thought it would make a wonderful movie. Then he suggested using it to demonstrate his ability to create an illusion. I never thought it would go this far. You were supposed to see the ghost and come running into the house to tell me about her. Then I could have my laugh, and we would move on. I never expected you to treat her as a patient. And I left a message for Harley when you became ill, telling him to stay away. But he never received it."

Olivia looked into his eyes and was surprised. The anger she expected to find there had already dissipated, and instead Olivia saw contentment.

"You needn't apologize, my dear," he replied. "I shouldn't be angry with you for giving me what I wanted. I've always desired to meet my first love. Now I have."

A twinge of jealousy surged through Olivia, but it was quickly tempered by her lingering guilt.

"Why do I always feel the need to settle accounts with everyone, even the one I love above all others?"

"It's because you're human, Olivia. And since I feel the same way about you, I find the trait to be eminently tolerable."

They embraced, and never spoke of the woman from the past again.

In everyone's mind there is a garden where a person's deepest emotions and desires are nurtured, free from the cumbersome burdens of reality. On the nights when Hollis Simms retreated to that special place, he looked out the window towards Fairhaven's garden to find it bathed in an unearthly glow.

Angie was there.

About the Author

J.E. Hall is a native of Long Island, New York. He is a graduate of the New York Institute of Technology. His interest in politics was very instrumental in shaping his first novel *The Wall*. Hall's concern for the environment influenced his second novel *Two Men With A Mission*. His third novel, *Angie of the Garden*, reflects the author's interest in history. He enjoys traveling to the unspoiled places in this world. But this author has discovered that a person's most fascinating journeys are often the ones taken with their minds alone. J.E. Hall is currently working on his fourth novel.